'Call off the march,' he demanded. 'It is too risky now. Stop it before it is too late.'

Allan turned away to stamp on his boots and don his waistcoat. He thrust his arms through the sleeves of his coat. The emotions between them filled the room like smoke from a blocked chimney.

Marian's voice was barely audible. 'Perhaps you ought not stay for dinner after all.'

Allan felt sick inside.

She laughed, but the sound was mournful. 'And again I free you from your obligation to marry me, Captain. I suspect that a threat to arrest and hang me is an indication we would not suit.'

'Marian,' he murmured, at a loss to say more.

She opened a drawer and pulled out a robe, wrapping it around her and walking to the door. 'Take what time you require to dress and then leave my house.'

AUTHOR NOTE

The soldiers' march depicted in this book is a mere figment of my imagination, although the plight of the soldiers after Waterloo was real enough. The Blanketeers and the Spa Field Riots did occur, and Lord Sidmouth, the Home Secretary, was accused of hiring provocateurs to cause the trouble at Spa Fields. Henry Hunt was a genuine liberal orator, but Mr Yost did not really exist.

Today we take for granted the freedom to criticise our government and demonstrate for causes, but with the Seditious Meetings Act of 1817 it was illegal for groups of more than fifty people to gather together. It also became illegal to write, print or distribute seditious material. Lord Sidmouth had been a strong advocate of these measures, but they proved to be a blight on Lord Liverpool's government and ultimately ushered in a more liberal Tory government in 1822.

Next in my *Three Soldiers* series is Gabriel Deane's story. From the moment he, Allan and Jack rescue a Frenchwoman from Edwin Tranville at Badajoz, Gabe is captivated by her. When he meets her again in Brussels they begin a scorching affair, but when Gabe asks her to marry him she refuses.

Then they meet a third time in London....

Look for Gabriel's story. Coming soon.

CHIVALROUS CAPTAIN, REBEL MISTRESS

Diane Gaston

First published in Great Britain 2010
by Mills & Boon, an imprint of Harlequin (UK) Limited,
Large Print edition 2011
Eton House, 18-24 Paradise Road, Richmond, Surrey TW9 1SR

© Diane Perkins 2010

ISBN: 978 0 263 22293 7

Harlequin (UK) policy is to use papers that are natural, renewable
and recyclable products and made from wood grown in sustainable
forests. The logging and manufacturing process conform to the
legal environmental regulations of the country of origin.

Printed and bound in Great Britain
by CPI Antony Rowe, Chippenham, Wiltshire

As a psychiatric social worker, **Diane Gaston** spent years helping others create real-life happy endings. Now Diane crafts fictional ones, writing the kind of historical romance she's always loved to read. The youngest of three daughters of a US Army Colonel, Diane moved frequently during her childhood, even living for a year in Japan. It continues to amaze her that her own son and daughter grew up in one house in Northern Virginia. Diane still lives in that house, with her husband and three very ordinary housecats. Visit Diane's website at http://dianegaston.com

Previous novels by the same author:

THE MYSTERIOUS MISS M
THE WAGERING WIDOW
A REPUTABLE RAKE
INNOCENCE AND IMPROPRIETY
A TWELFTH NIGHT TALE
   (in *A Regency Christmas* anthology)
THE VANISHING VISCOUNTESS
SCANDALISING THE TON
JUSTINE AND THE NOBLE VISCOUNT
   (in *Regency Summer Scandals*)
GALLANT OFFICER, FORBIDDEN LADY
   (*Three Soldiers* mini-series)

…and in eBook Mills & Boon Historical *Undone!*:
THE UNLACING OF MISS LEIGH

   Look for Gabriel's story. Coming soon.

To my Uncle Bob,
a veteran of World War II,
and my cousin Dick,
who served in Vietnam.

They are heroes still.

Prologue

1812—Badajoz, Spain

The heavy footsteps of the marauding mob were close, so close Lieutenant Allan Landon smelled their sweaty bodies and the blood staining their uniforms. Allan and his captain, Gabriel Deane, hid in the shadows as the mob moved past, intent, no doubt, on more plundering, more rape, more slaying of innocent civilians.

Was there anything more loathsome than men gone amok, egging each other on to more violence and destruction?

Fire ravaged a tall stone building and illuminated the rabble from behind. Brandishing clubs and bayonets, they rumbled past Allan, whose muscles were taut with outrage. These were not the enemy, but Allan's own countrymen, British soldiers, lost to all decency, all morality, in the throes of madness.

After the bloody siege of Badajoz, leaving thousands of their comrades dead, a rumour swept through the troops that Wellington had authorised three hours of plunder. It had been like a spark to tinder.

As the marauders disappeared around the corner, Allan and Gabriel Deane stepped back on to the street.

'Wellington should hang them all,' Allan said.

Gabe shook his head. 'Too many of them. We need them to fight the French.'

The loud crack of a pistol firing made them both jump back, but it was too distant to be a threat.

Gabe muttered, 'We're going to get ourselves killed and all for damned Tranville.'

Edwin Tranville.

Edwin's father, Brigadier General Lionel Tranville, had ordered them into this cauldron of violence. His son, who was also his aide-de-camp, was missing, and Allan and Deane were to find him and return him safely to camp.

'We have our orders.' Allan's tone sounded fatalistic even to himself, but, like it or not, his duty was to obey his superior officers. The rioting crowd had forgotten that duty.

Two men burst from an alleyway and ran past them, their boots beating sharply against the stones.

From that alleyway came a woman's cry. *'Non!'*

Women's screams had filled their ears all night, cutting through Allan's gut like a knife, always too distant for Allan and Gabe to aid them. This cry, however, sounded near. They ran towards it, through the alley and into a small courtyard, expecting to rescue a woman in distress.

Instead the woman held a knife, ready to plunge its blade into the back of a whining and cowering red-coated British soldier.

Gabe seized the woman from behind and disarmed her. 'Oh, no, you don't, *señora.*'

The British soldier, bloody hands covering his face, tried to stand. 'She tried to kill me!' he wailed before collapsing in an insensible heap on the cobblestones.

Nearby Allan noticed the body of a French soldier lying in a puddle of blood.

Deane gripped the woman's arms. 'You'll have to come with us, *señora.*'

'Captain—' Allan gestured to the body.

Another British soldier stepped into the light 'Wait.'

Allan whirled, his pistol raised.

The man held up both hands. 'I am Ensign Vernon of the East Essex.' He pointed to the British soldier collapsed face down on the ground. 'He was trying to kill the boy and rape the woman. I saw it. He and two others. The others ran.'

'What boy?' Gabe glanced around.

Something moved in the shadows, and Allan turned and almost fired.

Vernon stopped him. 'Don't shoot. It is the boy.'

Still gripping the woman, Deane dragged her over to the inert figure of the man she'd been ready to kill.

Deane rolled him over with his foot and looked up at Allan. 'Good God, Landon, do you see who this is?'

'Edwin Tranville,' the ensign answered, loathing in his voice. 'General Tranville's son.' Allan grew cold with anger.

They had found Edwin Tranville, not a victim, but an attempted rapist and possibly a murderer. Allan glanced at Ensign Vernon and saw his own revulsion reflected in the man's eyes.

'You jest. What the devil is going on here?' Allan scanned the scene.

The ensign pointed to Edwin, sharing Allan's disdain. 'He tried to choke the boy and she defended him with the knife. He is drunk.'

The boy, no more than twelve years old, ran to the Frenchman's body. *'Papa!'*

'Non, non, non, Claude,' the woman cried.

'Deuce, they are French.' Deane knelt next to the body to check for a pulse. 'He's dead.'

A French family caught in the carnage, Allan surmised, a man merely trying to get his wife and child to safety. Allan turned back to Tranville, tasting bile in his throat. Had Edwin murdered the Frenchman in front of the boy and his mother and then tried to rape the woman?

The woman said, *'Mon mari.'* Her husband.

Gabe suddenly rose and strode back to Tranville. He swung his leg as if to kick him, but stopped himself. Then he pointed to the dead Frenchman and asked the ensign, 'Did Tranville kill him?'

Vernon shook his head. 'I did not see.'

Gabe gazed back at the woman with great concern. 'Deuce. What will happen to her now?' A moment earlier he'd been ready to arrest her.

Footsteps sounded and there were shouts nearby.

Gabe straightened. 'We must get them out of here.' He signalled to Allan. 'Landon, take Tranville back to camp. Ensign, I'll need your help.'

To camp, not to the brig?

Allan stepped over to him. 'You do not intend to turn her in!' It was Edwin who should be turned in.

'Of course not,' Deane snapped. 'I'm going to find her a safe place to stay. Maybe a church. Or somewhere.' He gave both Allan and the ensign pointed looks. 'We say nothing of this. Agreed?'

Say nothing? Allan could not stomach it. 'He ought to hang for this.'

'He is the general's son,' Gabe shot back. 'If we report his crime, the general will have *our* necks, not his son's.' He gazed towards the woman. 'He may even come after her and the boy.' Gabe looked down at Tranville, curled up like a baby on the ground. 'This bastard is so drunk he may not even know what he did.'

'Drink is no excuse.' Allan could not believe Gabe would let Edwin go unpunished.

Allan had learned to look the other way when the soldiers in his company emptied a dead Frenchman's pockets, or gambled away their meagre pay on the roll of dice, or drank themselves into a stupor. These were men from the rookeries of London, the distant hills of Scotland, the poverty of Ireland, but no man, least of all an officer with an education and advantages in life, should get away with what Edwin had done this night. The proper thing to do was report him and let him hang. Damn the consequences.

Allan gazed at the woman comforting her son. His shoulders sagged. Allan was willing to risk his own neck for justice, but had no right to risk an already victimised mother and child.

His jaw flexed. 'Very well. We say nothing.'

Gabe turned to the ensign. 'Do I have your word, Ensign?'

'You do, sir,' he answered.

Glass shattered and the roof of the burning building collapsed, shooting sparks high into the air.

Allan pulled Edwin to a sitting position and hoisted him over his shoulder.

'Take care,' Gabe said to him.

With a curt nod, Allan trudged off in the same direction they had come. He almost hoped to be set upon by the mob if it meant the end of Edwin Tranville, but the streets he walked had been so thoroughly sacked that the mauraders had abandoned them. Allan carried Edwin to the place where the Royal Scots were billeted, the sounds of Badajoz growing fainter with each step.

He reached the general's billet and knocked on the door. The general's batman answered, and the scent of cooked meat filled Allan's nostrils.

'I have him,' Allan said.

The general rose from a chair, a napkin tucked into his shirt collar. 'What is this? What happened to him?'

Allan clenched his jaw before answering, 'He is as we found him.' He dropped Edwin on to a cot in the room and only then saw that his face was cut from his ear to the corner of his mouth.

'He is injured!' His father shouted. He waved to his batman. 'Quick! Summon the surgeon.' He leaned over his drunk son. 'I had no idea he'd been injured in the battle.'

The wound was too fresh to have been from the battle and Allan wagered the general knew it as well.

Edwin Tranville would bear a visible scar of this night, which was at least some punishment for his crimes. Edwin whimpered and rolled over, looking more like a child than a murderer and rapist.

The general paced back and forth. Allan waited, hoping to be dismissed, hoping he would not be required to provide more details.

But the general seemed deep in thought. Suddenly,

he stopped pacing and faced Allan. 'He was injured in the siege, I am certain of it. He was not supposed to be in the fighting.' He started pacing again. 'I suppose he could not resist.'

He was convincing himself, Allan thought. 'Sir,' he responded, not really in assent.

The general gave Allan a piercing gaze. 'He was injured in the siege. Do you comprehend me?'

Allan indeed comprehended. This was the story the general expected him to tell. He stood at attention. 'I comprehend, sir.'

A Latin quotation from his school days sprang to mind. Was it from Tacitus? *That cannot be safe which is not honourable.*

Allan shivered with trepidation. No good could come from disguising the true nature of Edwin Tranville's injury or his character, he was certain of it, but he'd given his word to his captain and the fate of too many people rested on his keeping it.

Allan hoped there was at least some honour in that.

Chapter One

June 18th, 1815—Waterloo

Marian Pallant's lungs burned and her legs ached. She ran as if the devil himself were at her heels.

Perhaps he was, if the devil was named Napoleon Bonaparte. Napoleon had escaped from Elba and was again on the march, heading straight for Waterloo and a clash with Wellington's army, and Marian was in the middle of it.

Already she heard the random cracking of musket fire behind her and the sound of thousands of boots pounding into the muddy ground to the drum beat of the French *pas de charge.* Somewhere ahead were the British.

She hoped.

The muddy fingers of the earth, still soaked from the night's torrential rains, grabbed at her half-boots. The field's tall rye whipped at her hands and legs. She glimpsed a farm in the distance and ran towards it. If nothing else, perhaps she could hide there.

Only three days earlier she and Domina had been dancing at the Duchess of Richmond's ball when Wellington arrived with news that Napoleon's army was making its way to Brussels. The officers made haste to leave, but, during a tearful goodbye, Domina had learned from her *most passionate love,* Lieutenant Harry Oliver, that, unless the Allies were victorious at a place called Quatre Bras, the Duke expected to defend Brussels near Waterloo. Domina spent two days begging Marian to come with her to find Ollie's regiment. Domina was determined to see the battle and be nearby in case Ollie needed her.

Finally Marian relented, but only to keep Domina from making the journey alone. Marian thought of them dressing in Domina's brother's clothes so it would not be so obvious they were two women alone. They'd ridden together on Domina's brother's horse for hours and hours in darkness and pouring rain, hopelessly lost until they finally heard men's voices.

Speaking French.

Domina had panicked, kicking the horse into a gallop so frenzied that Marian flew off and hit the ground hard, the breath knocked out of her. Afraid to shout lest the French hear her, Marian watched Domina and the horse disappear into the rainy night. She huddled against a nearby tree in the darkness and pouring rain, hoping for Domina to return.

She never did.

Marian spent the night full of fear that Domina had been captured by the French. What would French soldiers do to an English girl? But when daylight came, she shoved worries about Domina from her mind. The French columns had started to march directly towards her.

The farm was her only chance for safety.

A wooded area partially surrounded the farm buildings, and Marian had to cross a field of fragrant rye to reach it. The crop would certainly be ruined when the soldiers trampled on it, but for now the tall grass hid her from Napoleon's army.

Still, she heard them, coming closer.

Her foot caught in a hole and she fell. For a moment she lay there, her cheek against the cool wet earth, too tired to move, but suddenly the ground vibrated with the unmistakable pounding of a horse's hooves.

Domina?

She struggled to her feet.

Too late. The huffing steed, too large to be Domina's, thundered directly for her. Her boots slipped in the mud as she tried to jump aside. She threw her arms over her face and prepared to be trampled.

Instead a strong hand seized her coat collar and hoisted

her up on to the saddle as if she weighed nothing more than a mere satchel.

'Here, boy. What are you doing in this field?' An English voice.

Thank God.

She opened her eyes and caught a glimpse of a red uniform. 'I want to go to that farm.' She pointed towards the group of buildings surrounded by a wall.

'You're English?' He slowed his horse. 'I am headed there. To Hougoumont.'

Was that the name of the farm? Marian did not care. She was grateful to be off her weary feet and to be with a British soldier and not a French one.

The horse quickly reached the patch of woods whose green leaves sprinkled them with leftover raindrops. A low branch snagged Marian's cap, snatching it from her head, and her blonde hair tumbled down her back.

'Good God. You're a woman.' He pulled on the reins and his horse turned round in a circle. 'What the devil are you doing here?'

Marian turned to get a proper look at him. Her eyes widened. She'd seen him before. She and Domina had whispered about the tall and handsome officer they'd spied during a stroll through the Parc of Brussels. His angular face looked strong, his bow-shaped lips firm and decisive, his eyes a piercing hazel.

'I am lost,' she said.

'Do you not know there is about to be a battle?'

She did not wish to debate the matter. 'I was trying to reach somewhere safe.'

'Nowhere is safe,' he snapped. Instead of turning towards the farm, he rode back to where her cap hung on the tree branch, looking as if it had been placed on a peg by the garden door. He snatched it and thrust it into her hands. 'Put the cap back on. Do not let on that you are a woman.'

Did he think she was doltish? She repinned her hair as best she could and covered it with the cap. Behind them came the sounds of men entering the wood. A musketball whizzed past Marian's ear.

'Skirmishers.' The officer set his horse into a gallop so swift the trees suddenly became a blur of brown and green.

They reached Hougoumont gate. 'Captain Landon with a message for Colonel MacDonnell,' he announced.

Marian made a mental note of his name. *Captain Landon.*

The gate opened. 'There are skirmishers in the wood,' he told the men.

'We see them!' one soldier responded, gesturing to a wall where other men were preparing to fire through loopholes. A company of soldiers filed past them out of the gate, undoubtedly to engage the French in the wood.

The soldier took hold of Captain Landon's horse and pointed. 'That's the colonel over there.'

The colonel paced through the yard, watching the men and barking orders. Some of them wore the red coats of the British; others wore a green foreign uniform.

'Stay with me,' Captain Landon told her.

He dismounted and reached up to help her off the horse. Then he gripped her arm as if afraid she might run off and held on to her even when handing the message to the colonel and waiting for him to read it.

The colonel closed the note. 'I want you to wait here a bit until we see what these Frenchies are up to. Then I'll send back my response.' He pointed to Marian. 'Who's the boy?'

'An English lad caught in the thick of things.' Landon squeezed Marian's arm, a warning, she presumed, to go along with his story.

MacDonnell looked at her suspiciously. 'Are you with the army, boy?'

Marian made her voice low. 'No, sir. From Brussels. I wanted to see the battle.'

The colonel laughed. 'Well, you will see a battle, all right. What's your name?'

Marian's mind whirled, trying to think of a name she might remember to answer to. 'Fenton,' she finally said. 'Marion Fenton.' Her given name could be for a boy, and Fenton was Domina's surname. If anything happened to her, God forbid, perhaps Domina's family would be alerted. No one else knew she'd come to Brussels.

Captain Landon said, 'I'll come back to fetch him

after the battle and see he is returned to his family. Where should I put him in the meantime?'

The colonel inclined his head towards the large brick house. 'The château should do. Find him a corner to sit in.'

The captain marched Marian into the château. Green uniformed soldiers filled the hall and adjacent rooms, some gazing out of the windows.

'Why are they in green?' she whispered.

The captain answered, 'They are German. Nassauers.'

The soldiers looked frightened. Marian thought them very young, mere boys, certainly younger than she at nearly twenty-one.

'English boy,' the captain told them, pointing to her. 'English.'

An officer approached them. 'I speak English.'

Captain Landon turned to him. 'This boy is lost. He needs a safe place to stay during the battle.'

'Any room,' replied the officer, his accent heavy. 'Avay from vindow.'

The captain nodded. 'Would you tell your men sh— he's English.'

The officer nodded and spoke to his troops in his Germanic tongue.

Captain Landon led Marian away. They walked through the house, searching, she supposed, for a room without a window.

'I can find my own hiding place, Captain,' she said. 'You must return to your duties.'

'I need to talk to you first.' His voice was low and angry.

She supposed she was in for more scolding. She deserved it, after all.

They walked through a hallway into what must have been a formal drawing room, although its furniture was covered in white cloth.

Captain Landon finally removed his grip and uncovered a small chair, carrying it back to the hallway. 'You will be safest here, I think.' He gave her a fierce look and gestured for her to sit.

She was more than happy to sit. Her legs ached and her feet felt raw from running in wet boots.

He looked down on her, his elbows akimbo. 'Now. Who are you and what the devil are you doing in the middle of a battlefield?'

She met his gaze with defiance. 'I did not intend to be in the middle of the battlefield.'

He merely glared, as if waiting for a better answer.

She took off her cap and plucked the pins from her hair. 'I am Miss Marian Pallant—'

'Not Fenton?' He sounded confused.

She could not blame him. She quickly put her hair in a plait while his eyes bore into her.

'I gave that name in case—in case something happened to me. I was with my friend Domina Fenton, but we became separated in the night.'

'Your friend was with you? What could have brought you out here?' he demanded.

She pinned the plait to the top of her head. 'Domina is Sir Roger Fenton's daughter. She is secretly betrothed to one of the officers and she wanted to be near him during the battle.' It sounded so foolish now. 'I was afraid for her to come alone.'

His eyes widened. 'You are respectable young ladies?'

She did not like the tone of surprise in his voice. 'Of course we are.'

He pursed his lips. 'Respectable young ladies do not dress up as boys and ride out in the middle of the night.'

She covered her hair again with her cap. 'Dressing as boys was preferable to showing ourselves as women.'

He rubbed his face. 'I dare say you are correct in that matter.'

She glanced away. 'I am so worried about Domina.' Turning back, she gestured dismissively. 'I quite agree with you that it was a foolish idea. We became lost, and our horse almost wandered into a French camp. I fell off when we galloped away.' Her stomach twisted in worry. 'I do not know what happened to Domina.'

He gazed at her a long time with those intense hazel

eyes. Finally he said, 'Surely your parents and Domina's must be very worried about you by now.'

She gave a wan smile. 'My parents died a long time ago.'

Allan Landon took in a quick breath as his gaze rested upon her. At this moment Marian Pallant looked nothing like a boy. He could only see a vulnerable and beautiful young woman. Even though her wealth of blonde hair was now hidden, he could not forget the brief moment the locks had framed her face like a golden halo.

'Your parents are dead?' he asked inanely.

She nodded. 'They died of fever in India when I was nine.'

He noticed her voice catch, even though she was obviously trying to disguise any emotion. It reminded him anew that she was a vulnerable young woman, one trying valiantly to keep her wits about her.

'Is Sir Roger Fenton your guardian, then?' he asked.

'No.' She glanced away. 'My guardian does not trouble himself about me overmuch. He leaves my care to his man of business, who knew I was a guest of the Fentons, so I suppose you could say, at the moment, I am in Domina's father's charge.' Her worried look returned. 'I should have talked Domina out of this silly scheme instead of accompanying her. I am so afraid for her.'

She seemed more concerned for her friend than for

herself. He could give no reassurance, however. The French were not known to be gentle with captives, especially female ones—although Allan well remembered one instance when British soldiers were as brutal.

'I suspect the Fentons are frantic over the fate of both of you, then.'

She nodded, looking contrite.

He felt a wave of sympathy for her, even though she'd brought this on herself with her reckless behaviour.

Again her blue eyes sought his. 'Do you have anyone frantic over your fate, Captain?'

Odd that his thoughts skipped over his mother and older brother at home on the family estate in Nottinghamshire and went directly to his father, who had been so proud to have a son in uniform and who would have cheered his son's success, his advance from lieutenant to captain and other battle commendations.

His father had been gone these four years, his life violently snatched away. He had not lived to celebrate his son's victories in battle, to lament the horrors he'd endured, nor to shudder at the times he'd narrowly escaped death himself.

Miss Pallant's brows rose. 'Is it so difficult to think of someone who might worry over you?'

He cocked his head. 'My mother and brother would worry, I suppose.'

She gave him a quizzical look, making him wonder

if his grief over his father's death showed too clearly in his eyes. It was his turn to shutter his emotions.

She glanced away again. 'It must be hard for them.'

Was it hard on them? he wondered. He'd always imagined they were used to him being far away. He'd been gone longer than his father.

A German voice shouted what could only have been an order. The tramping of feet and cacophony of men's voices suggested to Allan that the French must be closing in on the farm.

'What does it mean?' she asked, her voice breathless.

He tried to appease her alarm. 'I suspect the Nassauers have been ordered out of the château. That is all.'

Her eyes flashed like a cornered fox. 'That does not sound good. I wish I had stayed in Brussels.' Her expression turned ironical. 'It is too late to be remorseful, is it not?'

'My father used to say it is better to do what one is supposed to do now than to be remorseful later.'

She kept her eyes upon him, and he realised he had brought up the subject he most wanted to avoid.

'A wise man,' she said.

'He was.' The pain of his father's loss struck him anew.

She regarded him with sympathy. 'He is deceased?'

'He was killed.' He cleared his throat. 'You heard,

no doubt, of the Luddite riots in Nottinghamshire a few years ago?'

She nodded.

'My father was the local magistrate. The rioters broke into our house and killed him.'

Her expression seemed to mirror his pain. 'How terrible for you.'

Suddenly muskets cracked and shouts were raised, the sounds of a siege.

She paled. 'The French are attacking?'

He paced. 'Yes. And I must go.' He hated to leave her. 'Stay here, out of the way. You'll be safe. I'll come back for you after the battle. With any luck I can see you returned to Brussels. Perhaps news of this escapade will not spread and your reputation will be preserved.'

'My reputation.' She gave a dry laugh. 'What a trifle it seems now.' She gazed at him with a new intensity. 'You will take care, Captain?'

Allan thought he would carry the impact of her glittering blue eyes throughout the battle. 'Do not worry over me.'

More muskets cracked.

He turned in the sound's direction. 'I must hurry.'

'Yes, you must, Captain.' She put on a brave smile.

'I'll be back for you,' he vowed, as much for himself as for her.

She extended her hand and he wrapped his fingers around it for a brief moment.

'Godspeed,' she whispered.

Allan forced himself to leave her alone in the hallway. He retraced their steps through the house, angry that her foolish act placed her in such danger, and angrier still that he could not extricate her from it.

He had his duty, his orders. Orders must be obeyed.

Allan's duty was to be Generals Tranville and Picton's messenger during the battle. He was paired with Edwin Tranville, the general's son, and both were given the same messages to carry so that if one was shot down, the other might still make it through. Unfortunately, right after the first message was placed in their hands, Edwin disappeared, hiding no doubt.

Edwin had hid from battle countless times on the Peninsula. Afterward he would emerge with some plausible explanation of his whereabouts. This time, however, his cowardice meant that Allan alone must ensure Tranville and Picton's messages made it through.

The outcome of the battle could depend upon it.

So he had no choice. He had to leave Miss Pallant here at Hougoumont, which could well become the most dangerous place in the entire battle. The French would need to attack the farm to reach Wellington's right flank, and Wellington ordered Hougoumont held at all costs.

Allan reached the entrance of the château, Miss Pallant's clear blue eyes still haunting him. The mixture of courage and vulnerability within her pulled at his sensibilities, making him ache to stay to protect her.

But the soldier in him had orders to be elsewhere.

This was more blame to lay at Edwin's feet. If Edwin possessed even half of Miss Pallant's courage, Allan could trust him to carry the generals' messages, and seek permission to take her back to Brussels.

Outside the château Allan stopped one of the Coldstream Guardsmen, the British regiment defending Hougoumont. 'What is the situation?'

'Our men have been driven back from the wood. The enemy is close by.'

Allan ran to the wall and looked through a loophole while an infantryman reloaded.

The woods below teemed with the blue coats of the French, their cream trousers brown with mud. As they broke into the open, British soldiers, firing from the walls, mowed them down. Their bodies littered the grass.

Allan searched for Colonel MacDonnell and found him inside the farmhouse at an upper window that provided a good view of the fighting.

MacDonnell said, 'You'd better wait a bit, Landon.'

'I agree, sir.'

The sheer number of Frenchmen coming at the walls and falling from the musket fire was staggering. The enemy regiment was one commanded by Prince Jerome,

Napoleon's brother, but the walls of the farm offered good protection. The French had no such advantage.

Allan turned to MacDonnell again. 'May I be of service in some way?'

The colonel looked proud. 'My men are doing all I could wish. I have no need of you.'

Allan could not merely sit around and watch. He returned to the yard and searched for any weakness in the defence. One soldier was shot in the forehead, the force of the ball throwing him back on to the ground. French ladders appeared at the gap created by the man's loss.

Allan seized the man's musket, powder and ammunition and took his place at the wall, firing through the loophole until the ladders and the men trying to climb them fell upon the ground already filled with dead and wounded.

'Look!' cried one of the guardsmen nearby. 'The captain knows how to load and fire a musket!'

Other guardsmen laughed, but soon forgot about him as another wave of blue-coated soldiers tried to reach the walls.

Allan lost track of time, so caught was he in the rhythm of loading and firing. Eventually the shots around him slowed.

'They are retreating!' a man cried.

The French were withdrawing, like a wave ebbing from the shore.

Allan put down the musket and left his place at the wall. He met MacDonnell near the stable.

'Get word to Wellington that we repelled the first attack, but if they keep coming we'll need more ammunition,' MacDonnell told him.

One of the soldiers brought out his horse and Allan mounted the steed. 'I'll get your message through.' He didn't know how to say what he most wanted MacDonnell to know. 'The boy is in the château, but have someone look out for him, will you?'

MacDonnell nodded, but one of his officers called him away at the same time.

Allan had to ride off without any assurance that MacDonnell would even remember the presence of the boy Miss Pallant pretended to be.

Chapter Two

The shouts of the soldiers and the crack of musket fire signalled a new attack. Marian's eyes flew open and she shook off the haze of sleep. Her exhaustion had overtaken her during the lull in fighting.

Now it was clear the French were attacking the farm again. The sounds were even louder and more alarming than before. So were the screams of the wounded horses and men.

She hugged her knees to her chest as the barrage continued. Had the captain made it through? With every shot in the first attack, she'd feared he'd been struck and now her fears for him were renewed. One thing she knew for certain. He was gone—either gone back to the British line or just…gone.

She cried out in frustration.

He must survive. To think that he would not just plunged her into more despair.

The hallway suddenly felt like a prison. Its walls might wrap her in relative safety, but each urgent shout, each agonised scream, cut into her like a sword thrust. To hear, but not see, the events made everything worse. She hated feeling alone and useless while men were dying.

She stood and paced.

This was absurd. Surely there was something she could do to assist. She'd promised Captain Landon that she would stay in the hallway, but he was not present to stop her, was he?

Marian left where the captain had placed her and made her way to the entrance hall.

The green-uniformed soldiers were gone, but several of the Coldstream Guards rushed past her. The sounds of the siege intensified now that she'd emerged from her cocoon of a hiding place.

The château's main door swung open and two men carried another man inside. Blood poured from a wound in his chest.

She rushed forwards. 'I can help. Tell me what to do.' She forgot to make her voice low.

They did not seem to notice. 'No help for this one, laddie,' one answered in a thick Scottish accent. They dumped the injured soldier in a corner and rushed out again.

Marian looked around her. Several wounded men leaned against the walls of the hall. The marble floor was smeared with their blood.

Her stomach rebelled at the sight.

She held her breath for a moment, determined not to be sick. 'I must do something,' she cried.

One of the men, blood oozing through the fingers he held against his arm, answered her. 'Find us some bandages, lad.'

Bandages. Where would she find bandages?

She ran back to the drawing room where the captain had found the chair for her. Pulling the covers off the furniture, she gathered as much of the white cloth as she could carry in her arms. She returned to the hall and dumped the cloth in a pile next to the man clutching his bleeding arm.

'I need a knife,' she said to him.

He shook his head, wincing in pain.

Another man whose face was covered in blood fumbled through his coat. 'Here you go, lad.' He held out a small penknife.

Marian took the knife, still sticky with his blood, and used it to start a rent in the cloth so she could rip it into strips. She worked as quickly as she could, well aware that the man the soldiers had carried in was still moaning and coughing. Most of the other men suffered silently.

She knew nothing about tending to the injured. It stood to reason, though, that bleeding wounds needed to be bandaged, as the wounded soldier had suggested.

Marian grabbed a fistful of the strips of cloth and turned to him. 'I'll tend that other man first, then you, sir.' She gestured to the moaning man who'd been so swiftly left to die. 'And you,' she told the man who'd given her the knife.

'Do that, lad. I'm not so bad off.' His voice was taut with pain.

Marian touched his arm in sympathy and started for the gravely wounded soldier.

Her courage flagged as she reached him. Never had she seen such grievous injuries. Steeling herself, she gripped the bandages and forced herself to kneel at his side.

He was so young! Not much older than Domina's brother. Blood gurgled from a hole in his abdomen. Her hand trembling, she used some of the cloth to sponge it away. The dark pink of his innards became visible, and Marian recoiled, thinking she would surely be sick.

He seized her arm, gripping her hard. 'My mum,' he rasped. 'My mum.' His glassy eyes regarded her with alarm, and his breathing rattled like a rusty gate. 'My mum.'

She clasped his other hand, tears stinging her eyes. 'Your mum will be so proud of you.' It was not enough to say, not when this young man would die without ever seeing his mother again.

The young man's eyes widened and he rose up, still gripping her. With one deep breath he collapsed and air slowly left his lungs as his eyes turned blank.

'No,' she cried. The faces of her mother and father when death had taken them flashed before her. 'No.'

The room turned black and sound echoed. She was going to faint and the dead young man's hand was still in hers.

The door opened and two more men staggered in. She forced her eyes open and took several deep breaths.

More wounds. More blood. More men in need.

She released the young soldier's hand and gingerly closed his eyes. 'God keep you,' she whispered.

Marian grabbed her clean cloth and returned to the man who had told her to get bandages. 'You are next,' she said with a bravado she didn't feel inside.

He gestured to the soldier who had given her the knife. 'Tend him first.'

She nodded and kneeled on the floor, wiping away the blood on the soldier's head so she could see the wound. His skin was split right above his hairline. Swallowing hard, Marian pressed the wound closed with her fingers and wrapped a bandage tightly around his head.

'Thank you, lad,' the man said.

She moved to the first man and wrapped his wounded arm. Not taking time to think, she scuttled over to the next man, discovering yet another horrifying sight. She took a deep breath and tended that man's wound as well. One by one she dressed all the soldiers' wounds.

When she'd finished, one of the soldiers caught her arm. 'Can y'fetch us some water, lad?'

Water. Of course. They must be very thirsty. She was thirsty, as a matter of fact. She went in search of the kitchen, but found its pump dry. There was a well in the middle of the courtyard, near the stables, she remembered. She found a fairly clean bucket and ladle on the kitchen shelf and hurried back to the hall.

'I'll bring you water,' she told the wounded men as she crossed the room to the château's entrance.

When she stepped outside, the courtyard was filled with soldiers. Men at the walls fired and reloaded their muskets, others repositioned themselves or moved the wounded away. The fighting was right outside the gate. She could hear it. French musket balls might find their way into the courtyard, she feared.

Gathering all her courage, Marian started for the well. Before she reached it, a man shouted, 'They're coming in the gate!'

To her horror a huge French soldier, wielding an ax, hewed his way into the courtyard followed by others. It was a frightening sight as they hacked their way toward the château. Several Guardsmen set upon them. The huge Frenchman was knocked to the ground, and one of the Guards plunged a bayonet into his back.

'Close the gate! Close the gate!'

Men pushed against the wooden gate as more French soldiers strained to get in. Without thinking, Marian dropped her bucket and added her slight strength to the effort to force the gates closed. Finally they secured it, but the fighting was still fierce between the British soldiers and the few Frenchmen who had made it inside.

Marian picked her way through the fighting and returned to the well. She pumped water into the bucket, her heart pounding at the carnage around her. When the bucket was full, one of the Guardsmen shoved a boy towards her, a French drummer boy, his drum still strapped to his chest.

'Take him,' the Guardsman said. 'Keep him out of harm's way.'

She took the boy's hand and pulled him back to the château with her.

'*Restez ici,*' she ordered. *Remain here.*

The drummer boy sat immediately, hugging his drum, his eyes as huge as saucers.

Marian passed the water to the men and told them about the gate closing and about the drummer boy. A moment later, more men entered the château, needing tending.

Eventually the musket fire became sporadic, and she heard a man shout, 'They're retreating.'

She paused for a moment in thankful relief.

'It is not over yet, lad,' one of the wounded men told her. 'D'you hear the guns?' The pounding of artillery had started an hour ago. 'We're not rid of Boney yet. I wager you could see what is happening on the battlefield from the upper floors.'

'Do you think so?' Marian responded.

'Go. Take a look-see.' The man gestured to the stairway. 'I'll watch the drummer.'

She could not resist. She climbed the stairs to the highest floor. In each of the rooms Guardsmen manned the windows. One soldier turned towards her when Marian peeked into the room.

'Where did you come from, lad?' the man asked.

She remembered to lower her voice this time. 'Brussels, sir. I came to see the battle.'

He laughed and gestured for her to approach. 'Well, come see, then.'

The sight was terrifying. On one side thousands of French soldiers marched twenty-four-men deep and one hundred and fifty wide. The rhythmic beating of the French *pas de charge* wafted up to the château's top windows. On the Allied Army side a regiment of Belgian soldiers fled the field. In between a red-coated soldier galloped across the ridge in full view of the French columns. Was it Captain Landon? Her throat constricted in anxiety.

Please let him be safe, she prayed.

'Where are the English?' There were no other soldiers in sight. Just the lone rider she imagined to be the captain.

'Wellington's got 'em hiding, I expect.' The soldier pointed out of the window. 'See those hedges?'

She nodded.

'Our boys are behind there, I'd wager.'

As the columns moved by the hedge, the crack of fire-arms could be heard. 'Rifles,' the soldier explained.

The columns edged away from the rifle fire and lost their formation. Suddenly a line of English soldiers rose up and fired upon them. Countless French soldiers fell as if they were in a game of skittles, but still others advanced until meeting the British line. The two sides began fighting hand to hand.

Marian turned away from the sight. 'Napoleon has too many men.'

'The Cuirassiers are coming.' Anxiety sounded in the soldier's voice. Cuirassiers were the French cavalry.

Marian felt like weeping, but she turned to watch the Cuirassiers on their powerful horses charging toward the English soldiers while the French drums still beat, over and over.

A battle was not glorious to watch, she thought, closing her eyes again. It was all about men wounded and men dying, not at all what she and Domina had imagined.

'They're breaking!' the soldier said.

Marian could not bear to see her countrymen running away like the French had run from Hougoumont. Her chin trembled and her throat constricted with unspent tears.

'I'll be damned.' The soldier whistled. 'If that is not a sight.'

Marian opened her eyes.

The French, not the British, had broken from their

lines and were running away. 'I don't understand. Why did they run?'

'Who can tell?' The soldier laughed. 'Let's be grateful they did.'

She was indeed grateful, but by now she knew not to ask if the battle was over. The French would try again and Napoleon was known to pull victory from the jaws of defeat.

Marian took a breath and mentally braced herself for whatever came next.

Allan rode the ridge. After taking MacDonnell's message to Wellington, he searched for Picton, who seemed nowhere to be found. He'd settle for Tranville, then, for new orders. From the distance he'd seen the second siege of Hougoumont and gave a cheer when the French had again been repelled.

He reached his regiment, the Royal Scots, just as the French attacked. Artillery pummelled the French columns, but still men in the front ranks fought hard in hand-to-hand combat. Allan unsheathed his sword and rode into the thick of it.

The fighting was fierce and bloody. Fists flew and bayonets jabbed and the air filled with the thud of bodies slamming into each other, of grunts and growls and cries of pain. Allan slashed at the French soldiers, more than once slicing into their flesh as they were about to kill. They came at him, trying to pull him from his horse.

He managed to keep both his horse and himself in one piece, but blood and mud splattered on to his clothing. By the time the French retreated his arm was leaden with fatigue, and he breathed hard from the effort of the battle.

For a mere moment he indulged in the relief of still being alive, but only for a moment. He quickly resumed his search for Picton and Tranville, but spied Gabriel Deane instead. He headed towards his friend. Gabe, too, would have fought without heed to his own survival and Allan said a silent prayer of thanks that he appeared unscathed. General Tranville had been always been unfair to Gabe, denying him promotion because Gabe's father was in trade.

'Gabe!' he called. 'Have you seen Picton?'

Gabe rode up to him. 'Picton is dead. Shot right after he gave the order to attack.'

Allan bowed his head. 'I am sorry to hear of it.' The eccentric old soldier might have retired after this. 'Where is Tranville, then?'

'Struck down as well,' Gabe answered.

'Dead?' Allan would not so strongly grieve if Tranville was lost.

Gabe shook his head. 'I do not know. I saw him fall and I've not seen him since.'

Orders came for the cavalry to advance upon the re-treating French. Allan and Gabe grew silent as they watched the Scots Greys ride out, like magnificent waves of the ocean on their great grey horses.

'Perhaps we will win this after all,' Gabe said.

They *must* win, Allan thought as they watched the cavalry pursue the French all the way to the line of their artillery. The Allies were on the side of all that was right. Napoleon had broken the peace, and too many men had already died to feed his vanity.

Gabe struck Allan on the arm and pointed to where French lancers approached from the side. 'This cannot be good.'

'Sound the retreat!' Wellington's order carried all the way to Allan and Gabe's ears.

The bugler played the staccato rhythm that signalled an order to retreat, but it was too late. The cavalry were too far away to hear and too caught up in the excitement of routing the French infantry.

Allan and Gabe watched in horror as those gallant men were cut down by the lancers, whose fresh steeds outmatched the British cavalry's blown ones.

'Perhaps I spoke too soon of victory.' Gabe's voice turned low. He rode off to prepare his men for whatever came next.

Allan asked several other soldiers if they had seen Tranville. No one could confirm his death or his survival. He found the officer who had assumed Picton's command.

'I have messengers aplenty, Landon,' the man said. 'Make yourself useful wherever you see fit.'

Allan glanced towards Hougoumont, now being pounded by cannon fire. Dare he go there? See to the safety of one foolish woman over the needs of the many? He frowned. Cannon fire made Hougoumont even more dangerous, but perhaps if she stayed put as he'd asked she'd stay safe.

The cannon were also firing upon the infantry, and Wellington ordered them to move back behind the ridge and to lie down. Allan spied a whole regiment of Belgian troops deserting the field.

The cowards. Could they not see? The battle was far from over. Victory was still possible. The British had already captured thousands of French soldiers and were marching them toward Brussels.

Allan turned back again to Hougoumont, still being battered relentlessly.

Heading to the château became instantly impossible. A shout passed quickly through the ranks. 'Form square! Form square!'

A battalion of men stood two to four ranks deep, forming the shape of a square and presenting bayonets. Cavalry horses would not charge into bayonets, so, as long as the square did not break in panic, cavalry were powerless against them.

Allan rode to the crest of the ridge to see what prompted the order. Masses of French soldiers rode towards him, their horses shoulder to shoulder, advancing at a steadily increasing pace.

What was Napoleon thinking? There was no infantry marching in support of the cavalry. This was insanity.

But it was very real. The French advance was so massive, it shook the ground like thunder. The vision of a thousand horses and men was as awe inspiring as it was foolish. Allan stood rapt at the sight. He almost waited too late to gallop to the nearest square.

The square opened like a hinged door to allow him inside.

Another officer rode up to him. 'Captain Landon, good to see you in one piece.'

It was Lieutenant Vernon, whom he'd first met that ill-fated day at Badajoz. Vernon had been a mere ensign then. He had also been in the fighting at Quatre Bras two days ago. Gabe and Allan had run into him afterwards.

'Same to you, Vernon,' Allan said.

The roar of the French cavalry grew louder and shouts of *'Vive l'Empereur!'* reached their ears. A moment later the plumes of the Cuirassier helmets became visible at the crest of the ridge.

'Prepare to receive cavalry,' the British officers shouted.

Horses and riders poured over the crest, some slipping in the mud or falling into the ditch below, but countless numbers of them galloped straight for the squares. The men in the front line crouched with bayonets thrust forwards; the back line stood ready to fire a volley.

All depended upon the men remaining steady in the face of the massed charge.

Allan rode to one side of the square. 'Steady, men,' he told them. 'They cannot break you. Steady.'

The riders might have been willing to ride into the square, but the horses balked at the sight of the bayonets pointed towards them. They turned and galloped past, the men on their backs only able to fire a single pistol shot each.

The British infantry raked them with a barrage of musket fire, and the British cannon fire was unceasing. Smoke was everywhere, and through it the cries of wounded men.

Finally the cavalry retreated, but it was a short respite. They reformed and attacked again.

The squares held.

After the second attack, Allan left the square to ride to the ridge to reconnoitre. His attention riveted not on the French cavalry regrouping, but on Hougoumont.

The château at Hougoumont was on fire, the château he'd forbidden Miss Pallant to leave.

He immediately urged his horse into full gallop, risking interception from the French. He was hell-bent on reaching Hougoumont, praying he had not forced Miss Pallant into a nightmare from which she could not escape.

The gate did not open to him, even though there were only a few Frenchmen firing at the men on the walls.

'How can I get in?' he called as soon as he was close enough.

One of the soldiers pointed to another entrance, well protected by muskets.

He rode into heat and smoke. The barn was afire as well as the château and some soldiers had run in to pull the horses to safety. One of the animals broke free and ran back into the fire.

Allan tied his horse to a post and went to the door of the château, sure that during the rigours of battle the *boy* he'd brought there would have been forgotten. He prayed the fire had not yet consumed the hallway.

As he reached the door, he almost collided with someone dragging a man out. Someone dressed in boy's clothes.

'Miss Pallant!' he cried, forgetting her disguise.

She glanced at him as she struggled to get the man, too injured and weak to walk, out of the door, away from the fire. 'Help me, Captain.'

He took one of the man's arms and pulled him outside to the middle of the courtyard. As soon as she let go of the man, she started for the château's entrance again.

He caught her arm. 'What are you doing?'

She wrenched it away. 'There are more men in there.' She dashed inside again.

Allan followed her straight into an inferno. She ran

to a corner and pulled a man by the collar of his coat, sliding him across the hall. Allan glanced up. The fire swirled above them and pieces of ceiling fell, one narrowly missing her. She paid no heed. Allan hurried through and found another man trying to crawl away from the flames. He flung the man over his shoulder and helped pull Miss Pallant's soldier at the same time. 'Hurry!' he cried. 'Now!'

They made it out of the door just as the ceiling collapsed.

'No!' She turned and tried to rush back in.

Still holding the wounded man, he caught her arm. 'You cannot go in there.' He gripped her hard. 'Now get the man you have saved to the courtyard.'

She nodded and pulled her charge away from the burning building, while the agonised screams of the trapped men pierced Allan's very soul. As soon as he lowered his injured soldier to the ground near the other men she had saved, Miss Pallant ran towards the château again. He tore after her, catching her around the waist before she charged into the inferno.

She struggled. 'There are men in there. Can't you hear them?'

He held her tight, his mouth by her ear. 'I hear them, but there is nothing we can do to save them.'

She twisted around and buried her face into his chest, only to pull away again. 'The little boy! The drummer boy! Is he still in there?'

One of the men on the ground answered her, 'He escaped, lad. I saw him. He's unharmed.'

Allan pulled her back into his arms and she collapsed against him.

'How many did you pull out of there?' he asked her.

'Only seven.' Her voice cracked.

Seven men? How had she mustered the strength? The courage? 'Those seven men are alive because of you.'

She shook her head. 'It was not enough. There are more.'

'They are gone.' He backed her away from the château where the flames were so close and hot that he feared they would combust like the château's walls. 'Come take some water.'

The well was busy with men drawing water to fight the fire and Allan had to wait to draw water to drink. She cupped her hands and scooped water from the well's bucket. Allan drank as well. One of the soldiers held out his shako and Allan filled it, passing it around to the rescued men. Allan's horse, tethered nearby, pulled at its reins, its eyes white with fear.

While the fire raged the French infantry attacked Hougoumont again. Colonel MacDonnell shouted orders to the men at the walls to keep firing. He and his officers moved through the area alert for weaknesses, ordering them reinforced.

Allan sat Miss Pallant on the ground, forcing her to rest. He lowered himself beside her.

'Will it never end?' she whispered, echoing Allan's own thoughts. As the sounds of the siege surrounded them, she glanced at him as if noticing him for the first time. 'Why are you here, Captain? You said you would come when it was over.'

He rubbed his face. 'No one had need of me. General Picton is dead and Tranville, too, most likely—'

Her eyes widened in surprise. 'Tranville!'

'General Lord Tranville. My superior officer.' What did she know of Tranville?

'Surely he did not return to the army?' Her voice rose.

'Are you acquainted with him?'

She pressed her hand against her forehead. 'He is my late aunt's husband. And my guardian.'

'Your guardian!'

'I—I have had no direct contact with him since my aunt died.' She averted her gaze. 'I never imagined he would return to the army, not since he inherited his title.'

Tranville had become a baron before the Allies left Spain. Both he and his son Edwin returned to England then and did not rejoin the regiment until Napoleon escaped from Elba a few months ago.

She bowed her head. 'He is dead?'

Allan put his hand on hers in sympathy. 'It appears

so. Several of his men saw him struck down. No one has seen him since.'

She paused before speaking. 'You must know my cousin Edwin. Is—is he still alive?'

Of course Edwin was alive, safely hiding out of harm's way. 'I suspect he is. I've not heard otherwise.'

She put on a brave face, but clearly she was battling her emotions. 'Well. I have rested enough. I must see if the wounded need attending.' She rose.

Allan rose with her and gripped her arm. 'No. It has become too dangerous for you here.'

The buildings still burned, but the Coldstream Guards, the Nassauers and the others had again set the French into retreat. How many more times could the French be repelled, though?

'I'm getting you out now.' Allan's duty was clear to him now. The army did not immediately need him, but this woman, the ward of his superior officer, did.

'But the wounded—' she protested.

'You've saved them. You have done enough.' Besides, he did not know how much more she could stand. She looked as if she might keel over from exhaustion at any moment.

She allowed him to lead her away. Allan took her to his horse, still skittish from the fire around them.

He lifted her on to the horse's back and called to one of the soldiers. 'Which way out?'

The man pointed. 'The south gate.'

At the gate Allan mounted behind her and spoke to the soldier who opened it for them. 'Tell MacDonnell I am taking the boy out of here now.'

Once through the gate Allan headed towards the Allied line, determined to at least get her beyond where the fighting would take place. The smoke from Hougoumont obscured his vision, thinning a bit as they proceeded through the orchard.

Suddenly pain shot through his shoulder, followed by the crack of rifle fire. He jerked back and his shako flew from his head. It was all he could do to stay in the saddle.

He pushed Miss Pallant down on the neck of his horse and covered her with his body. 'Snipers! Stay down.' He hung on with all his strength. 'I am hit.'

Chapter Three

Marian felt the captain's weight upon her back and sensed his sudden unsteadiness. The horse fled the orchard and galloped across a field towards a ridge where a line of cannons stood. Just as they came near the cannons fired, each with a spew of flames and white smoke and a deafening boom.

The horse made a high-pitched squeal and galloped even faster, away from the sound and the smoke, plunging into a field of tall rye grass, its shoots whipping against their arms and legs.

'Captain!' Marian worried over his wounds.

'Hold on.' Pain filled his voice. 'Cannot stop her.'

'Are you much hurt?' she yelled.

He did not answer at first. 'Yes,' he finally said.

Marian closed her eyes and pressed her face against the horse's neck, praying the captain had not received a fatal shot.

The horse found a dry, narrow path through the field and raced down its winding length, following its twists and turns until Marian had no idea how they would find their way out. The explosions of the cannon faded into some vague direction behind them until finally the horse slowed to an ex- hausted walk.

'We're safe, at least,' the captain said, sitting up again.

She turned to look at him. Blood stained the left side of his chest and he swayed in the saddle.

'You need tending,' she cried.

'First place we find.' His words were laboured.

They wandered aimlessly through farm fields that seemed to have no end. The sounds of the battle grew even fainter.

Finally Marian spied a thin column of smoke. She pointed to it. 'Look, Captain.'

It led to a small hut and barn, at the moment looking as grand as a fine country estate.

Marian called out, 'Hello? Help us!'

No one responded.

She tried saying it in French. *'Au secours.'*

Nothing but the distant sounds of the battle.

She turned around. Captain Landon swayed in the saddle. 'I must see to your wounds, Captain. We must stop here.'

The door to the hut opened and a little girl, no more than four years old, peered out.

'There is someone here!' Marian dismounted and

carefully approached the little girl, who watched her with curiosity as she reached the door.

'Where are your parents?' she asked the child.

The little girl popped a thumb in her mouth and returned a blank stare.

Marian tried French, but the child's expression did not change. Thumb still in her mouth, the little girl rattled off some words, pointing towards a dirt road that led away from the hut.

It was not a language Marian understood. Flemish, most likely.

'This isn't going to be easy,' she muttered. 'We each of us cannot make ourselves understood.' She crouched to the child's level. 'Your mama? Mama?'

'Mama!' The child smiled and pointed to the road, chattering again.

Marian turned from the doorway to Captain Landon. 'Her mother cannot be far or I think she'd be in distress. She's not at all worried.' Perhaps her mother had merely gone to the fields for a moment. 'We need to stay. At least long enough for me to look at you.'

Allan winced. 'I agree.'

He started to dismount on his own, nearly losing his balance. Marian ran to him, ready to catch him if he fell, but he held on to the horse for support.

He made a weak gesture to the barn. 'In there. Won't see us right away. Just in case.'

'Just in case what?'

His brows knit. 'In case French soldiers come by.'

The sounds of battle had disappeared completely, but they did not know which side would be the victor.

He led the horse into the barn.

It was larger than the hut, with three stalls. In one a milk cow contentedly chewed her cud. The other stalls had no animals, but were piled with fresh-smelling hay. A shared trough was filled with clean-looking water. The captain's horse went immediately to the water and drank.

Holding on to the walls, the captain made his way to one of the empty stalls. He lowered himself on to the soft hay, his back leaning against the wood that separated this stall from the other, and groaned in pain.

'I need more light if I am to see your wound.' The sun was low in the sky and the barn was too dark for her to examine him. She glanced around and found an oil lantern. 'I can light it from the fireplace in the hut. I'll be right back.'

The little girl had stepped outside the hut, her thumb back in her mouth. Marian gestured with the lantern and the child chattered at her some more, but Marian could only smile and nod at her as she walked inside.

The hut was nothing more than one big room with a dirt floor, a table and chairs and a big fireplace with a small fire smouldering beneath a big iron pot. Curtains hid where the beds must be. Marian found a taper by the fireplace and used it to light the lantern.

Back in the barn, Marian hung the lantern on a nearby peg and knelt beside the captain. He was wet with blood. 'We must remove your coat.'

He nodded, pulling off his shoulder belt and trying to work his buttons.

'I'll do that.' Marian unbuttoned his coat.

He leaned forwards and she pulled off the sleeve from his right arm first. There was as much blood soaking the back of his coat as the front. He uttered a pained sound as she pulled the sleeve off of his left arm. 'I am sorry,' she whispered.

She reached for his shirt but he stopped her. 'Not proper.'

Proper? She nearly laughed. 'Do not be tiresome, Captain.' She quickly took his shirt off too.

The wound, a hole in his shoulder the size of a gold sovereign, still oozed blood, and there was a corresponding one in his back that was only slightly smaller.

'The ball passed through you,' she said in relief. She would not have relished attempting to remove a ball from a man's flesh. 'I need a cloth to clean it.'

'In my pocket.'

There was a clean handkerchief in the right pocket. She dipped it in the water trough and used it to clean the wound.

Even as she worked Marian could not fail to notice his broad shoulders and the sculpted contours of his chest. Beneath her hand his muscles were firm. She and

Domina had admired his appearance in uniform what seemed an age ago when they'd first glimpsed him in the Parc. *You should see him naked, Domina,* she said silently to herself.

Marian had stuffed rolls of bandage in her pockets before the fire. She pulled them out and wrapped his wound.

'Where did you learn to tend wounds?' he asked.

She smiled. 'At Hougoumont.'

He looked shocked. 'At Hougoumont?'

'It was all I could do.' The sounds and smell and heat of the fires at Hougoumont returned. Tears stung her eyes as she again heard the cries of men trapped inside.

She forced herself to stop thinking of it. 'I really have been a gently bred young lady.' At least since leaving India, she had been. In India she remembered running free.

She tied off the bandages. 'How does that feel, Captain?'

'Good.' His voice was tight.

She made a face. 'I know it hurts like the devil.'

His lips twitched into a smile that vanished into a spasm of pain. 'We should be on our way.' He tried to stand, but swayed and fell against the stall. 'Ahhhh!' he cried.

She jumped to her feet and caught him before he slipped to the ground. 'You cannot ride.'

His face was very pale. 'Must get you to Brussels.'

'Or die trying? I won't have it!' She pointed to his horse, now munching hay, coat damp with sweat and muscles trembling. 'Your horse is exhausted and you have lost a great deal of blood.'

Captain Landon tried to pull out of her supporting arm to go towards his horse. 'She needs tending. Rubbing down.'

She held him tight. 'You sit. I will look after your horse.'

He frowned. 'You cannot—'

'I can indeed. I know how to tend a horse.' This was a complete falsehood, of course, but he would not know she never paid much attention to horses except to ride them.

With her help, he sat down again and she found a horse blanket clean enough to wrap around him. A further search located a piece of sackcloth that she used to wipe off the horse's sweaty coat. She removed the horse's saddle and carried it and the saddlebags over to the captain.

His eyes seemed to have trouble focusing on her. 'Is there some water?'

Water. She could suddenly smell it from the trough, and became aware of her own thirst. Surely there must be somewhere to get water without sharing it with the animals. 'I'll find some.'

There was a noise at the doorway. The little girl was watching them.

Marian gestured to her, pointing to the water and making a motion like a pump. *'L'eau?'*

The child popped her thumb into her mouth again and stared.

Marian rubbed her brow. 'I wish I knew how to say *water.'*

'Water?' The child blinked.

'Yes, yes.' Marian nodded. 'Water.'

The little girl led her to a pump behind the hut. Marian filled a nearby bucket and cupped her hands, drinking her fill. The child left her, but soon returned with a tin cup and handed it to her.

'Thank you,' she said.

The girl smiled. *'Dank u. Dank u. Dank u.'*

Marian carried the bucket and cup to the barn. The captain opened his eyes when she came near.

'Water.' She smiled, lifting the bucket to show him. She set it down and filled the cup for him.

His hand shook as he lifted the cup to his lips, but he swallowed eagerly. Afterwards he rested against the stall again.

And looked worse by the minute.

'When Valour is rested, we'll start out again.' Even his voice was weaker.

'Valour?'

'Valour.' He swallowed. 'My horse.'

She laughed. 'But she was not valorous! She bolted away from the cannons.'

He rose to the horse's defence. 'The fire frightened her. She's used to cannon.'

Then it must have been the flash of flame from the cannonade that had set the horse on her terrified gallop.

And brought them to this place.

She sat next to him, suddenly weary herself.

He seemed to be having difficulty keeping his eyes open. 'The cannon stopped. It is over.' He took a breath. 'I wonder who won.'

'We shall learn that tomorrow.' Marian tried to infuse her voice with a confidence she did not feel. Back in England one day had always seemed much like the last, but here, who knew what tomorrow would bring?

The captain coughed and cried out with the pain it created. It frightened Marian how pale he looked and how much it hurt him to simply take a breath. Soon his eyes closed and his breathing relaxed.

Let him sleep, she told herself, even though she felt very alone without his company. Memories of the day flooded her mind. The face of the dying soldier. The fire.

Eventually even those images could not keep her eyes from becoming very heavy. She'd just begun to doze when she heard voices outside. The parents returning?

She shot to her feet and peeked out of the door.

A man and a woman in peasant garb led a heavily laden mule. The little girl ran out to meet them. She pointed towards the barn.

Marian stepped outside. The man and woman both dropped their chins in surprise. She supposed she looked a fright, black with soot, clothing torn and stained with the captain's blood and the blood of other men she'd tended. She was dressed as a boy, she must recall. They would think her a boy.

'*Bonjour,*' she began and tried explaining her presence in French.

Their blank stares matched their little daughter's.

She sighed. '*Anglais?*'

They shook their heads.

There was no reason to expect peasants to speak anything but their own language. What use would they have for French or English? At least Marian knew one word of Flemish now. *Water.* She almost laughed.

Her gaze drifted to the mule. She expected to see it carrying hay or harvested crops or something, but its cargo was nothing so mundane. The mule was burdened with French cavalry helmets and bundles of red cloth.

Loot from the battlefield. Marian felt the blood drain from her face. They had been stripping the dead.

Bile rose into her throat, but she swallowed it back and gestured for them to follow her into the barn.

She pointed to Captain Landon. 'English,' she said.

'Injured.' Maybe they would understand something if she happened upon another word their languages had in common. 'Help us.' She fished in the pocket of her pantaloons and found a Belgian coin. She handed it to the man, who turned it over in his hand and nodded with approval.

He and his wife went outside and engaged in a lively discussion, which Marian hoped did not include a plan to kill them in their sleep. People who could strip the dead might be capable of anything. As a precaution she went through the captain's things and found his pistol. Hoping it was loaded and primed, she stuck it in her pocket.

Finally the man stepped back in. He nodded and gestured about the stall. She understood. They were to remain in the barn.

'Food?' she asked.

His brows knit.

'Nourriture,' she tried, making as if she were eating. 'Bread.'

He grinned and nodded. *'Brood.'*

'Yes. Yes. *Brood.'*

He gestured for her to wait.

She sank down next to the captain. 'We will have bread anyway.' Her brow furrowed. 'At least I hope *brood* is bread.'

The captain opened his eyes briefly, but closed them

again. He needed sleep, she was certain, but it made her feel very alone.

First the mule was unloaded and returned to the barn, then the wife brought Marian bread and another blanket. After eating, Marian piled as much straw as possible beneath her and Captain Landon. She pulled off his boots and extinguished the lantern. Lying down next to him, she covered them both with a blanket. With the pistol at her side, she finally fell into an exhausted sleep.

Pain. Searing pain. A throbbing that pulsated up his neck and down the length of his arm.

Allan could make sense of nothing else. Not the sounds, the smells, the lumpy surface upon which he lay. He didn't wish to open his eyes, to face more pain.

He tried to remember where he had been, what had happened. He remembered pulling Miss Pallant from the burning château. He remembered being shot and Valour running amok.

Valour nickered. He opened his eyes.

'Miss Pallant?' His throat was parched and speaking intensified the pain.

She had fallen asleep next to him. 'Captain?'

Her face, smudged with soot, was close, framed by a tangle of blonde hair. Her blue eyes dazzled.

He caught a lock of her hair between his fingers. 'Where is your cap?'

She looked around and found it on the floor. He watched her plait her hair and cover it.

Sunlight shone through cracks in the wood. He frowned. 'How long have we slept?'

She stretched. 'All night, I suppose.'

'All night!' He sat up straighter and the room spun around.

'The child's parents returned.' Her voice seemed tense. 'I gave them a coin so we could stay in here.'

A stab of pain hit his shoulder again. He held his breath until it faded. 'Did they know who won the battle?'

'Perhaps, but they could not tell me.' She grasped her knees to her chest. 'They speak Flemish. I don't suppose you speak Flemish, do you?'

'No.' But he knew many Belgians were on the side of the French and despised the Allies.

The door to the barn opened and the peasant farmer walked in. Allan noticed Marian pick up his pistol and put it in her pocket.

The peasant's expression was as guarded as Marian's. He nodded. *'Goedemorgen.'*

'Good morning,' she responded in a tight voice.

The man lifted a pail and spoke again, but this time Allan could not decipher the words. The farmer walked over to another stall and began milking the cow. The smell of fresh milk filled the barn. He was hungry, Allan realised.

'Brood?' Marian walked over to the peasant and showed him a coin from her pocket.

The man nodded and pointed to the door.

She placed the pistol next to Allan and covered it with the blanket. From a basket she handed him a small piece of bread. 'This is from last night. I am going to get some more for us. Take care. I do not entirely trust these people.'

Allan silently applauded her cleverness.

She left and the man finished milking his cow. When he walked past Allan carrying the bucket of milk, he paused. Turning back, he picked up the tin cup and dipped it into the milk, handing the cup to Allan. *'Drink de melk.'* The peasant gestured, and Allan easily understood him.

'Thank you.' He took the cup, cream swimming at the top and sipped. His hunger urged him to gulp it all down, but he knew better.

'The battle?' he tried asking the peasant. 'England or France?'

The man tapped his temple and shook his head. Did he not know the battle's outcome or did he not understand the question? The man shrugged and walked out.

To be unable to converse was a frustration. To not know who won the battle was worse.

Had Wellington won?

It seemed essential to know. Had Napoleon been

vanquished at last or were his victorious soldiers now pillaging the countryside? Was Miss Pallant safe here? Should he return her to the safety of her friends or was Brussels under Napoleon's control?

Allan tried to take stock of his injuries. It seemed a good thing that the ball had passed through his shoulder, although it burned and ached like the very devil.

He flexed his fingers. Despite a sharp pain that radiated down his arm, they worked well. More good news.

He rested his head against the stable wall, exhausted from the mild exertion. He felt hot and dizzy. Feverish, God forbid. He needed to regain his strength so they could ride out of here. He broke off a piece of the stale bread and dipped it in the milk, making it easier to eat. Even chewing exhausted him, but he slowly managed to finish it.

The door opened again, and Miss Pallant came to his side.

She sat by him. 'I have some more bread.'

'In a minute.' He handed her the cup of milk. 'Have some. It is very much like ambrosia, I think.'

She laughed. 'I do not know when I have been so hungry.'

He waited for her to finish drinking. 'Tell me why you do not trust our host.'

She tore off a piece of bread. 'I think they went to the battlefield and robbed the dead.'

He gritted his teeth. It happened after every battle. Oftentimes the very men who'd fought beside the dead returned to deface their final rest. Most of the officers turned a blind eye to the practice. In fact, most of them were not averse to purchasing some interesting piece of booty. A Frenchman's sword, perhaps. Or a fine gold watch.

'But they have fed us and didn't kill us during the night,' she added. 'That is something in their favour.' She nibbled on a crust.

'We must leave today.' Allan ignored the dizziness that intensified and his increasing difficulty breathing.

She regarded him intently and placed her fingers against his forehead. She felt cool. 'You have a fever, Captain.'

He feared as much. 'It is nothing of consequence. I just need a moment and we can go on our way.'

She watched him, arms crossed over her chest. He needed to prove he could do it.

'Help me stand.' If he could get to his feet, he'd be able to ride, he was certain of it.

She helped him struggle to his feet, pain blasting through his chest and down his arm. He lost his footing and she caught him, his bandaged and naked chest pressing against her as if in an embrace.

Allan cursed his weakness, cursed that he had placed her in this uncomfortable situation. To undress a strange man. To bind his gruesome wounds. To learn one of the horrid secrets of war.

He gained his balance and leaned against the stable wall.

Marian did not remove her hands from the skin beneath his arms. 'You are too weak for this.'

It seemed an obvious observation, but he made a dismissive gesture. 'Saddle Valour. We can ride to Brussels. It cannot be far.'

She did not move, but, instead, stared at him. His eyes betrayed him as surely as his body. No matter how hard he tried, he could not keep her in focus.

Finally she said, 'You cannot ride to Brussels.'

'You cannot go alone.' He managed to disguise the extent of his pain and his growing disorientation.

She nodded. 'I agree. I do not know what these people would do to you if I left you here alone.'

That was not what he meant. He meant a woman could not wander alone through a countryside that might be teeming with French soldiers.

She glanced away, but finally she met his gaze again. 'We must stay here until you are well enough to ride. I have your pistol and your sword in case these people try to hurt us and I have some coins to pay them for food. We shall just have to take care.'

His strength had failed him. He might have started the previous day as her protector, but at the moment she was acting as if she was his.

He could not allow it. 'I can ride.'

She gazed at him firmly. 'No, Captain. You must lie down again. Let me help you.' She moved to his side, wrapping one of his arms around her shoulder so that he could lean on her while she lowered him to the floor.

'No.' He wrenched away. 'Cannot do it. Must get you to safety.' He tried to ignore the pain and the spinning in his head. He could endure a few hours on a horse.

He took a step, keeping one hand on the stable wall.

'Captain,' her voice pleaded.

'I will saddle the horse.' He stepped out of the stall. His horse walked up to him. He grabbed her mane to steady himself.

But the room turned black.

The last thing Allan felt was the hard surface of the barn floor.

Chapter Four

'Captain!' Marian rushed to his side.

He opened his eyes. 'I passed out.'

'Now will you listen to reason? Please. We must stay here until you are well.' With all the strength she could muster, she helped him up again and settled him back on to the bed of hay. She made a pillow of his saddle by covering it with one of the blankets.

His breathing had turned laboured. 'I am sorry, Miss Pallant. I cannot get you out of here.'

'Considering I am the reason you were shot, I should apologise to you.' She tucked another blanket around him.

'A Frenchman shot me, not you,' he said.

She brushed damp hair off his face. 'Remain still, Captain. Rest.' His determination to take her back to Brussels was foolish. He was too ill.

He gave a wan smile. 'I seem to have little choice.'

She knelt next to him, tucking a blanket around him. 'I thought soldiers were realistic.'

He laughed. 'I do not know where you would get that notion. If we were realistic, we would never march into battle or try to storm a fortress.'

'You do have a point.'

He closed his eyes, and she was free to watch him for a moment. A fine sheen of perspiration tinged his face, evidence of his fever, but he looked as if he wished to fight it, as he might fight the enemy. She would wager by the afternoon he would tell her he was ready to ride, even if his fever had worsened.

When her father had contracted the fever in India, he'd merely sunk into despair, lamenting that he'd brought the illness upon his household. His wife. Even at nine years old, Marian knew her father had simply given up. Her mother was dead and a daughter was apparently not enough to live for.

'Do not leave me, Captain,' she whispered.

He opened his eyes. 'I will not leave you. We both shall ride out of here this afternoon.'

She smiled and blinked away tears. *God keep him alive,* she prayed.

Valour whinnied and blew out a noisy breath.

Marian rose. 'She heard you, I expect, and thinks you meant now.' She released Valour from her stall and the mare immediately found the captain, lowering her head to nuzzle his arm.

'Ow, Valour, stop.' He shuddered from the pain, but stroked Valour's neck. 'Nothing to fret over.'

Marian smiled. 'She is trying to tend you.'

He returned her gaze. 'I already have an excellent nurse.'

She could only hope she would be good enough to pull him through. Marian led Valour away. 'I will feed her.' She found the feed and Valour soon forgot about her master.

Marian glanced around the barn. The door was open, providing plenty of light and fresh air, but living with animals and wearing dirty clothes still assaulted the nostrils. She took a broom from against the wall and performed a task she had never done before in her life—she swept the barn.

'What are you doing?' The captain could not see her.

'Sweeping out the dirty hay,' she responded.

'You should not have to perform such a task.' He sounded breathless and disapproving.

It stung. She very much wanted him to admire her, to value the fact that she was not missish or helpless.

She swept over to where he could see her. 'I prefer this work to the smell.'

'I should be doing the task,' he rasped.

Perhaps he merely felt guilty. That would certainly be like him.

'It is a simple enough task,' she remarked.

He looked up at her. 'You do whatever needs to be done, do you not, Miss Pallant?'

She felt herself go warm all over, as if the sun had chosen to shine only on her. 'As do you, Captain.' She held his gaze for a special moment. How alike they were in some ways. 'Your turn will come when you are better.'

He nodded and closed his eyes again.

Marian hummed as she finished the task, sweeping the dirty hay from the floor to the outside. Two chickens pecked at the soil around the hut. She glimpsed the farmer and his wife in the side yard sorting through the bundles they'd brought in the day before.

Their bounty from the dead.

Her good spirits fled, and she remembered that men had died in the battle, some in her arms.

Death had robbed her of almost everyone she cared about. Her parents. Her Indian amah. Her aunt. All she had left was her cousin Edwin and Domina, and she did not know if Domina had survived.

She glanced back at the captain, the light from the door shining on him. He would not die, she vowed, not as long as she drew breath. She turned back to see what else needed doing in the barn.

Marian was pitching fresh hay into the horse's stall when the farmer walked in and glanced all around. *'Wat is dit?'*

She could guess what he asked. 'I cleaned it.'

He raised his brows and tapped his head.

'I know.' She sighed. 'You do not understand.'

But he looked pleased and she felt a surge of pride that her work had been appreciated. He smiled. *'Brood?'*

She almost laughed. *'Brood.'* She nodded. Bread was to be her reward. 'Thank you.'

He looked down at the captain and frowned. *'Slaapt hij?'*

'Sleeping?' Her smile turned wan. 'Yes.' A fever-ish sleep. She fished into her pocket and held out a coin to the peasant. She pulled at her dirty coat. 'Clean clothes?'

He stared.

She repeated, this time pointing to the stains on the captain's trousers, as well.

'Ah.' The man nodded vigorously.

A few minutes later he brought back a basket of bread and cheese and an armful of folded clothes.

'Thank you,' she cried.

After he left, she set the food aside for later and ex-amined the clothes. There were two sets consisting of shirts, coats and trousers. One set was very large, for the captain; one smaller, for her. She held one of the shirts up to her nose and smelled the bitter odour of gunpowder.

The peasant had brought her plundered clothing. The large trousers were white, like the trousers of the French soldiers who had stormed the gate at Hougoumont.

These were pristine, however, obviously tucked away in some poor Frenchman's pack.

A wave of grief for the poor fellow washed over her. It seemed dishonourable to don his clothing and be glad of its cleanliness, but what choice did she have?

They would wear these garments only until she could wash and dry their own. And she would say a prayer for the poor men who died to clothe them even temporarily.

Marian carried the bucket to the well to draw clean water, which she brought back to bathe the captain as best she could. She supposed a lady ought to try to get the farmer to undress the captain, but she was pretending to be a boy.

She knelt beside him. 'Captain, I have clean clothes for you, but first I must bathe you.' He was already shirtless, so there was nothing to do but remove his trousers. It should be no more difficult to pull off his trousers than to undress a doll.

He opened his eyes. 'Bathe?'

'Yes. It will cool you, as well.' She dipped the cloth in the water and wrung it out.

She started with his face, wiping off soot and dirt. Rinsing the cloth, she wiped his hair and rinsed again. She cleaned around his bandages, careful not to get them wet.

'I should not let you…' he murmured.

She made a face at him. 'I know. I know. My reputation

and all that is proper.' She moved the cloth across his nipple and felt a strange surge of sensation inside her. She lifted the cloth, then rinsed it again, trying to regain composure. 'I suspect if you were feeling better you would give me a lecture.'

A wan smile formed on his lips. 'Indeed, I would.'

'Would it not be ridiculous for me to leave you dirty in soiled clothing merely because I am an unmarried miss?' Perhaps if she kept talking the fluttering inside her would cease. 'It would be nonsensical. Much of what one must do to preserve one's reputation is nonsensical, is it not?'

'Nonsensical,' he murmured.

'Yes…like—like being alone with a man. A few minutes alone and one's parents or guardian force a betrothal even if the gentleman and lady despise each other. Ridiculous.'

He leaned forwards and she washed off his back.

'Sometimes men are not to be trusted.' He spoke with difficulty.

It pained her. 'I know that.'

The teachers at the school she and Domina had attended explained such things very carefully, how men could behave if alone with a woman. 'But surely there are exceptions.' Such as one finding herself in the middle of a battle and a man saving her.

'Now I must remove your trousers,' she said, as if that

were the most natural thing in the world. She reached for the buttons fastening them.

The captain put his hand over hers. 'That seems too much—'

She looked him straight in the eye. 'Blood has soaked through your trousers and, I expect, through your drawers as well. It is beginning to smell.' She exaggerated about the smelly part, but she wanted his cooperation.

His eyes were still feverish. 'I'll do it. Step away.'

She stepped out of his sight, but watched as he removed his trousers and drawers, just in case he needed her. With some effort he wiped his skin with the cloth.

This was her first glimpse of a totally naked man, she realised. She and Domina used to wonder how they would ever see a naked man. Never would they have guessed it would be under these circumstances. Marian's eyes were riveted upon his masculine parts, so different from those on the statues of Roman gods she'd seen in elegant houses in Bath and London. His was living flesh, warm and vari-coloured, more fascinating than attractive. She tilted her head as she examined him.

Once, when she and Domina were pressing one of the maids for some forbidden information, the woman described how men's parts grew bigger during lovemaking. Gazing at the captain, Marian's heart raced. *Bigger?*

She remembered the maid's description of lovemaking.

What would it be like to do that with a man? With the captain?

She shook off her hoydenish thoughts and turned to hand him the French soldier's drawers.

The captain covered himself with the blanket and looked exhausted. 'The clothing?'

'You must let me help,' she insisted. 'Do not fuss.'

She put the drawers on his legs and pulled them up as far as she could, her hands under the blanket and very near his male parts. For a moment her gaze caught his and the fluttering inside her returned. His hands touched hers as he took the waistband of the drawers from her grip and pulled them up the rest of the way. Next she did the same with the trousers.

She cleared her throat. 'I will get the shirt.'

He leaned back against his saddle, pressing his hand against his wound.

She set the shirt aside and knelt down. 'Let me see your wound.' She moved his hand aside and carefully pulled the bandage away from his skin.

It looked inflamed and swollen and smelled of infection. The layers of cloth closest to the wound were moist with pus.

'You need a clean bandage,' she told him, but how she would ask the peasants for a bandage, she did not know. 'Lean forwards.' His back wound was not as nasty.

'Leave off the shirt,' he said, touching her arm. 'A new bandage would be good.'

'I'll get some clean water, then change my clothes. I'll see to it quickly.' She hurried out of the barn.

At the water pump she rinsed the bucket and the piece of cloth he'd used as a wash rag. She refilled the bucket with clean water and returned to the barn. Choosing the empty stall next to where the captain lay, she quickly removed the bloodstained clothing she'd worn for almost two days straight. She unwrapped the long scarf she'd used to bind her breasts to disguise that she was a woman. Bare from the waist up, Marian bent down to the bucket and scrubbed the blood from the fabric. She hung it over the wall of the stall, hoping it would dry a little before she had to put it back on. Using the cloth she rubbed her skin clean of blood and grime. No steaming hot bath in a copper tub with French-milled soap had ever felt as wonderful.

Eager to feel clean all over, she removed her breeches. Completely naked now, she turned and saw his face through a gap in the wood that separated the two stalls. Had he been watching her? She could not tell. Every nerve in her body sparked.

Heart pounding, she grabbed the clean shirt and held it against her chest. 'Captain?'

'I am still here,' he replied.

She quickly donned the clean trousers and reached for the scarf to begin rewrapping her breasts.

A sound made her turn.

The peasant woman stood at the opening to the stall, gaping open-mouthed. *'U bent een vrouw.'*

Marian could guess what the woman said. 'Yes. A woman.'

She quickly pulled on the shirt, her mind racing to provide an explanation, something the woman would accept and understand. Her vocabulary of fewer than five words was insufficient to explain why she was in the company of a wounded soldier.

She pointed to Captain Landon. 'I am his wife.'

'Wat?' The woman did not comprehend.

'Wife,' Marian repeated. She pointed to Landon. 'Husband.'

The woman shook her head.

'Married. Spouse,' she tried.

'She does not understand you,' the Captain said. *'Épouse. Mari.'*

Marian pointed to Landon again and hugged herself, making kissing sounds. She tapped her ring finger, which, of course, had no ring.

'Gehuwd!' The woman broke into a smile.

'Yes!' She nodded. Whatever *gehuwd* meant, it caused the peasant woman to smile.

Marian pointed to the door, then put her finger to her lips. 'Shh.' She gestured to herself. 'Shh.'

The peasant woman nodded. 'Shh,' she repeated. She walked over to Marian and clasped her hand.

A friend, Marian thought. At least for the moment.

She walked her new friend over to the captain. 'I want to show her your wound.'

'Excellent idea.' There was a catch in his voice. 'Maybe she will have bandages.'

Marian pointed to his bandage and pulled it away. She touched the bandages again. 'New bandages. Clean.'

The woman leaned down and examined the wound for herself. *'Zeer slecht.'*

'Zeer slecht?' Marian repeated. That did not sound good.

'Ja.' The woman nodded. She patted Marian's arm reassuringly and uttered a whole string of words Marian could not understand. She raised a finger as if to say 'wait a moment' and walked out the door.

After she left Marian sank to the floor next to the captain. 'I hope she understood.'

He touched her hand. 'We'll find out soon enough.'

'How are you feeling?' She felt his forehead.

'Better,' he said.

He looked worse, flushed and out of breath. She dipped the cloth in the water and wiped his brow.

He released a breath. 'That feels uncommonly good.'

'I'm worried your fever grows worse.' She dipped the cloth again and held it against his forehead.

'It is nothing.' He coughed and winced in pain, but managed to smile. 'So you are my wife now.'

Surely it was a harmless lie. 'I wanted her to approve of us.'

'Clever.' His voice rattled. 'Worked a charm.'

She beamed under the compliment. 'We must remain in their good graces. We are totally dependent on them.'

'Food. Clothing. Shelter,' he agreed.

She pulled at her shirt. 'I try to remember we would not have clean clothes if they had not stolen from the dead soldiers, much as I detest the thought. They are poor. It was generous of them to share what little they have with us.'

'And you gave them some coins,' he said.

She smiled. 'Yes.'

The peasant wife bustled in, bandages and folded towels in one hand and a small pot in the other. She knelt down at the captain's side, chattering and gesturing for Marian to unwind his old bandage. The captain tried to cooperate.

The woman dipped a cloth into the water and bathed around the wound. That done, she opened the pot. The scent of honey filled the air.

'Honey?' His eyes widened.

'Ja.' The woman nodded. *'Honing.'*

Honing. Another word for Marian to learn, but why?

The woman poured the honey directly into his wound and he trembled at its touch. After placing a cloth compress over it, she gestured for Marian to help him lean forwards. She dressed the exit wound in the same manner. Then she wrapped the cloth bandage around him to keep everything in place. She smiled and chattered at them both.

Marian helped him into his shirt. 'Honey.'

'Let us hope she knows more about healing than we do.' The captain glanced at the farmer's wife. 'Thank you, *madame*.'

Marian had been moved by the tenderness of the woman's care.

When the woman stood to leave Marian walked her to the door. She pointed to herself. 'Marian.'

The woman grinned and tapped her own chest. 'Karel.'

The two women embraced. Marian wiped away tears. She had an ally.

The rest of the day proved that comfort was fleeting.

The farmer left with the mule laden with plunder. Marian had neither the means nor the opportunity to ask him to carry a message to someone—anyone—English.

Captain Landon's fever steadily worsened and he slept a great deal of the time.

Marian busied herself by washing their soiled clothes, which dried quickly in the warm afternoon sun. She spent the rest of the time at the captain's side, talking when he wished to talk, bathing his face to cool him, or merely just sitting next to him.

Late in the afternoon he became even more fitful. The little girl carried in another basket of bread and cheese, this time with the addition of a tankard of ale.

The girl stared wide-eyed at the captain while Marian took the food and drink from her tiny arms.

'Fetch your mama,' Marian asked her. 'Mama.'

The little girl ran off and her mother showed up soon afterwards kneeling down to check the captain. She clucked her tongue and furrowed her brow and said… something. She rushed off again.

Several minutes went by before she returned with a pot of some sort of tea, leaves and pieces of bark floating in the liquid. She handed Marian a spoon and gestured for her to give the tea to the captain.

'Thank you, Karel,' Marian said.

She spooned the tea into the captain's mouth.

He roused. 'What is this?'

'Tea,' she responded. 'To make you feel better.'

By the time darkness fell, he was sleeping uneasily, their old clothes were dry and folded, and the farmer had still not returned. Marian surmised wherever he'd gone had been too far to return in a day.

She continued her ministrations as the moon rose in the sky, lighting the stable with a soft glow that gave her enough light to see by. The captain mumbled and moved restlessly.

Exhausted, Marian fell asleep at his side, the wet cloth still in her hand.

'No!' the captain cried.

She woke with a start.

He rose to a sitting position. 'You bloody bastard. You ought to be hanged.'

He swung a fist at an imaginary enemy. His eyes flashed in the moonlight and he tried to rise.

'Captain, stay down!' Marian held him from behind and tried to keep him still.

'I ought to kill you myself.' His voice was low and dangerous and frightening.

'You are dreaming, Captain,' she told him. 'There is no one here but you and me. I am Marian Pallant. Remember me?'

He reached around and easily wrenched her off his back. Suddenly he held her in front of him, her legs straddling his, his face contorted in anger. 'I ought to kill you myself for what you did.'

Marian trembled with fear. While he still held her, she managed to cup his face between her hands and to keep his head steady enough to look at her. 'I'm Marian, Captain. You are dreaming. You are sick. You must lie down again.'

Her hair came loose and tumbled down her back. His face changed, but he seized her hair and with it drew her close so that her face was inches from his. 'Foolish woman,' he murmured, his other hand feeling her bound chest. 'Not a boy at all. A foolish woman.'

Her fear took a new turn, her heart beating so hard she thought it would burst inside her. Forcing him to look at her again, she made her voice steady and firm although she felt neither inside. 'Yes, I am foolish, but you are very sick and you are hurting me. Release me and lie back down this instant.'

For a brief moment he seemed to really see her, then his eyes drifted from her like a boat that had lost its sail.

He released her and collapsed against the saddle, shivering so hard his whole body convulsed. 'Cold,' he murmured. 'So cold.'

She gathered up all the blankets and wrapped them around him. Then she moved to the other side of the stable, watchful lest he would again mistake her for whomever he wished to kill. Or to seduce.

A rooster crowed.

Allan lifted his eyelids, seeing first the weathered grey wood of the barn stall, then the hay, the light from the window and finally Miss Marian Pallant.

She sat against the wall opposite him, her hair cascading on to her shoulders, her eyes closed. He examined her sleeping face.

How could she have thought such features would pass

for a boy's? Her complexion was like fresh cream, her brows delicately arched, lips full and pink and turned up at the corners. Even with her hair loose and in a man's shirt and breeches, she looked as if she belonged in the finest ballroom, not sleeping in a peasant's barn.

He struggled to sit, but pain shot through his shoulder. Pressing his hand against his wound, he felt a bandage securely in place. It was damp with sweat.

No wonder. Blankets were piled at his feet. He kicked them away and made another effort to sit, trying to bear the pain. A cry escaped. 'Ah!'

Miss Pallant jumped and seemed to recoil from him. 'Captain?'

She looked at him as if he were the bogeyman himself while she plaited her hair.

His cry must have alarmed her. 'Forgive me. I put too much strain on my shoulder.' He rubbed his face. 'Is it afternoon?'

'No, morning.' Her wariness did not abate.

'Morning? Do you mean I slept all of yesterday?'

'You were very feverish,' she responded in a defensive tone. 'And, yes, you did sleep on and off. Do you not remember any of it?'

Bits and pieces of the previous day returned. Miss Pallant undressing him, stroking him with a cool cloth. Miss Pallant naked, her skin glowing and smooth against the dark rough wood of the stable, like a goddess thrust off Mount Olympus.

He glanced away from her. 'I remember some of it.'

'You were feverish all day,' she said. 'And all night.'

He touched his forehead. 'I feel better today. I hope I did not cause you any distress because of it.'

Her voice rose. 'No distress, Captain.'

She was like a skittish colt. What had happened?

She stood. 'Are you thirsty?'

He was very thirsty, come to think of it, but he shook his head. 'I am determined to no longer be a burden to you. I will get the water today. Tell me where to go.' Surely he could rise to his feet today.

'You will do no such thing.' She gave him a scolding look. 'Karel left some ale.' She handed him the tankard. 'Drink it if you are thirsty.'

It was reddish brown in colour, tasted both sweet and tart, and Allan thought it was quite the most delicious ale he'd ever consumed.

He drank half the contents. 'Karel is the wife's name?'

Miss Pallant nodded, still watching him as if he were a wildcat about to pounce.

He touched his shoulder. 'I remember. She dressed my wound.' The pain was finally fading.

'Are you hungry?' She reached for a basket and placed it near him. 'There is bread and cheese.'

He chose only one piece of bread and one square of

cheese and handed the basket back to her. 'You must eat as well.'

She hesitated before taking the basket from his hand. What had caused this reticence towards him? A battle, a fire, and an escape had not robbed her of courage. What had? 'Miss Pallant, when I was feverish, did I do something to hurt you or frighten you?'

'Not at all.' Her response was clipped. 'You merely had a nightmare.'

There was more to it, he was certain, but it seemed she didn't want him to pursue it. 'The farmer packed up the plunder and left us yesterday, I remember. Did he return?'

She tore off a piece of bread and chewed it before answering, 'He has not.'

He wanted to ask her more, but even the minor exertion of sitting up and eating had greatly fatigued him. He could not even finish his bread. 'If you give me the basket again, I'll wrap this up.'

She reached for the bread instead. 'I will do it.'

Their fingers touched, and her gaze flew to his face. He could not find words, but tried to show his regret for whatever he had put her through.

Her expression softened.

He leaned back and tried not to show how much he enjoyed merely gazing upon her.

She rose. 'I believe I will sweep the barn.'

He remembered her doing so the day before. He tried to stand. 'Perhaps I can do it today.'

He made it to his feet, but his legs felt like rubber. She rushed over to lend her shoulder for support. She smelled of hay and a scent all her own, a combination that was pleasant to his nostrils.

The door to the barn swung open and the farmer's wife walked in, a little girl trailing her. *'Goedemorgen.'*

'Good morning, Karel,' Miss Pallant responded.

The woman broke into a smile and put her palms to her cheeks when she saw Allan and Miss Pallant with arms around each other. She immediately began talking and advanced on Allan, touching his face and gesturing that she wanted to check his bandage. Miss Pallant backed away and he braced himself against the stable wall.

The farmer's wife lifted his shirt and examined the wounds under the bandages. She turned to Miss Pallant and nodded approvingly. Still talking, she walked over to the cow and milked the animal while the little girl watched. Miss Pallant took the broom and began to sweep.

Allan refused to do nothing while the women worked. Using the wall for support, he made his way to Valour's stall.

The mare's eyes brightened and she huffed and nickered in excitement. 'Ready to ride, girl?' he murmured.

Valour moved her head up and down.

He smiled. 'I am eager to be off as well.' He found a brush with which to groom her.

Miss Pallant, still holding her broom, rushed over. 'You mustn't do that. You need to rest, Captain.'

'I need to regain my strength,' he countered.

They needed to leave this place. They needed to discover what had happened in the battle, whether it was safe for him to return her to her friends in Brussels. If possible, he would like to get her back to Brussels today. Each day away meant more damage to her reputation.

From outside the barn came a man's voice. *'Engels! Waar ben je?'*

'Jakob?' The farmer's wife stood up so fast the milk stool clattered on to the floor. She left her bucket and ran out of the barn, her little daughter at her heels.

'Toon jezelf, Engels!' Apparently the farmer had returned.

'Help me to the door,' Allan demanded.

Leaning on Miss Pallant, he reached the barn's door.

Gesturing for Marian to remain behind him, he stepped into the light.

The farmer, his eyes blazing, pointed to him. *'Engels, bah! U won—'* He ranted on, and Allan caught both Wellington's and Napoleon's names in the foreign diatribe.

Two words stood out. *U won.* The Allies won. Wellington had done it, by God!

But this peasant farmer did not cheer about it. He carried an axe and shook it in the air.

His wife seized his arm and tugged on it. *'Nee!'* she pleaded. The little girl clung to her skirts and wailed.

Allan was no match for this man, not in his debilitated state.

The farmer, face crimson with anger, advanced, raising the axe high.

Chapter Five

'Stop!' Miss Pallant cried.

She emerged from the barn, Allan's pistol in her hand. *Smart girl,* he said to himself.

She aimed it at the farmer. 'Back away.'

The farmer halted and pointed at her. *'Een vrouw?'*

'Back!' Miss Pallant repeated.

The farmer gripped the axe even tighter.

'Marian, nee.' His wife started towards her.

'No, Karel!' Miss Pallant's voice turned pleading. 'Stay back.' Her expression turned firm again as she pointed the pistol at the husband and glanced nervously at Allan. 'What now, Captain?'

His mind worked quickly. 'Give the pistol to me.' He extended his hand. 'We leave now. Can you saddle the horse?'

'I can.' Her voice was determined. She inched towards him and gave him the pistol.

The farmer cast a worried look to his wife. They exchanged several tense words. Planning to overpower him, perhaps? If they guessed how close his legs were to buckling beneath him, they might succeed. Allan held the pistol with both hands, supporting his weary arms against his body.

The farmer and his wife continued their argument, the man pointing towards the mule bucolically watching this scene unfold. Was the man worried they might report him for stealing from the dead? The French would not have cared; the French army survived on plunder, but Wellington might not be so forgiving. If the farmer killed them, no one would ever know. They would simply have disappeared.

'Mama!' The little girl pulled at her mother's skirts as the woman tried to shield the child with her body.

Allan would not kill a child. He was not Edwin Tranville.

His long-standing anger at Edwin strengthened Allan's arms. He lifted the pistol higher, but sweat dripped from his brow. Miss Pallant had better hurry.

He heard her moving around behind him, and Valour's hooves stamping the ground, as if as impatient as he.

'Your boots, Captain?' she called to him.

'Bring them. I'll don them later.'

Marian led the horse to him, saddled and with his boots sticking out from the bags slung across the horse's back.

'Hold the pistol while I mount.' He handed the pistol to her, and prayed for the strength to seat himself on the horse. His wound now throbbed in agony and the muscles in his legs were trembling with the effort of standing so long.

He grabbed the pommel and put his stockinged foot in the stirrup. Taking a deep breath, he swung his leg over the horse.

And cried out with pain.

But he made it into the saddle, even though his vision momentarily turned black.

'Farewell, Karel,' Miss Pallant cried as she mounted the horse. She clutched Allan's arm with one hand and held the pistol in the other. 'Go now.'

Valour sped off as if she'd understood the need to hurry. The farmer ran after them, shouting and swinging the axe, but Valour galloped faster, down the same path on which the farmer had undoubtedly just arrived. Allan gave Valour her head until they were a safe distance away and the path opened on to a larger road. He slowed the mare before she was blown.

They passed fields and wood, all blurring into shades of green and brown. Allan's muscles ached and his wound throbbed, but he hung on. Miss Pallant, seated behind him, clung to his back.

The road on which they travelled showed no signs of leading anywhere. Allan tried to keep them heading in a north-easterly direction, surmising they would either find a road that led to Brussels or they'd reach the Dutch border. Either way they would be travelling away from

France and would be unlikely to encounter a retreating French army.

'We should stop, Captain,' Miss Pallant said to him.

'Not yet,' he managed. He swayed in the saddle.

'Captain—'

'I am well enough.' The day was not far advanced. They might reach a town soon if he held on a little longer.

The road twisted to follow a stream flowing alongside. Valour turned toward the water.

'She is thirsty, Captain. Let her drink.'

'Very well.' He could not argue, even though he had no assurance he'd have the strength to mount the horse again once off her back.

Miss Pallant slipped off, landing on her feet. Allan's legs nearly gave out on him when he dismounted.

Marian had guessed he'd been holding on by a thin tether. She'd felt the tension in the muscles of his back as he rode.

'You must rest, too,' she insisted.

'We are too exposed here,' he said. 'I do not think the farmer would pursue us, but if I am wrong—' He glanced around and pointed to some thick bushes across a very narrow section of the stream. 'Come. We can hide over there.'

She helped him cross the stream to the shelter of the

foliage before returning to lead Valour over. The sanctuary was ideal. There was even a pool of water perfect for Valour to drink unseen.

The Captain collapsed to the ground and leaned against a tree trunk, his eyes closed, breathing hard from the walk. How had he managed to ride so far? she wondered. Only the day before she'd feared he would die.

Marian reached into the saddlebags and pulled out the tin cup she'd packed along with their clothing. Walking a bit upstream from where Valour stood she filled the cup and drank, then refilled it and carried it to the captain. 'Drink this.'

He returned a grateful look as he wrapped his fingers around the cup.

His stockings were shredded from the stirrup. 'It is time you put on your boots.'

He lowered the cup. 'My feet will welcome them.'

It was the closest he'd come to complaining throughout this ordeal. She retrieved his clean stockings and boots from the saddlebags. 'Shall I put them on for you?'

'My stockings, if you do not mind. The boots I must do myself.' His voice was weary, though he seemed to be making an effort to disguise it.

She took his foot in her hand, brushing off the leaves and removing the torn stockings. She gently slipped on the clean one, pulling it up and smoothing out the wrinkles. She glanced at his face.

He gazed at her with an expression that made her go warm all over. She quickly turned her attention to his other foot.

When she finished, he said, 'Thank you, Miss Pallant.' His voice, low and raspy, seemed to reach deep inside her, making her want—something.

'Has your fever returned?' She moved closer to place her palm on his forehead. 'You feel cool.'

'On the mend.' He smiled. His hand closed around hers. 'I hope to give you no more trouble, Miss Pallant. You have endured enough already. You have done extremely well.'

Her heart swelled at his praise, although she suspected it was his courage that fed her own. 'I am not about to complain of the need to tend you. Where would I be without you?'

He laughed. 'Shall we take turns admiring each other?'

He admired her? Her insides fluttered at the thought.

'Sit and rest, Miss Pallant. You were right to make us stop. We should be safe enough here.'

She leaned against the same tree trunk as he, her shoulder touching his. 'Surely the farmer will not come after us.'

'I think not.' He paused. 'Did you hear him? I believe he said the Allies won the battle.'

'How very glad I am of it.' She sighed. 'Was that what angered him, do you think? Was he angry that Napoleon lost? I heard talk in Brussels that some of the Belgians preferred Napoleon.'

'Perhaps that was the reason.' His voice had a hard edge. 'Or he feared we would charge him with theft.'

She faced him. 'You will not do that, will you? You will not charge him with theft? They were so poor. His wife was kind to us. You might not have survived without the help she rendered.'

His eyes softened. 'I will say nothing.'

She reached for him, but withdrew her hand and sat back again.

'I do not know what awaits you in Brussels, though.' His voice turned low.

'Do you mean about Domina?' A wave of guilt washed over her. She had forgotten that Domina might not have encountered a chivalrous man like the captain.

'Your friend, as well, but I was primarily thinking of your reputation.'

She felt like laughing. 'Really, Captain, I am grateful to be alive. Nothing else seems as important.' Except, perhaps, knowing he also was alive.

Their conversation fell away and soon his breathing slowed to the even cadence of sleep. Valour contentedly chewed on a patch of grass. The air was warm, and the sound of the trickling stream and the rustling leaves lulled Marian until her eyes, too, closed and sleep overtook her.

She woke to a touch on her shoulder. The Captain stood over her, boots on. 'We should be off.'

She quickly stood. 'How long did I sleep?'

'Two hours. Perhaps a bit more, I would guess.' He glanced at the sun, which had dipped lower in the sky. 'But we need to make the most of daylight.'

They mounted Valour again and returned to the road.

The landscape did not change for miles but as the sun dipped low in the sky the spire of a church steeple came in sight.

'A village, Captain,' she cried.

He turned his head. 'At last, Miss Pallant.'

It was near dark when they reached the village streets and found an inn. They left Valour to the care of the stable workers and entered the inn.

The innkeeper's brows rose at their appearance. They must have looked strange, indeed, in their plundered clothing, wearing shirts and no coats, and looking weary from all they'd been through.

'Do you speak English?' the captain asked.

The innkeeper straightened. *'Français, monsieur.'*

Marian tapped the captain on the arm. 'We have very few coins left.'

The captain spoke French to the innkeeper, negotiating the price of the room and board. At this point Marian would have been happy to sleep in the stable with Valour. She'd become used to stables.

The captain procured the room and ordered a hot meal to be brought to them. The arrangements complete, the innkeeper grabbed a lighted candle and led them up a stairway.

Captain Landon leaned down to her ear. 'I was afraid we would not have enough for two rooms.'

She nodded. 'I am certain we do not.'

He faltered on the step and clapped his hand against his wound. She offered her shoulder, but he shook his head. They had another flight to climb and a long hallway before finally being escorted into a very small room with a tiny window and only enough space for the bed and a small table and chair.

The innkeeper lit a candle on the table from the one he carried. He inclined his head very slightly and spoke in French. 'Your meal will be delivered directly.'

When the door closed behind him, Captain Landon clasped the bedpost.

Marian hurried to his side. 'You must lie down, Captain.'

'The chair will suffice.'

She would not hear of it. 'Nonsense.' She gently manoeuvred him to the bed, and he gave no further argument.

He sat with numb acceptance as she pulled off his boots. 'Lie down for a bit,' she murmured.

He moaned as he lowered himself against the pillows. She had no wish to disturb him further, either by helping him remove his shirt or trousers or even by covering him.

Wanting nothing more than to lie next to him, she instead busied herself with unpacking their own clothing from the saddlebags. She hung the clothes in layers over the chair, hoping the wrinkles would fall out. When she finished, a knock on the door brought their food.

A maid carried in the tray and already the scent of the food made Marian's mouth water. There were two large bowls of stew, and a dish piled with potatoes cut into long rectangles. As soon as the maid left, Marian picked up one of the potato pieces. It tasted fried on the outside but soft and full of flavour on the inside.

She glanced to the captain, too deeply asleep for even the scent of the food to wake him. She was tempted to eat the whole plate of potatoes without him.

Shaking her head in dismay over her selfishness, she turned to him. 'Captain?'

He did not rouse.

'Captain?' She touched his unwounded shoulder.

His eyes opened, softening into a look that made her knees turn to melted wax.

'Our food is here,' she told him.

He sat on the bed and she on the chair as they ate,

too hungry for conversation. Along with the stew and potatoes were large tankards of beer. Marian drank the entire contents of one. By the time they had finished their dishes were almost as clean as if scrubbed by a scullery maid. She felt calmer than she'd felt in days, even since before the Duchess of Richmond's Ball.

She was also very sleepy.

She stacked the dishes on the tray and set them outside the door. When she came back in the room, the Captain pointed to the clothing hanging on the chair. 'Are those clean?'

She nodded.

'I believe I would prefer sleeping in clean clothing than in these.' He looked down at himself.

Now that he mentioned it, Marian could well agree. She was also anxious to remove the clothing of the dead soldiers.

'I will help you.' She separated her clothing from his.

His gaze caught hers. 'I will be grateful.'

Her body flooded with sensation again and this time she understood it had nothing to do with tending to an injured soldier, but everything to do with him being a man. She pulled off his shirt, dusty from the road, and helped him on with the laundered one, which sported a tattered hole where the musket ball had torn through. She reached for the buttons on his trousers.

He stopped her. 'I will manage this part.'

She turned away.

When she turned back he lay against the pillows, eyes already closed. She sat in the chair and rested her head on the table, using her arms for a pillow.

'Miss Pallant.' His voice intruded. She'd almost fallen asleep. 'Share the bed or I'll insist we change places.'

She glanced over at him. His eyes were still closed. She should not sleep with him, but the chair was so hard and the bed so temptingly soft. She and Domina had shared a bed on occasion when travelling with Domina's family, and she and the captain had slept in the same stall the past two nights, after all. And he was not delirious.

She pushed the chair away from the table and pulled off her cap, removing the pins and setting them carefully aside. Again lamenting the lack of a comb, she redid her plait and quickly changed back into Domina's brother's clothes.

One last moment of decision. She hesitated only a second longer before climbing under the covers next to him. Even though careful not to touch him, she felt the warmth of his body nearby. He faced her and she watched him in repose, the pain gone from his features, his strong face softened and shadowed with a three-day growth of whiskers. She was tempted to touch his beard, to discover how it felt. Soft like the hair on his head? She slid her hand towards him, but made herself roll over away from him instead.

Sleep eluded her. He moved closer and took her in his arms, spooning her against him. She ought to be shocked. She ought to push away and return to the chair.

Instead she nestled against him and instantly fell asleep.

Marian woke to the morning sun warming her face. The captain faced her, one of his arms resting across her shoulder. The other lay over her hair, now loose and splayed over the pillows.

She gasped and tried to edge away.

His eyes fluttered open and gazed into hers. His lips widened into a sleepy smile. 'Good morning, Miss Pallant.'

'Morning,' she managed.

He smoothed her hair off her face. 'We seem to be still in one piece.'

His stroking hand sent waves of sensation all through her. 'One piece,' she repeated.

She'd danced with gentlemen and even had kisses stolen by one or two, but never had she felt the nearness of a man more acutely than this. She felt naked next to him, even though they were both fully clothed. At the same time she felt completely at ease with him.

His expression sobered and his hand rested against the back of her neck. 'I am glad you are here.'

She opened her mouth to tell him she, too, was glad

they were safe in the inn, but he drew her forwards until their bodies touched. His lips were so close she tasted his breath the moment before his lips met hers. His kiss, so gentle at first, seemed to reach down to the most female part of her. A needful sound escaped and she pressed against him.

His arms tightened around her and she felt the firm shape of him beneath his trousers. Remembering how close her fingers had come to touching him there, she sighed, and his tongue slipped into her mouth.

This was a completely surprising experience, but she lost herself in the pleasure of such a kiss from this man. The pleasure that radiated throughout her body and made her desire so much more from him.

She suddenly understood how men and women needed to couple, to join together in that carnal way. She understood it because she felt it with Captain Landon.

His hand reached under her shirt and rubbed against her breasts, though they were still bound up by her scarf. He might as well have been touching her bare flesh, the sensation was so acute. She wanted to cry out.

She writhed against him, feeling the evidence of his male member. It had grown bigger, just like the maid described. What harm would there be in letting him bed her? Her reputation was already likely in tatters. Why resist this—this promise of unknown delights? They were already connected by their shared ordeal—why not be connected in flesh?

His hand journeyed lower. She covered it with her own and directed his hand lower still to the place between her legs where she was needing him to touch her. He complied, bringing intense sensation. As if a part of him, her body moved against his fingers. The sensation grew into exquisite rapture, supreme joy and suddenly, exploding pleasure.

She seized his shoulders to steady herself.

He cried out and rolled away from her, grasping his shoulder.

She'd touched his wound.

'I am sorry. I am sorry.' She sat up and reached for him, fearful she'd done some irreparable damage.

He covered the wound with his hand. 'Do not touch it!' he cried. Breathing heavily as if he'd run a league, he made a mollifying gesture with his hand. 'Give me a moment.'

Pain had thrust Allan back to reason.

By God, he'd been about to make love to her! He'd already touched her in ways a gentleman would never touch a respectable female who was not his wife. What was he thinking?

He had not been thinking, merely feeling, revelling in her beauty, her nearness and his need. He'd taken advantage of her in the most abominable way.

The pain subsided enough for him to sit next to her. 'It is I who should apologise,' he rasped. 'I took advantage.'

He shook his head. After all she had done for him, he'd engaged in selfish indulgence. 'It will not happen again.'

'You are sorry that happened between us?' Her question was asked in a tone he could only interpret as dismay. She turned away from him and straightened her clothing.

How could he explain it to her? He had aroused her, seduced her so well that she would have easily allowed him to deflower her. How did he admit to this valiant woman who had saved his life that he had been selfish enough to abandon all propriety with her?

As he watched her, his senses merely flamed anew and he could think only of tasting her lips again or feeling her convulse against his fingers. He was in danger of repeating his behaviour and more. He spun away, got up and walked to the window.

The window faced the stable and the scent of horse, leather and hay wafted the great distance to their third-floor room. The scent reminded him of the peasant's stable, of Miss Pallant bringing him water and food and tending his wound, of her aiming a pistol at a huge man with an axe a man who could have cut her down as easily as chopping wood for winter.

And he would repay her with dishonour.

Her half-boots sounded against the wooden floor. 'I will go below and see to some food and clean bandages for your wound.'

'Wait,' he cried, intending to tell her he alone was at fault, intending to ask her forgiveness. Instead, below he spied a man.

A man in a red coat.

A red uniform.

He turned to her, so quickly that pain shot through his shoulder again. He clutched it and laboured to speak. 'There are English soldiers down there.' Three men in red coats entered the stable. 'I can get you back to Brussels at last.'

Chapter Six

By late afternoon they were on the road to Brussels, a wide, flat, well-travelled road very unlike the ones they'd ridden the previous day. They rode in a carriage and Valour remained at the village stable. The English soldiers had lent them the money for the trip and for stabling Valour. Captain Landon had given them his vowel, although Marian was determined to pay for all of it.

She glanced out of the carriage window and watched wounded soldiers, in wagons and on foot, head towards Brussels. Even three days after the battle there were still great numbers of wounded on the road.

She turned to Captain Landon. His eyes were closed and his head rested against the side of the carriage. He was still weak, but insisted upon escorting her back to Brussels.

It would have been much easier if he would have allowed her to make the journey alone. Then their goodbyes would have already been spoken, and she could make him a memory or perhaps forget altogether that he regretted nearly making love to her.

She knew that men needed to bed women. The teachers at the boarding school had explained that to her and Domina. They'd explained that men visited brothels and kept mistresses and seduced maids because men must bed women. Men's urges were very strong. Once aroused, they must be satisfied.

This was the reason a young lady must never be alone with a man and must never titillate his carnal desires. Alarming tales reinforced this lesson, tales of respectable girls bearing babies out of wedlock, being tossed out of their homes and winding up as women of the street.

Marian understood perfectly now.

At the time she had listened to these lessons with an arched brow. Certainly *she* would be able to handle any man who dared make unwanted advances towards her.

What she had not understood was that she, too, could be overpowered by irresistible urges. And that one man could arouse them.

Captain Landon.

Marian flushed with shame at the memory of what happened between them, Yet at the same time she yearned to repeat the experience.

She sighed. It was all too confusing.

'What is it?' His eyes were open and gazing at her.

'Nothing.' Surely he could not read her mind. 'Why do you ask?'

'You sighed.'

She turned back to the window so he could not see her pink cheeks. 'I was looking at all the wounded soldiers. Why are they still on the road? Why are they not cared for?'

'They said at the inn there were many casualties.' He glanced out the window and swore softly. 'Good God.'

'They have been on the road for miles. So many of them,' she whispered.

He leaned further out of the window. 'I can see Brussels ahead.'

'We are near?' They had been on the road for five hours, but she was still not ready. She looked into his eyes. 'Then we will be saying goodbye soon.'

His expression sobered. 'As soon as you are safely returned to your friends.'

Her friends? She could hardly remember them. 'It will seem odd.'

'To be with your friends again?'

'No.' Her throat tightened. 'To not be with you.'

His eyes darkened. 'Indeed.'

Tears pricked her eyes. 'Perhaps we can see each other? In Brussels, I mean?'

He averted his gaze. 'That may not be advisable.'

She felt crushed. Had her wanton behaviour caused

so great a dislike he wished to avoid her? Then why had he not simply sent her back to Brussels alone?

'I see.' Her voice came out sharp.

He turned back to her. 'Maybe news of your escapade can be kept quiet. At Hougoumont and at the village you were disguised as a boy. No one knew you. You may be able to return with your reputation intact.'

'My reputation.' She thought of the previous night. 'Perhaps my wanton behaviour deserves a bad reputation.'

He took her hand. 'That was my fault. My dishonor. I ought to offer—'

'No!' She pulled her hand away. 'I will not make you pay for what was my fault. It was all my fault. I came to the battlefield. I joined you in bed. I—I made you touch me.'

He shook his head. 'It is just that right now. I have nothing to give you. No wealth. Nothing.'

Did he think she cared about such things? No, she cared about love. She'd seen marriage without love and wanted none of it.

The Captain went on. 'We stopped before we went too far. If we can protect your reputation, it will be as if this whole time did not happen.' He lowered his gaze. 'If not, I will offer—'

She waved a hand. 'Enough, Captain. You are not obligated to marry me. Take me back to the Fentons. We will both of us act as if nothing happened.'

Outwardly she might be able to pretend that her life was unchanged, but truly her time with Captain Landon had changed everything inside her. All the frivolity that had consumed her and Domina before—the routs, the balls, the latest ladies' fashions—seemed meaningless to her now.

They soon entered the city. Soldiers were everywhere, sitting on the pavement or leaning against buildings, all wounded, all looking as if they needed a bed and much doctoring.

'Look at them.' Marian cried in alarm. 'Is there no shelter for them? No care for them?'

The captain, too, looked affected by the sight. 'There must be too many.'

'You have a room, though, do you not, Captain?' she asked. 'You have a place to stay in Brussels?'

'Not in Brussels,' he responded. 'I will go back to the village inn where we were last night. I have to get Valour, after all. And when I am a bit more healed, I must return to the regiment.'

She glanced out the window again at the numbers of homeless soldiers. 'But the coachman said he will return there *tomorrow*, not tonight.'

He gave a not-too-reassuring smile. 'I'll find something for tonight.'

'Where?' she cried. If there were rooms available, no men would be on the streets. 'Do you have friends in Brussels?'

He shrugged. 'Likely not. My regiment is probably already on the march.'

Marian felt distraught. She would stay on the street with him, to care for him, rather than have him be alone.

'Do not worry about me.'

The carriage entered the more fashionable part of the city, where London society had chosen housing. Even on these familiar streets, soldiers were languishing.

The Fentons' rooms were nearby. Marian took a breath against a sudden pang of anxiety. 'We are almost there.' She could not leave him without knowing he had a place to stay.

The carriage stopped.

'Is this the place?' he asked.

They were practically in front of the Fentons' door. 'Yes,' she murmured.

Climbing from the carriage caused him pain, but the captain insisted upon helping her out.

He spoke to the driver. 'Where will I find you?'

The coachman named the stable where he would refresh the horses. 'I'll take whatever passengers I can find and leave tomorrow morning by eight.'

'Thank you,' the Captain replied.

As the carriage rolled away, he glanced at Marian. 'Which door?'

She pointed. 'This one.'

He did not move, instead stood looking down upon her.

'Oh, Captain,' she whispered. 'I cannot bear for us to be parted.'

He enfolded her in his arms and she buried her face against his chest, feeling the bandage beneath his clothing.

'Nor I,' he murmured, holding her even tighter. 'We will meet again some day.'

Marian wished she could believe him, but it felt like she would be parted from him for ever.

He released her slowly, caressing her face before knocking upon the Fentons' door.

A manservant opened it.

'Captain Landon escorting Miss Pallant,' the captain said.

The manservant gaped first at the captain, then Marian. She looked down at herself, still in Domina's brother's clothes, now torn and shabby. The captain's coat was ripped where the musket ball had pierced it.

'Come in.' The manservant stepped aside. 'I'll announce you.'

He left them waiting in the hall. The captain pressed his hand to his shoulder again and pain flitted across his face.

At least they had had shelter in the Belgian farmer's stable—where would the captain be this night, before returning to the inn and Valour?

She glanced around the hall, at the marble table holding a vase of flowers, at the silver tray, now empty, that had once held piles of invitations. There was no chair for the captain. She'd never noticed the lack of a chair before.

A quarter of an hour passed before the servant returned to escort them above stairs to the Fentons' drawing room. When they entered, both Sir Roger and Lady Fenton were present.

Lady Fenton glared at Marian. 'You have some nerve returning here big-as-you-please.'

Marian's face burned as if it had been slapped. She had not expected a warm welcome, but this was no welcome at all.

Captain Landon stepped forward. 'Allow me to explain—'

Sir Roger raised his quizzing glass to his eye. 'Who are you?'

'Captain Landon, sir,' he responded. 'Miss Pallant has been through a great deal. She deserves your every consideration.'

Lady Fenton laughed. 'Consideration? She has dishonoured us! Acted totally against anything we could wish—'

Marian broke in. 'Is Domina safe?'

'Domina?' the lady huffed. 'Safe from your bad influence, I can tell you. She told us you ran off during the night—off to be with some soldier, we could guess.'

Lady Fenton turned to Captain Landon. 'You, sir? Did she run off with you?'

The captain's eyes turned flinty. 'You misunderstand.'

Sir Roger pursed his lips. He turned away from Marian and addressed himself to the captain. 'Our son's horse came back, obviously having been ridden hard. Some of our son's clothing was missing.' He gestured to Marian. 'Domina eventually admitted Marian had run off.'

Lady Fenton added, 'At first our daughter would not tell us where she had gone. We soon wore her down—'

Sir Roger went on. 'Our daughter said Marian wished to witness the battle, but we do not credit that.'

'What well-bred young lady would even think to witness a battle?' His wife shook her head. 'Not that she is as well bred as she pretends, born in India and all that. This behaviour is hoydenish in the extreme.'

'Domina is unhurt?' All the abuse of her character washed over Marian for the moment. None of it mattered if her friend had come home in one piece.

Lady Fenton shot daggers at her. 'She is vastly hurt by your behaviour and by how you abused her friendship and took advantage of us all.'

The captain straightened. 'You have been misled. Miss Pallant did not—'

Lady Fenton held up a hand. 'Do not say a word. I will not believe it.'

It finally dawned on Marian that Domina had blamed the entire escapade on her. She swallowed. 'Leave it, Captain. They will not hear you.'

Lady Fenton glared at her. 'Your trunk is packed. Take it now or send instructions where to deliver it.'

The captain stepped forwards. 'Wait a moment. You accepted responsibility for this young lady. You are still responsible for her.'

Lady Fenton laughed in his face. 'It seems *you* have accepted responsibility for her. It is you who have dishonoured her, is it not, sir?'

His eyes blazed at the woman. 'Miss Pallant has done nothing that requires apology.'

Marian felt her face burn. He was wrong and he knew it. 'I do not wish to stay here. I will go back in the carriage.'

The captain turned to her. 'You will not leave. These people brought you to Brussels and they will not abandon you now.'

'She will go,' Sir Roger said.

The Fentons had been like a mother and father to her. Domina had been like a sister. Or so she'd thought.

How easily they turned her out.

'It is near dark.' The captain spoke in a firm voice. 'There is no guarantee of finding accommodations so late.'

Not for him either, she thought.

'Tomorrow I will make other arrangements for her,'

he went on. 'Tonight she stays with you or a story will soon circulate about how respectable young women cannot trust you to chaperon them.'

'You would not dare speak against us.' Lady Fenton looked as if she would explode.

The captain glared.

'Very well.' Lady Fenton's shoulders slumped. 'She must confine herself to her room. I do not wish to set eyes on her again.'

He nodded and turned to Marian, reaching over to steady himself on the back of a chair. 'I'll come for you in the morning.'

She could not help but feel relief. She would be parted from him for only a night.

Her brows knit. 'But you have no place to stay tonight.' She turned to the Fentons. 'There is room in this house. He must stay here.'

'I will not hear of it!' cried Lady Fenton.

The captain looked directly into Marian's eyes. 'I will manage. It is only one night.' With a fortifying breath he released his grip on the chair and bowed to Sir Roger and Lady Fenton. 'I will call for Miss Pallant in the morning.'

He walked to the door, but needed to hold on to the doorjamb a moment before proceeding to the stairs.

'Captain!' Marian ran after him.

From the top of the stairs she watched his descent. The manservant waited at the bottom step.

The captain faltered. Seizing the banister, he bent slightly as if seized with pain.

'Captain!' Marian hurried to him, but the manservant reached him first and assisted him the rest of the way.

Sir Roger and Lady Fenton came to the top of the stairs.

Marian looked back at them. 'You heartless people. Can you not see he is wounded? A Frenchman's musket ball went through him, and still he helped me return to you. He said he'd return me safely *home.*' She choked back an angry sob.

She turned to the manservant. 'He has no place to stay.'

The man's expression was sympathetic.

The captain waved them off. 'I am quite back to rights again.'

Marian glared at the Fentons. 'He must stay here as well. Otherwise he will be on the streets like the others.'

'It is not our concern,' said Lady Fenton.

'Now, dear…' Sir Roger looked uncertain.

The manservant spoke up. 'If I may be so bold, sir. This soldier may use my bed and I'll make up a cot for myself.'

'Very well.' Sir Roger looked relieved. 'Take him below. He may stay.'

The Captain did not protest when the man offered his shoulder to assist him. Marian watched them make their way to the door down to the servants' quarters. The manservant glanced back at her. 'Do not fret, miss. I'll see he is well tended.'

She waited until they closed the door behind them before climbing the stairs to the room where she once so happily spent her nights. When she passed Sir Roger and Lady Fenton on the first landing, she refused to even look at them. Her room was one flight up, but she deliberately set a slow pace. Let them not see the distress burning inside her. When she reached the room, she still did not hurry.

After she closed the door behind her she leaned against it for a moment. By God, she would not give in to tears now, not even angry ones.

With a groan of frustration she removed her half-boots, all scratched and worn, and tore off the cap that had hidden her hair. At least she would finally be able to brush out its tangles.

There was a faint knock at the door. Domina's maid peeked in. 'I came to help you, if you wish, miss.' Becky was young, but aspired to be a fine lady's maid some day.

At least her face was friendly. 'Oh, Becky, I do not wish to get you in trouble.'

The maid shrugged. 'We won't tell them, then, will we?' She picked up the cap and jacket off the floor. 'What happened to you, miss?'

Marian glanced away. 'I wound up in the middle of

the battle for a while, and have since been trying to get back.' She lifted her gaze to the girl. 'Miss Fenton told them I went alone, but that was not the truth. She must have found her way back; I do thank God for that.'

'I think she came in before dawn,' Becky admitted, folding the jacket. 'But there is time to talk of that later. What might I do for you now?'

'I do not know what to request.' She put her hand in her hair. 'All I really want is to wash myself and my hair, but I dare not request a bath.'

Becky smiled. 'Let's get you out of the rest of those clothes and into a wrapper. We'll sneak you down to the kitchen for a bath. Lady Fenton will never know.'

Marian hugged her. 'I cannot think of anything that would be more generous.'

'I'll come back for you when the water is ready,' Becky said.

Marian shed the rest of her clothing and nearly cheered aloud when she freed herself from the scarf binding her chest. She rolled the garments into a ball, intending to burn them. She'd send Domina's brother new ones.

Standing in the room naked felt better than wearing those clothes. She could still smell the blood and smoke of Hougoumont upon them even though she'd tried to scrub them clean.

She turned to the trunk and opened it, searching through to find her nightrail and her brush and comb.

She wrapped the robe around her, tied the sash, and sat in the chair in front of her dressing table. Starting from the ends, she combed the tangles from her hair.

Half an hour had gone by before she could pass the comb through without it catching on a knot.

Becky returned. 'We can sneak you down to the kitchen now. We've set up a tub in the scullery. It will be quite private there.'

Marian followed her down the servants' staircase to the area below stairs where, as well as the kitchen, the housekeeper's and the manservant's rooms were located. Marian had never been in this part of the house.

When they entered the kitchen, Captain Landon was the first person she saw. He sat at the table, a huge plate of food in front of him. Also in a robe, he was clean-shaven and his wet brown hair gleamed almost black. He'd obviously also been offered a bath.

She warmed at the idea he'd been so well tended. 'Captain, they appear to be taking good care of you.'

'They are indeed.' His gaze flickered over her.

She wrapped her nightrail tighter and touched her hair, wishing she had tied it back with a ribbon.

'Enjoy your bath,' he said.

She might have, except with every stroke of the wash cloth against her skin, she thought of his hand stroking her. The look he had just given her when gazing on her dishabille had been unreadable.

* * *

When she finished her bath, he was no longer in the kitchen, but the cook insisted she eat a meal. Not nearly as hungry as she thought she might be, she ate enough to show Cook how grateful she was for the kindness. Afterwards she climbed the servants' stairs to her room with no one to see her.

She entered her room and found Domina sitting on the bed.

Domina jumped off. 'Oh, Marian! I've been waiting ages for you.'

Marian felt cold. 'Domina.'

The short auburn curls that framed Domina's round face bobbed as she hurried towards Marian. 'I expect you are angry because of what I said to Mama and Papa, but I had to do it. They were so angry.' Her eyes filled with fat tears. 'Marian, it is so dreadful. So terribly dreadful.' She threw her arms around Marian and sobbed. 'Ollie is dead! His name was on a list. He was killed in the battle.'

Lieutenant Harry Oliver had proudly worn the uniform and gleaming Grecian helmet of the Inniskilling Dragoons, and Domina had fallen head over ears in love with him. She and Ollie were secretly betrothed, because Ollie had no title and Domina's mother would never have approved the match, but they were in *love*.

Now Ollie, the reason they'd ridden off to be near the battle, was dead.

Marian set her anger aside. 'I am so sorry, Domina.' She held her grieving friend.

Domina sniffled. 'Mama and Papa do not understand. But you do, don't you, Marian?'

Marian had never understood Domina's infatuation with the rather ordinary Harry Oliver, but she did understand loss and now she knew the horror of a soldier's death.

She coaxed her friend back to the bed and sat next to her. 'I am so sad for you.'

Domina went into great detail about how devastated she was, how perfect a man Ollie had been, and how her life was over. 'And...and the worst of it is—' tears streamed down her cheeks '—I have not had my monthly courses.'

'What?' Marian gaped at her.

Domina blew her nose into a soggy handkerchief. 'I may have Ollie's child inside me.'

'Do not say you bedded him, Domina.' Marian shook her head.

Domina sighed. 'How could I resist? We had such a passion for each other.' She collapsed against the pillow with fresh sobs.

Marian lifted her so Domina was forced to look at her. 'Do your parents know?'

Domina's eyes widened as if she thought Marian had lost her wits. 'Certainly not.'

Marian held her firmly. 'You must tell them. If you are increasing, they will have to make plans—'

'I will never give up Ollie's baby!' Domina cried.

Marian shook her. 'Then you had better tell your parents so they can make plans for both of you. Your reputation and your child's future are at stake.'

Domina sobered. 'My child's future. Yes, you are right.' She gave Marian a quick hug and hopped off the bed. 'I will tell them directly.' Her curls danced as if she were still a carefree débutante as she ran to the door. She turned to wave at Marian before she fled into the hallway, never once asking about Marian's health or about what had happened after Marian fell off the horse.

Soon the sound of raised voices reached Marian's ears, Lady Fenton's shrill cries, Sir Roger's booming tones and Domina's strident wails.

Domina had taken her advice.

Marian donned her nightdress and crawled into bed and fell asleep quickly in spite of the verbal battle being waged. She slept soundly until a knock on the door woke her.

Becky entered carrying a candle. 'Miss Pallant, I came to tell you we are leaving as soon as it is light.'

'Leaving?' Marian sat up.

Becky nodded. 'Sir Roger and Lady Fenton have ordered a carriage. We are to return to England posthaste, but you are not to come with us.' The candle illuminated the maid's worried face. 'What will you do, miss?'

The Fentons had already planned to abandon her, so this came as no great surprise.

'Do not worry over me.' The Captain would not desert her, that much she knew.

'Then, goodbye, miss.' Becky turned to leave.

Marian rose from the bed. 'Wait a moment.'

She ran to her trunk and rummaged through it until she found her coin purse. She dropped several coins into the maid's hands.

Becky stared at the money. 'Oh, miss, it is too much.'

Marian gave her a quick embrace. 'Your kindness deserves reward. If you ever need any assistance at all, you must find me.'

The girl stared at her hand again before curtsying and rushing out of the room.

Marian sat upon the edge of the bed to wait until dawn and the Fentons' departure. After that, she and the Captain would decide what to do.

Glad as she was to delay saying goodbye to him, she knew it was only a matter of time.

Perhaps he would find her a way to return to England. Or maybe he would locate her cousin Edwin and place her in Edwin's care. Edwin would want to return to England. He would inherit his father's title and estate and there would be much for him to arrange.

Marian had almost forgotten that her Uncle Tranville had also lost his life at Waterloo. She had never been close to him, so it was difficult to feel grief. He had rarely been in her company. If he hadn't been away at war, he had been with his mistress, breaking her aunt's heart and, Marian believed, hastening her death.

Marian remembered seeing Uncle Tranville once in Bath, strolling in the square with the woman who'd been his mistress for years. Her uncle had touched the woman as if to remove a bit of lint from her spencer. The woman had pressed his hand against her breast.

Another memory flashed through her mind, one more painful, a memory of her father. In India she'd been out in the market with her *amah* when she glimpsed her father in a carriage, his arms around an exotic creature draped in colourful silks. The woman slipped on to her father's lap and put her lips on her father's mouth.

Later when her parents became sick with the fever, her mother accused her father of catching it from *that woman*. Marian, though a child, somehow she knew who her mother meant, just as she knew *that woman,* and later her Uncle Tranville's mistress, had chosen to be carnal with a man.

Marian gave a cry and lay back on the bed, covering her face with her hands.

She'd never understood before what would drive a

woman to abandon all morality and be carnal with a man not her husband.

Not until now. Not until Captain Landon.

Chapter Seven

'Captain!'

The man's voice roused Allan from a sleep so deep and welcome he did not wish to leave it.

'Captain, wake up.' He recognised the voice as Johnson's, the manservant who had given up his bed for him.

Allan opened his eyes to the man's Spartan room.

Johnson stood over him. 'I must leave, Captain. We depart within the hour.'

Allan sat up. 'Depart?'

'For England, sir. Sir Roger and Lady Fenton decided quite abruptly. The Belgian cook and housemaids remain, but the rest of us travel with the family.' He stepped forwards. 'If you rise now, I have time to change your bandage and assist with your dress.'

'What of Miss Pallant?' Returning to England would be best for her. He must see her, though, before she departed.

'She is not to travel with us.'

Allan rose from the bed. This was outrageous. 'They would leave her here? What sort of people are they?'

The man frowned. 'It is not my place to criticise my employers, sir.'

Allan lifted a hand. 'Forgive me. I did not mean for you to speak against them.'

The manservant untied the bandage.

Allan asked, 'Why the haste in leaving? Are you able to tell me that much?'

'I do not know, sir,' the man admitted. 'It came after heated words with their daughter.'

About Miss Pallant? Allan wondered. Perhaps the daughter had told the truth, but, if so, how could these people leave Miss Pallant alone in Brussels? It was unconscionable no matter what she had done.

He sat still as Johnson re-bandaged his wounds. There was still the problem of finding someone to take charge of Miss Pallant before irreparable damage was done to her reputation.

The bandaging completed, the manservant brought Allan's clothes, freshly laundered and brushed. Mended, as well. There were no longer holes in his shirt and coat, no stains on his trousers.

'This is indeed a kindness.' Allan fingered the mended area of his coat. Even his wounds felt on the mend. After Johnson helped him dress, Allan spoke. 'I want to show you my appreciation, but I have no money with me.'

The manservant looked embarrassed. 'No need, sir.'

He handed Allan his boots, polished to gleaming black. 'I must be off, sir. I'll be needed by now.'

None the less, Allan would not forget this kind man. As soon as he could arrange it, a token of his gratitude would be sent to him. 'I am very grateful to you.'

The servant bowed his head. 'We are all grateful to *you*, sir, and to the rest of our soldiers.' He hurried out.

After donning his boots and buttoning his coat, Allan climbed the stairs and watched from the recesses of the hall as the Fentons' trunks and bandboxes were carried out the door. Lastly Sir Roger, Lady Fenton and a young woman Allan presumed was their daughter bustled down the stairway, followed by a grumbling boy of about fourteen years.

'I still do not see why we have to leave,' the boy complained.

The family reached the front door. Only the daughter, her face shrouded by a hooded cape, turned back and glanced towards the top of the stairs.

As soon as the door closed behind them, Allan stepped out into the hall. He, too, glanced to the top of the stairs.

Miss Pallant stood there.

Gone was the scruffy lad or the dishevelled nurse or the alluring creature dressed in nothing but a robe. All were replaced by a woman who ought to have been decorating London's finest drawing rooms. Her blonde hair was pulled on top of her head with curls framing her flawless complexion. Her lips were full and her cheeks tinged with pink. She wore a filmy white gown, like an angel might wear, and her shoulders were draped with a colourful shawl.

'Captain.' To his surprise, her voice was excited and her sapphire-blue eyes sparkled. 'I have a wonderful notion.' She started down the stairs, and he felt riveted to the spot waiting for her. 'The Fentons have left for England, but I know they paid for these rooms for another month, at least. We can use the house for the injured soldiers.'

And he'd expected her to lament being abandoned.

'You can stay here, as well. You need a place to recuperate.' She reached the bottom step. 'Have you eaten? Come to the kitchen. If we can convince the cook and the maids to stay, we should be able to offer good care to a great many of them.'

He held up a hand. 'One moment, Miss Pallant—'

But she continued past him. 'I will need your help, because I have no idea who to contact or which of the soldiers are most in need. There are several rooms here. And if we could find extra bedding—'

He seized her arm. 'You cannot do this!'

She lifted her chin. 'After the manner in which Sir Roger and Lady Fenton treated me, I have no qualms about using rooms for which they have already paid.'

'That is not what I meant.' Allan felt like shaking her. 'You cannot care for wounded soldiers.'

She gaped at him. 'Why not? I have cared for you, have I not? And the men at Hougoumont?' Her voice cracked and he realised her high spirits hid more painful emotions.

He suddenly had the urge to hold her, to comfort her for all she had seen and endured.

But he did not. 'Can you not see?' he said instead. 'I gave you no other choice. Besides, you were disguised as a boy then. No one knew you were a respectable young lady. In Brussels your identity will become known. You must consider your reputation—'

'Oh, do not prose on about my reputation again.' She pulled away with a scornful laugh. 'Am I to pit my reputation against their suffering? Do not be nonsensical, Captain.' She walked towards the servants' staircase.

He followed her. 'I do not dispute that using this house would be a great service to those men, only that you should not provide their care.'

She stopped and again pain flitted through her eyes. 'My chaperons have abandoned me, Captain. I do not know anyone who might take me in. Indeed, I know of no one but you upon whom I may depend. Let me be of some use.' Her expression turned pleading. 'I will ask Cook and the maids. If they do not object to helping the soldiers, then neither should we.'

The cook and the maids, all women with grey hair

and lined faces, spoke enough French and English that Miss Pallant was able to communicate her plan. While Cook fed them breakfast, Miss Pallant explained to them, 'I will pay you and pay for the food and other supplies the soldiers will need.'

'Can you afford such an expense?' Allan asked her.

She made a dismissive gesture. 'I have wealth enough. My father made a great deal of money in the East India Company. Neither Lord Tranville nor his man of business bothered overmuch with the amounts I drew out, so I have plenty with me to pay for what we need.'

She had wealth? A woman with wealth had excellent prospects—if she preserved her good name.

The cook and two maids enthusiastically agreed to help care for the wounded soldiers. Apparently these women were not among the Belgians supporting the French.

Miss Pallant gazed at him from across the kitchen table. 'Will you help, Captain? You must know where to go or who to speak to about this.'

He knew her well enough now to be certain she could not be persuaded to abandon this idea. 'I will assist only if you agree not to personally provide care to the men.'

Her gaze did not waver. 'I will do what is required.'

Blast her. Her stubborn streak had already created more trouble for her than she deserved.

He stood. 'Miss Pallant, would you be so good as to speak with me above stairs.'

Allan walked out, hearing with relief her footsteps behind him. He climbed the stairs to the drawing room, the room where the Fentons had so cruelly turned her away. He held the door open for her and caught the scent of roses as she walked by him.

She whirled on him as he closed the door. 'You are going to try to talk me out of this.'

He felt no need to apologise. 'I certainly am. Will you sit?'

She merely walked over to the window and looked out, arms crossed over her chest.

He cleared his throat. 'Very well. Do not sit.' He walked over to stand behind her, wanting to put his hands on her shoulders, remembering how soft and warm she'd felt in his arms when they'd shared the bed—

He dared not think of that. 'Consider this carefully. It is generous of you to pay for the care of the soldiers, and I've certainly no objection to using this house, but you cannot be a lone woman caring for men.'

'The cook and the maids will be helping,' she responded defensively.

'But they are not proper chaperons for you. We must find you a respectable place to stay.' He was distracted by the graceful shape of her neck and by the golden tendrils that caressed its nape.

She turned and was inches from him. 'Where, Captain? I have no friends here who were not friends of the Fentons. My guardian is dead and my cousin, if he is alive, surely is in no position to help me at the moment. Why would anyone take me in when Sir Roger and Lady Fenton have cast me off?'

Her gaze reached his eyes and he forgot for a moment to breathe.

'Perhaps they have said nothing to their friends,' he managed, though his voice turned husky. 'To speak of it would reveal their failure to properly chaperon you, and, do not forget, everyone would have been preoccupied by the battle. We can invent a story to protect your reputation.'

'Do I deserve the protection, Captain?' she whispered. 'Have I not demonstrated all the wanton behaviour of which I have been accused? Should you, of all people, not know how little I deserve a good name?' Her eyes filled with tears, but she ruthlessly blinked them away.

Not before one fell on to her cheek.

Allan brushed it away with the pad of his thumb. 'My fault,' he murmured. He leaned down, closer, so close he felt her breath on his lips.

She made a tiny, yearning sound, tilting her head up to his.

No! He had hurt her enough with his seduction.

He moved away. 'Heed me.' He was unable to more

than glance at the surprised expression on her face. 'If we say nothing, no one will know you and I shared the—the time together.'

She turned back to the window, but her breathing quickened. 'I am already lost. Let me at least stay busy. Do some good. After it is all done, perhaps Edwin will be free to take me back to England.'

Edwin.

Allan would be damned if he put her in the care of such a man. She could not know the despicable behaviour of which Edwin was capable.

But Allan's own behaviour deserved censure, as well, did it not? Guilt tore at his insides. He had not forced her, perhaps, but he certainly had taken advantage of her.

And almost did so again in this room.

He straightened. 'I will go to the Place Royale and see if there is someone else with whom you can stay. I must go there and report in, in any event.' He started for the door but turned back. 'I will inform the authorities that there are accommodations for several soldiers at this address.'

She looked over her shoulder. 'Thank you, Captain.' Her voice seemed sad. 'I doubt you will find anyone willing to accept me, but would you also enquire of my cousin Edwin? I should like to know if he is alive and how I might contact him to inform him I am here?'

He nodded, but enquiring of her cousin did not mean he would ever put her into Edwin's care.

The walk to the Place Royale tired Allan more than he expected, and the sheer number and condition of the wounded on the streets tore at his emotions.

The Place Royale was all chaos. There was no question of finding an English family in Brussels who might offer Miss Pallant their hospitality. He could find no one even willing to discuss the matter. Most English families, it seemed, had fled to Antwerp and those who remained apparently had been prevailed upon to house wounded soldiers. News of another house available for the wounded was welcomed, however. He was told to expect arrivals that very day.

Allan reported to the regimental office, another place fraught with confusion. He was able to report in and be listed as wounded. He gave the Fentons' house as his direction.

He also learned that the battle cost about forty thousand lives, both Allies and French. The men in the office were too busy for him to ask about Edwin Tranville or, more importantly, whether Gabe and his other friends had survived. He was too exhausted to pore through the lists posted of all the dead and wounded officers. The regiment had already marched for France and, until he was well enough to rejoin it, he would not discover how many of the soldiers had survived, men who'd fought at his side throughout Spain and France and now Waterloo.

He walked into the square.

Forty thousand men lost. The battlefield must have been thick with bodies. At least Miss Pallant had been spared that sight.

In the square vendors were selling the casualty list. Allan used one of his last coins to purchase a copy to peruse later when he was alone. He'd discover then who among his friends he must grieve.

As he crossed the square, the faces of his men flashed through his mind. He stopped to catch his breath and looked around him. Soldiers slept on the pavement, others sat on the benches, still others sat with their backs against the stone walls. They all stared vacantly.

You are right, Marian, he said to himself, using her given name for the first time. *You are right to help them.*

He spied a uniform of the Royal Scots, a man lying on a spot of grass. With one hand clasped to his wounded shoulder, he hurried over.

It was a corporal from his old company. 'Reilly!'

The man's uniform sleeve was stained with blood and his face was flushed with fever.

He opened his eyes. 'Captain?'

Allan crouched down. 'Can you stand, Reilly? I'm taking you with me.'

Allan helped him to his feet, his own wound aching

with the effort. Had Allan been stronger, he would have carried Reilly, but, taking frequent rests, they hobbled back to the Fentons' house. Allan knocked upon the door.

Marian—he'd turned a corner; she was no longer Miss Pallant in his mind—answered the door, her arms laden with bed linens. She dropped them to the floor.

'Oh, my!' She rushed to assist him.

'This is Corporal Reilly from my regiment,' he said as the three of them stepped into the hall. 'I could not pass him by.'

'Ma'am.' Reilly inclined his head to her.

'Can we get you above stairs, Corporal Reilly?' She turned to Allan. 'We can put him in one of the bedrooms.'

With Marian on one side and Allan on the other they struggled up the stairs and led the corporal into the first bedroom they came upon.

'This was Lady Fenton's room,' Marian told Allan in a conspiratorial tone.

He nodded. Lady Fenton would certainly suffer a fit of vapours if she knew her bed was to be occupied by a simple soldier.

They sat Reilly upon the mattress.

'Do not worry, Captain,' she said with a smile. 'I changed the linens.'

He laughed, but was stifled by a spasm of pain. He grasped the bedpost.

Her forehead furrowed. 'Sit, Captain. You have over-taxed yourself.'

He did not protest, lowering himself into a nearby cushioned chair.

She turned to Reilly. 'Now, Corporal, I am going to unbutton your coat and pull off your boots, and you certainly may lie down, but I must send one of the servants to undress you and tend your wounds.' She glanced towards Allan. 'Your captain will not allow me to do more.'

'Thank you, ma'am,' Reilly mumbled.

When she was done, Allan accompanied her below stairs, all the way to the kitchen where she found one of the maids.

'I will go, *tout de suite*,' the maid responded, bustling out, looking as eager as Marian to tend their first patient.

'Now you, Captain,' Marian said. 'You must rest.' She helped him to the manservant's room where he'd spent the night.

He sat on the bed. His shoulder ached and his legs felt like rubber. She knelt and pulled off his boots, then, placing herself between his legs, reached up to unbutton his coat. What had seemed businesslike and efficient, when performed for Reilly, now was nothing but erotic to his senses. He wanted to press his exhausted body against hers, to savour her softness and her strength.

Instead he touched her hand.

She paused for only a moment. 'I will help you remove your coat.' She gave him a look that suggested she knew precisely what he had been feeling. 'Just your coat and your shirt. I want to check your wound.'

He tried to remain very still while she unbuttoned his coat and pulled it off him. He controlled himself when she lifted his shirt over his head.

She looked beneath his bandage. 'It looks black and blue. Does it pain you?'

He took her hand in his and held it against his heart. 'Not so much now.' His nostrils filled with her rose scent; he savoured her nearness.

He leaned forwards and touched his lips to hers. The kiss grew in intensity. Her arms encircled his neck and she pressed herself against him, powerfully arousing him.

And forcing himself to his senses. 'Enough, Marian.'

She blinked and her cheeks flushed pink.

He averted his gaze. 'I have crossed the bounds of propriety again.'

Her smile was tight. 'Calling me by my given name is hardly a serious breach of propriety.'

His gaze touched hers. 'You know what I mean.'

She whispered, 'I like it...you calling me Marian, that is.'

He touched her cheek and desire grew in her expressive eyes. Now he had aroused her. The idea both thrilled him and made him angry at himself.

He turned away. 'Go now,' he said in a harsh voice.

She hurried out.

Marian ran all the way up the stairs to the hallway, grabbing the linens she'd dropped earlier. She busied herself with making beds, anything to keep her from dwelling upon her body's reaction to the captain.

She feared she'd go mad thinking about him and re-experiencing her body's reaction to him, an aching that was both pleasurable and terribly unsettling.

The Fentons had labelled her lost to all propriety. They were correct. Her reaction to the captain was proof.

She could not be ashamed of it, though, nor was she ashamed of her efforts to help the soldiers. Both seemed right, as if destiny had decreed she act in such a manner.

It mattered only that the captain again regretted her wanton response to him. Had his voice not been harsh after she ground herself against him, after she had almost induced him to lay with her again?

More wounded soldiers arrived and soon she was busy directing where each should sleep, what each needed in order to be comfortable, who was most in need of care. The most severely injured received beds, and the others cots on the floor or a sofa. Eleven men came to them and they filled every room, fed them all and, thanks to some old trunks in the attic, made certain all had clean nightclothes to wear while their clothing was laundered and mended.

The captain slept through all this activity. Marian checked on him whenever she could, fearful the exertions of the day might bring back his fever, but his forehead was always cool to her touch. He was merely exhausted.

When night fell and everyone had gone to their beds, Marian made her way to the kitchen. It was quiet and peaceful as she fixed herself a pot of tea by the light of the embers in the oven and a single candle. As she waited for the tea to steep she lay her head down on the table, feeling a satisfied weariness.

'Marian?'

She glanced up. The captain was framed in the doorway.

'You are awake.' She tried not to sound as tired as she felt. 'Are you feeling unwell?'

'Not at all.' He strolled in and took a seat in the chair opposite her at the bare wooden table. 'Very rested, however.' He smiled, and it felt like butterflies were set free inside her.

'Are you hungry?' she asked.

His smile widened. 'Starving.'

She rose and found some cold meat and cheese for him to eat. She poured him a cup of tea.

He took an eager bite of the cheese. She enjoyed watching him eat, so ordinary and comfortable an event, so unlike the anxious times they'd spent together.

'How did you fare while I slept the day away?' he asked between bites.

She smiled proudly. 'We have eleven more patients.'

As he ate, she told him all they'd done that day to make the men comfortable.

'I did not dress wounds,' she added, pouring him more tea.

He nodded in approval and sipped from his cup. 'It must be very late. Why are you in the kitchen?'

'After midnight?' She yawned. 'Cook has given me her room. She will sleep on the sofa in the drawing room so she will hear the soldiers if they need her. The maids are on the third floor.'

'And we are on this level,' he said, his warm eyes resting on her like a caress.

Her heart skipped. 'Yes.'

He stared down into his tea. 'I owe you an apology.'

She felt a pang of disappointment at losing that warm gaze. 'For what?'

His eyes lifted. 'When I walked to the Place Royale, there were wounded soldiers everywhere. You were right. How could we not help them?'

She smiled. He'd said *we*.

He went on. 'I was not able to enquire for your cousin. There was no opportunity.'

'Later, then.' She hoped Edwin was alive, but what if he wanted her to leave Brussels now, when so much needed to be done?

Marian gazed at Captain Landon through her lashes.

She did not wish to leave. She was precisely where she wanted to be at the moment.

As he finished his meal and she, her tea, they chatted about practical things. Supplies they needed. How to feed all the men. How the tasks should be divided.

He walked her to the cook's room, and carried the candle inside to light the one next to her bed. She stayed near the door, fearful that her wantonness would overtake her again. As he passed her to leave, he stopped and stared down at her.

Marian felt a spiral of sensation twirl through her. With his free hand he tilted her face to his and touched his lips to hers. She seized the cloth of his shirt and clenched it in her fists, her body meeting his as if she had no control.

He stepped away. 'Goodnight, Marian.'

And was gone.

Chapter Eight

The next few days formed a routine that almost gave Allan an incongruous sense of peace. Marian, the cook and the maids were kept busy seeing every man was well tended and well fed. One of the maids, a widow who'd borne and reared many children, proved very skilled at tending the men's wounds. The other maid learned fast. Cook was kept busy feeding them all.

Marian did whatever else was needed, and, like the colonel of the regiment, she kept everyone organised and on task.

If Marian was the colonel, Allan was the quartermaster. He made certain they had all necessary supplies, going out each day to procure something with Marian's seemingly unlimited funds. It was a good task for him, helping him regain his strength and his stamina.

He'd been able to access some of his pay and immediately sent for Valour to be stabled nearby. He'd just visited the stable to make certain the horse was properly tended, and had purchased a bag of flour for Cook. He placed it on the table for her.

'*Merci, Capitaine,*' Cook said, clapping her hands in appreciation.

He asked, '*Où est Madamoiselle Pallant?*' Marian would want to know Valour had arrived safely.

'*Votre chambre,*' Cook replied.

His room? He hurried down the corridor and found her seated on the bed, a large piece of paper in one hand and a feather duster in the other. Her expression was distressed.

He forgot about Valour. 'What is it?'

She blinked up at him. 'A list of the casualties from the battle. I found it under the bed.'

Where he had tossed it after reading it. Too many good men were dead. Too many maimed. Some survived at least. Gabe, for one. Allan was grateful Gabe had survived.

'Domina's betrothed is listed.' Her voice wobbled.

They had not discussed the man for whom her friend had convinced her to run off to a battlefield. In fact, they had discussed nothing about the battle at all. Waterloo had sometimes seemed more like a former nightmare than a memory.

'Was he killed?' he asked.

She looked down at the piece of paper and nodded. 'Domina told me so that first night, but it seems real to see his name on a list.'

Perhaps that explained the Fentons' quick departure from Brussels. It made him slightly more sympathetic towards them.

'I remember some of the others listed as well.' Her voice went up a pitch as if she were battling emotion. 'We attended many of the same social events.'

'I am sorry for them.' He was sorry any of them were lost.

She turned the list over. 'At least Edwin is not listed.'

Allan felt a twinge of guilt. 'I never asked about him for you.' Possibly because he did not want Edwin near her.

She waved a dismissive hand. 'I confess to having forgotten about him as well. I hope this means he is unharmed.' She looked down at the piece of paper again. 'It lists my guardian as missing.'

Allan had never searched the list for Tranville's name. 'Missing?' Perhaps his body was never found. It happened sometimes. 'This list was printed soon after the battle. It may not be accurate.'

She dropped the paper on to the bed. 'I should not have read it. It brings back how horrible it all was.'

He sat next to her and put his arms around her. 'Let us hope Waterloo was the last big battle.'

She pressed her face against his chest and it was all he could do to keep from pulling her on to his lap and tasting her lips once again. He just held her close, trying to content himself with as much.

She pulled away. 'Enough feeling sorry for myself.'

He brushed a stray strand of hair away from her face. 'Would you like for me to enquire about your cousin today? I can go out again.'

She gently touched his wounded shoulder. 'You have already been out today. You mustn't do too much.'

He took her hand and squeezed it. 'I am feeling rather fit.'

She sighed. 'I would like to know if Edwin is in Brussels. I just do not want him to take me away before our soldiers are well.'

'Then we will not allow him to do so.' He rubbed the palm of her hand with his thumb.

Her eyes darkened and her lips parted slightly, pulling him towards her.

He caught himself. 'I'll go directly.'

Without another word or another glance back at her, he walked out of the room and back outdoors, making his way to the Place Royale.

He had walked too fast across the Parc of Brussels and was winded by the time he entered the regimental offices.

'Are you fit to rejoin the regiment?' the officer in charge asked him.

If he became winded by a walk through the streets of

Brussels, he doubted he would be able to join a march. 'Not as yet.' Besides, he did not wish to leave Brussels yet.

The man eyed him sceptically.

'I am looking for one of the Royal Scots' officers,' Allan told him.

The man looked down at his papers. 'Who?'

'Captain Edwin Tranville.'

The officer's brows rose. 'The General's son? Why?'

'I enquire for a friend.' That was as much as he wished to explain. 'Is he in Brussels?'

The man laughed. 'Search the taverns. You will find him.'

Allan frowned. 'Where is he staying?'

He jabbed his finger on a stack of papers. 'I will have to go through this whole pile before finding that answer. Just search the taverns. It will be faster.'

Allan started with taverns nearest the Place Royale. The officer was correct. He found Edwin in the third place he entered, a nearby inn.

'Oh, Lawd.' Edwin looked up as Allan approached the table where he sat alone. 'I heard you were dead.'

Allan's greeting was just as friendly. 'I, on the other hand, knew you would make it through without a scratch. Tell me, where did you go after we were dispatched with that first message?'

Edwin smirked. 'My horse went lame. I had no choice but to withdraw to the rear.'

It was one of Edwin's typical excuses and they both knew it.

Edwin waved his hand. 'Well, sit down. It hurts my neck to look up at you.' His words were slurred. 'Have some beer. Belgian beer.' He laughed and rubbed the scar on his face, the one he'd received at Badajoz. 'It is not half bad.'

Allan sat, but ordered nothing. 'I have been searching for you.'

Edwin put his tankard down with a loud clap. His jaw dropped. 'Gawd. Do not tell me my father sent you.'

Allan straightened. 'Your father?'

Edwin took another swig. 'Just like him to send you, all *sober* and everything.'

'But—your father was killed in the battle.' He gripped the edge of the table.

Edwin lifted the tankard again and his voice echoed. 'Not killed. Wounded. What do they say? *Fallen in battle.*' He gulped down more beer. 'Seems he was picked up again. Literally. He's rusticating at the Hôtel de Flandres under the care of his loving mistress, a woman I despise, by the way. Her son, whom I also despise, was the big hero. Carried my father off the battlefield. Curse him! He's been a thorn in my side since we were boys. Probably did it to keep me from inheriting.'

Allan could not believe his ears. 'Your father is alive and in Brussels?'

'I believe I just said that.' He wagged a finger at Allan. 'Perhaps you are not as sober as I thought.'

'What happened to him?'

'You require details?' Edwin rolled his eyes. 'He was struck down from his horse, his leg broken from a musket ball. He was quickly covered over, under other bodies, I suppose. Why that damned fellow went looking for him is beyond me.'

Allan glared at him. 'You were disappointed he did not die?'

Edwin laughed and touched his scar again. 'Oh, I did not wish my father dead, I assure you. I merely dislike seeing him in the clutches of that woman and her son. She'll squeeze more money out of him, you mark my words.'

Edwin Tranville sickened him. He'd be damned if he told this drunken coward about Marian now.

There was no need. His father, her guardian, was alive.

Allan stood. 'Are you also staying at the Hôtel de Flandres? In case I need to find you again.'

Edwin pointed to the ceiling. 'I have a room in this very inn. Handy, I admit.'

Allan had enough. He gave Edwin a curt nod, before striding away.

Edwin's voice followed him. 'Wait! You did not tell me why you were looking for me!'

Allan left the inn and made his way across the Parc.

General Tranville was alive? This changed everything. He might be able to avoid informing Edwin of Marian's presence in Brussels, but he could not hide it from her guardian.

General Tranville was legally responsible for Marian's welfare. Most importantly, he could provide the protection Marian needed. Tranville could prevent any damage to her reputation.

The longer Allan remained under the same roof with her, the closer he came to completely compromising her. And even if he kept his hands off her, each day she risked it becoming known by some member of society that she was living unprotected in a household of men.

This might be her only opportunity to erase any harm their time together could cost her.

Even though it meant leaving her in the care of a man Allan despised.

The more Marian thought about it, the more she decided that Edwin had probably already left for England. It had been over two weeks since the battle. Certainly he would have tied up his army affairs in that time.

She was glad. If she were required to travel to England

with him, it would stop her from seeing her soldiers recovered.

And would part her from the captain.

Their parting was inevitable, though. He grew stronger every day. Soon he would be required to return to his regiment. She dreaded the thought of it.

She climbed the stairway to the upper floors and knocked upon Corporal Reilly's bedroom door.

'Come in,' he responded.

He sat by the window in a patch of sunlight, his arm bandaged and in a sling.

'How good to see you up, Corporal.' She smiled at him.

He struggled to his feet. 'Good afternoon, Miss Pallant.'

She gestured for him to sit. 'I've come with fresh linens.'

He lowered himself in the chair again, a frown on his face. 'Doesn't seem fitting for a lady such as yourself to be making beds.'

She pulled off the old linens. 'Now you are sounding like Captain Landon.'

Reilly grinned. 'He is a stickler for what's proper.'

She laughed. 'Indeed.'

He sobered again. 'He is a good 'un, though. Brave as they come.'

She covered the mattress with a clean sheet and thought of him carrying a soldier out of the burning château and covering her with his body after he was shot. 'Indeed,' she repeated more softly.

'I've known him since he was a green lad. Didn't know the first thing about being an officer. He learned quick, though. Has lots of pluck, that one.'

She tucked in the corners of the sheet.

Reilly went on, 'I remember when General Tranville ordered Landon and Captain Deane into Badajoz during the pillaging. His son was lost and the general thought he'd gone into the town.' He paused and so did she. 'Any road, a sane man would have removed himself from Tranville's sight for a couple hours rather than enter those streets. Soldiers were deranged in there.' He shook his head. 'But, no, before you know it, here comes Captain Landon, carrying the general's son over his shoulder.'

She finished smoothing the blankets. 'That is quite a story.' One the captain had never told her. She patted the bed. 'There. Clean linens. Is there anything else you need?'

He stood and bowed his head. 'I'm pampered enough. I thank you, Miss Pallant.'

Marian walked out of the room.

The captain had rescued her cousin? Another brave and wonderful thing to add to a list of many. Filled with pride for him, she hummed as she walked down the stairs. When she reached the hall, the front door opened.

The captain walked in.

Marian felt her whole body come alive. 'Captain!'

His gaze rose to her. His expression was grim.

'What is it?' She turned cold. 'Is it Edwin?' Do not say her last blood relative was dead.

'Where can we talk?' Even his tone was grim.

She could think of nowhere to be private but his bed chamber. When they entered the room, he signalled her to sit and he closed the door.

Her heart raced painfully. 'Tell me, please, Captain, is Edwin dead?'

He raised his hand as if to stop her. 'He is unharmed, do not fear. He is here in Brussels. I spoke to him.'

'Thank God.' She pressed her hand against her chest. 'I was so frightened.'

'That is not what I must tell you.'

Her eyes widened. 'What then?'

'Listen to me.' He swallowed. 'Your uncle. He is alive. He wasn't lost, Marian. He is alive.'

'Uncle Tranville?' Her heart started racing again.

He paced in front of her. 'He was found alive and carried off the battlefield after the battle was over.' He frowned. 'I do not know all the details. Someone known to him carried him out. He broke a leg.' He waved a hand as if these details were of no consequence. 'He is here in Brussels, recuperating.'

'In Brussels?' Marian's mind whirled.

She must be glad his life was spared, mustn't she?

Even if she had no familial affection for him. She just did not want him here. She wanted nothing to interfere with her caring for her soldiers.

But, then, how likely was it that Uncle Tranville would trouble himself over her?

'Perhaps you could call upon him,' she said to the captain. 'I should like to know if he is recuperating well or if he is in need of anything I could provide.'

His pacing ceased. '*You* must call upon him, Marian.'

'I do not want him to know I am here.'

His brows rose. 'He is your guardian. He must know you are here. He is responsible for you.'

She stood. 'He cares nothing for me. For my aunt's sake, I would like to know if he needs my help, but otherwise I prefer to have nothing to do with him.'

He gave her an even look. 'He is *legally* responsible for you.'

She tossed her head. 'What do I care for that? I am well able to take care of myself.'

He grasped her arms. 'You do not comprehend. You are no longer a stranded orphan needing protection. You have a guardian who can assume your care.'

She tilted her head back so she could look him in the eye. 'You do not comprehend, Captain. I want nothing to do with my uncle.'

He brusquely released her. 'I must insist upon this. You must go to him. Place yourself in his charge.'

It shocked her that he would send her away. 'I am needed here, Captain. We have men to tend, whose health and well-being are in our hands. I cannot leave them. Not for *him*.'

'Marian, it is not for him. It is for you. If you are under the care of your guardian and his party, there can be no taint to your character.' He spoke in an earnest tone. 'Only the members of this household know what you have been doing and none of them will besmirch you. This is your only chance.'

Her insides twisted. 'You cannot make me go.'

He pierced her with his gaze. 'I must.'

'Why?' She felt close to tears. 'Because he is your superior officer?'

Something flickered in his eyes. 'No. Because this is the only way to preserve your good name and your future. No other reason.'

It still felt like betrayal. 'You will give me no choice. You will force me.'

His eyes hardened again. 'Yes.'

The captain took her that very afternoon.

The beauty of the Parc was lost on Marian as they walked through it to reach her uncle's hotel. The tension between them clouded her vision to the green shrubbery, white statues and colourful flowers. All she saw were more injured soldiers sitting upon benches and resting beneath trees. Could they not take more men into their care?

Could the captain not see that she needed to take care of the soldiers? It angered and disappointed her that he considered the needs of the men less important than the preservation of her reputation.

Even more painful, being forced to stay with her uncle meant being parted from the captain. Each day she'd shared with him made it more like he was the very air she must breathe, essential to life. She knew eventually his duties to his regiment would take him away, but even a few more weeks, a few more days, would be more precious than the finest jewels.

In her daydreams they would meet again away from war, somewhere in England where he was free to choose being with her rather than feeling it an obligation. There he would court her and perhaps they could kiss without her feeling she had seduced him into it.

Perhaps then he would not find anything about her of which to disapprove.

Her mind filled with all the ways he disapproved of her as they continued across the Parc. It helped fuel her anger.

And dampen the pain of parting with him.

Too quickly they arrived at the elegant Hôtel de Flandres, and the captain enquired after her uncle Tranville. The hotel's attendant showed them into a small drawing room to wait while he announced their arrival.

After a brief time a lovely woman entered the room. 'Miss Pallant? Captain Landon?' She extended her hand to them.

Marian did not miss the stunned expression on Allan's face at the sight of this chestnut-haired beauty. She felt inexplicably jealous.

'I am Ariana Blane,' the captivating creature said.

'Ariana Blane?' Marian's eyes widened in surprise.

Ariana Blane was the actress who had posed as Cleopatra in a scandalous painting that had been engraved and widely printed to publicise the play. When Marian left for Brussels, all of London had been clamouring for tickets to the performance.

'I saw you play Juliet at Drury Lane,' she told Miss Blane.

'That seems a long time ago.' Miss Blane looked wistful. 'I am afraid we did not know of your presence in Brussels, Miss Pallant, or we would have sent word about your uncle. I will take you to him right away.'

As she led them out of the drawing room and up the stairway, the Captain asked, 'Miss Blane, what connection do you have with Lord Tranville?'

She gave him a coy look. 'I might ask the same question of your connection to Miss Pallant.'

His eyes narrowed. 'I am her escort.'

She laughed. 'My connection is not so simple.' She

paused on the stairs. 'I am betrothed to a man whose mother is a friend of Lord Tranville. When we learned Lord Tranville had been injured, she assumed his care.'

The captain seemed to relax.

'How bad are his injuries?' Marian asked, hating herself for hoping they were severe enough that he could not bother with her.

They continued up the stairs.

'He has a badly broken leg and has just recovered from fever and an infection of the lungs,' Miss Blane said. 'He is weak, but much improved, certainly well enough to receive you.'

Marian felt a pang of disappointment.

They walked down a hallway and Miss Blane knocked upon a door. 'Are you ready for us?' she called.

The door was opened by a manservant, a man who looked familiar to Marian, but she could not work out why.

Her uncle was propped up in a large bed, wrapped in a colourful banyan. He looked smaller than she recalled and pale, but alert. His hair had turned white in the two years since she'd last seen him, just after her aunt died.

An older woman approached. 'Miss Pallant, I do not know if you know me—'

This was another surprise. 'Mrs Vernon! I remember you. From Bath.'

Mrs Vernon had been the mistress Marian's aunt had so despised, the woman her aunt had said lured her uncle away. The manservant had then been in her employ.

'Oh, my goodness.' Marian turned back to Miss Blane. 'Jack Vernon! Is Jack Vernon your betrothed?'

Jack was Mrs Vernon's son. When they'd been children, Edwin used to pick fights with Jack, and Marian would try to stop him. Otherwise Edwin would come home with a black eye and a bloody nose, and his father would bellow at him for being a ninny.

'He is indeed.' Miss Blane smiled.

'Jack Vernon?' The captain looked equally incredulous. 'Lieutenant Jack Vernon of the East Essex?'

Mrs Vernon answered him. 'That is my son. Do you know him?'

'I do.' The captain sounded surprised.

The connections made Marian's mind swirl. The captain was connected to her uncle and cousin and to Jack Vernon, as well.

'You just missed him,' Miss Blane said. 'Jack left to rejoin his regiment yesterday.'

Marian nearly forgot her manners. 'Mrs Vernon, allow me to present Captain Landon.'

'Landon!' Her uncle's voiced boomed from the bed, feeling neglected, Marian thought. 'Attend me.'

The captain stiffened before approaching her uncle's bedside. 'Yes, sir.'

'Why are you not with the regiment?'

Marian hurried over. 'He was injured, Uncle.'

'Injured?' Her uncle huffed. 'I was not informed of this.'

'Sir.' The captain's voice had a hard edge. 'We only today learned of your presence in Brussels.'

'*We?* What do you mean by *we*, Landon?' His expression was contemptuous. 'What do you have to do with my niece?' He turned to Marian. 'What the devil are you doing in Brussels, girl? You have no call to be here.'

She fought to hold her temper. 'I came with Sir Roger and Lady Fenton. You do recall their daughter is a great friend of mine.'

'Sir Roger brought you?' He looked indignant. 'I gave no such permission.'

Marian met his eye. 'Your man of business gave permission for me to stay with the Fentons.' As if his man of business cared any more than her guardian did where she went or what she did. 'Did you not put him in charge of me?'

He leaned forwards in bed. 'Do not be impertinent.'

Impertinent? Marian had no intention of allowing her uncle to intimidate her.

He turned back to the captain. 'What is your part in this, Landon?'

Marian held her breath, hoping the Captain would lie, hoping he would see now how awful her uncle could be.

Hoping he would not leave her.

The captain straightened. 'I am recuperating in the house Sir Roger leased in this city.'

Marian could have kissed him. He had not lied, precisely; merely withheld the whole truth. *Well done, Captain!* She applauded silently.

'I've a mind to ring a peal over Sir Roger's head, bringing my niece here. Damned fools, all these English flocking to Brussels when Napoleon was about to attack.'

Miss Blane rolled her eyes and Mrs Vernon lowered hers. These two English women, of course, had flocked to Brussels and had probably nursed him back to health.

Tranville pointed at Marian. 'You, girl, you tell Sir Roger I wish him to call upon me posthaste.'

Marian kept her voice steady. 'I will inform him of your request the next time I see him.'

She heard a breath escape the captain's mouth.

Please keep quiet, Captain.

Her uncle turned his attention back to him. 'What news of the regiment, Landon?'

'I know little, except they were bound for France,' he responded.

'Has Edwin gone with them?' he asked.

A muscle in the captain's jaw tensed. 'No, sir.'

Mrs Vernon came to Tranville's side and took his

hand. 'Remember, Lionel? Edwin is staying nearby until you are well.'

'Fool,' he huffed. 'His duty is to the regiment.' He pointed to the captain. 'I told him to befriend you. Said he could learn a thing or two from you. But Edwin never did anything I told him to do—' His voice broke off into a fit of coughing.

Marian felt angry on Edwin's behalf. He'd accepted a commission in the army to please his father even though Edwin had been totally unsuited to it.

Her uncle's coughing subsided and he leaned back against the pillow, looking weak and tired.

Unfortunately he roused again. 'Landon, you should have insisted Sir Roger or his wife accompany my niece. This is family business, not regimental business. It is not your affair.'

Marian spoke before the captain could respond. 'Captain Landon came at my request, Uncle,' she replied sharply. 'You have no call to scold him for it—'

Her uncle's eyes bulged. 'See here, girl!'

She kept on. 'He was being a gentleman, which is more than I can say for—'

The captain put a hand on her arm. 'Enough, Marian.'

She glanced at him in alarm and mouthed, 'No.'

He turned to her uncle. 'I will tell you why I have escorted your niece.'

'Go on.' Her uncle gave her a smug look.

Marian felt ill.

The captain set his chin. 'Sir Roger and Lady Fenton left for England several days ago. Your niece remained and opened the house for wounded soldiers.'

'What?' Uncle Tranville sat upright. 'She is acting as a nurse? Shameful. That is only for lowlife.'

'We are acting as your nurses,' Miss Blane muttered, but Uncle Tranville seemed to take no notice.

Marian lifted her chin. 'It is true Sir Roger left and I stayed behind. And it is true Captain Landon is one of the soldiers in my care, the only officer, which is why I chose him to escort me. I have not acted the nurse, however. Those tasks have been performed by the Fentons' Belgian servants. I have merely managed the house.'

'Managed the house,' her uncle muttered in disdain. 'You make it sound like a brothel.' His thoughts seemed to drift for a moment, then caught on some idea. He peered at the Captain and spoke in the most matter-of-fact tone. 'You spent the night under the same roof with my niece without a proper chaperon?'

Captain Landon straightened and held her uncle's gaze. 'Yes, sir. She kept me alive.'

Her uncle waved those words away as if Captain Landon's life was of no consequence. 'That is very improper. Very improper indeed.'

When had her uncle ever cared about where she went or what she did? 'You are being nonsensical, Uncle.'

He tapped his fingers on his mouth. 'He compromised a decent young lady.'

'He did not compromise me,' Marian cried. It would be more accurate to say that she had compromised him. 'Besides, you are not one to pass judgement, Uncle.'

When had he ever acted with propriety? He'd never taken any steps to conceal his relationship with Mrs Vernon. All of Bath knew. Marian's aunt had been greatly shamed by it. He'd not even remained faithful to Mrs Vernon, which caused even more talk.

'Perhaps this is not the best time to discuss this,' Miss Blane broke in. 'Are you not becoming fatigued, Lord Tranville?'

'I am as fit as you are.' His eyes shot daggers at her.

Miss Blane seemed unaffected.

'Listen.' The captain stepped forwards. 'I can resolve this—'

'Indeed you can, Landon!' Her uncle laughed as if in triumph. 'You can marry her.'

'Marry me!' Marian cried.

'Marry her.' The older man's expression turned smug. 'It is the perfect solution. He compromised her; he must marry her.'

'He did not compromise me!'

Her uncle paid her no heed. 'I must admit, I once thought that I'd marry you to Edwin, but now that Edwin will be a baron one day he needs to look a great deal higher. Landon will be perfect, though. He's a younger son, perfectly respectable, but needing to marry a fortune. You, my girl, have an excellent fortune.'

None of Marian's fantasies of how a gentleman might propose marriage had ever included her uncle. She would not go along with this no matter what. She'd already refused when the captain tried to propose out of duty; she certainly would not accept when the proposal came through her uncle. She was speechless with rage. How dared he?

The captain wore a thunderous expression. Mrs Vernon looked as if she might cry. Miss Blane looked disgusted.

'Sir.' The captain's voice was taut. 'It is not your place to propose—'

'Of course it is my place to propose,' her uncle interrupted. 'I am her guardian. I am supposed to see her married. This way I am saved the trouble of finding someone to bring her out into society.'

'I had my come-out in Bath with Domina,' Marian said to no avail.

Her uncle was beyond listening. 'I am correct that you have no fortune, am I not?' he demanded of the captain.

Allan was consumed with rage. Of all the manipulative, self-centred things Tranville had done, this was the pinnacle.

'I have no fortune,' he admitted stiffly. 'But that is of no consequence. You have no right to force—'

'Oh, I do not *force*.' Tranville's self-congratulatory tone turned threatening. 'I insist. If you do not do right by my niece, I will ruin your career in the army. I will make certain the parents of every marriageable young lady in the *ton* learn you are a callous seducer of respectable women.'

'You will do nothing of the sort!' cried Marian.

Tranville turned his malevolent gaze on her. 'Will I not, you ungrateful wretch!'

Allan could endure this no longer. He surged forwards, ready to put his face into Tranville's and tell him exactly what he thought of him.

Miss Blane pulled him back.

Tranville continued to address Marian. 'If you do not do what I say, young lady, you will not get a penny of your money until you inherit. How will you live then, eh? You'll be in the first man's bed who will have you. By the time you inherit, no decent man will want you.'

Allan pulled away from Miss Blane. 'This is beyond everything. Apologise this instant!'

Tranville was unstoppable. 'Is it not a bit late to play the champion, Landon? You have been sharing quarters with her for days.'

'Say and do what you want about me,' Allan seethed, 'but your niece has done nothing to deserve these high-handed threats. Her behaviour is to be admired, not punished.'

The General's eyes narrowed. 'You know what I am capable of, Landon. If you value your army career, your good name and your future, you will do as I say.' He tilted his head towards Marian. 'And if you defy my wishes, she will be ruined.'

'Lionel—' Mrs Vernon pleaded.

His head whipped around to her. 'Stay out of this, woman!'

Allan held up his hands. 'Enough!' He turned from Tranville to Marian. 'We will marry. Even though I detest your uncle's interference in the matter, marriage has always been the only honourable option.'

'No,' she rasped, so low only Allan could hear.

Tranville laughed like a demon. 'I knew he would agree the moment I said you were rich.'

Allan glared at him, his fingers curled into fists. It was all he could do not to strangle the life out of him.

'Let us leave now, Marian.' He took her arm and backed away from the bed. 'We can discuss this as we walk back.'

They started towards the door.

'Not so hasty, girl,' her uncle called after her.

Now what?

'You are not going back to perform menial tasks to a house full of men. You stay here.'

'No!' she cried.

Allan could not leave her with Tranville. Not after this. 'If you say I've already compromised her, what does it matter? She comes with me.'

'Do not add arrest to the list of things I might do to you, Landon,' Tranville countered. 'I am her legal guardian. She must do as I tell her and I tell her she is to stay here.'

'She can share my room,' Miss Blane offered. 'Come. I'll accompany you both out. You can have her things sent here later, Captain.'

'You see she returns, Ariana,' Tranville shouted.

Miss Blane hurried them out of the door.

When they were out of earshot, she stopped them both. 'Retreat was necessary. It is sometimes, is it not, Captain?'

He did not answer her.

'He is horrible,' Marian cried. 'I refuse to do as he says. I do not care what he does to me.'

Miss Blane raised a finger. 'Ah, but you do care what he does to Captain Landon.'

Marian averted her face.

'Let him do what he wants to me.' Allan touched Marian's hand. 'I will not let him hurt her.'

Sympathy warmed Miss Blane's eyes. 'The more you defy him, the worse he will become. Do you not know this to be true, Captain?'

'Yes,' he had to admit.

Miss Blane went on, 'Idleness is bringing out the

worst in him. I suggest you act as if you intend to do as he says. Give it a little time. You will be able to do as you wish once he has something else to think about.'

'You sound as if you know him well,' Marian said.

She smiled. 'Jack and I have been targets of his manipulation, but Jack made threats of his own. Tranville heeded them. We will renew those threats on your behalf, if necessary.'

'I do not fear a confrontation with him,' Allan said, his anger still blazing too hot to allow her to douse the flames.

'I am certain you fear nothing, Captain,' she responded. She shooed them to the stairway. 'Talk together privately, but do not do anything hasty.' She turned to Marian. 'I will wait for you in the drawing room. Rest assured, you will be away from Lord Tranville's company in my room.'

The Captain nodded in gratitude. 'Come outside with me,' he said to Marian, taking her arm.

They descended the stairs and continued through the hall out the front door of the hotel.

Outside the Hôtel de Flandres, he faced her. 'Forgive me, Marian. I was wrong to bring you here.'

She clutched the sleeves of his coat. 'Take me home, Captain. I do not want to stay here. I want to be with you and our soldiers.'

He shook his head. 'I cannot. The cost to you is too

great. We must do as Miss Blane suggests. Retreat for the moment and allow emotions to calm down.'

'He cannot make us marry.' Her face filled with anger again.

'When do you inherit?' he asked.

She looked at him suspiciously. 'In a little more than a year's time, when I turn twenty-one.'

'Twenty-one?' He was surprised. Most heiresses did not receive their inheritance until at least twenty-five.

'I know it is unusual,' she said. 'But that was how my father wrote the will. Why do you ask?'

'I propose we become betrothed, but we postpone marriage until after you are twenty-one. Once you have inherited, you can decide to cry off if you wish.' This way they could play Tranville's game and win.

Her brow furrowed. 'You propose to become betrothed only to thwart my uncle's manipulations?'

He still believed that marrying her was the only honourable thing he could do, but he could not tolerate her thinking he had done so to appease Tranville. Indeed, he could not quite imagine life without her. He believed that fate had brought them together. All they had to do was the right thing, the honourable thing and all would work out well.

He cupped his hand against her cheek. 'There is so much we have endured together that was not under our control. Let us put the issue of whether we marry or not into our hands and no one else's.'

Chapter Nine

Edwin Tranville lounged on a bench, trying to muster enough energy to wander back to the inn that had become his home in Brussels, the one with the excellent Belgian beer. He'd come from there to the Hôtel de Flandres, shamed by Landon into the notion that he owed his father a visit.

Thank God he had talked himself out of it before crossing the threshold. He glanced over at the hotel's entrance.

A British officer stood there with a woman. The two were engaged in an intense conversation and lots of intimate embraces. Lawd. It was probably some doxie trying to squeeze out more coin by making him more ruttish.

Would the man fall for her trick? The army seemed to breed men who were easily duped into paying a princely sum for a common whore.

'Do not heed her,' he said aloud, as if the officer was

Chapter Nine

Edwin Tranville lounged on a bench, trying to muster enough energy to wander back to the inn that had become his home in Brussels, the one with the excellent Belgian beer. He'd come from there to the Hôtel de Flandres, shamed by Landon into the notion that he owed his father a visit.

Thank God he had talked himself out of it before crossing the threshold. He glanced over at the hotel's entrance.

A British officer stood there with a woman. The two were engaged in an intense conversation and lots of intimate embraces. Lawd. It was probably some doxie trying to squeeze out more coin by making him more ruttish.

Would the man fall for her trick? The army seemed to breed men who were easily duped into paying a princely sum for a common whore.

'Do not heed her,' he said aloud, as if the officer was

of using her money for Valour, though. Only for the others. 'I will send your trunk.'

She nodded.

'We should say goodbye,' he murmured.

She ran into his arms again. 'Goodbye, Captain.'

He squeezed her as tightly as he could. 'I will call upon you as soon as I can.'

With a quick brush of his lips against hers, Allan backed away and turned to walk from her.

She nodded and flew into his embrace, her arms wrapped around his neck, her face against his heart. 'This is not the proposal of which I have dreamed. I do not know if you want to marry me or want to be released from the obligation.'

He held her. 'I know you do not want to marry me. You have said so more than once, but one thing I do know.'

'What is that?' she murmured against his chest.

He released her and lifted her chin with his finger. 'My proposal is vastly superior to General Tranville's.'

A laugh escaped her. 'Do not jest.'

He held her against him again. 'Be betrothed to me. For now. Perhaps even before I must leave Brussels we will be free to know our own minds.'

'I do not want to stay here.' She pulled away from him. 'I want to be with our soldiers.'

'I know.' He glanced towards the hotel. 'Avoid Tranville, but if you must see him, avoid a confrontation.'

She gave him a steady gaze. 'I promise to avoid him.'

He smiled. 'And I promise to see that your soldiers receive the best care possible.'

Her eyes glistened with tears. 'Deep in the left-hand corner of my trunk is a purse. Keep its contents to pay for food and the servants' wages and for Valour, if you need it. I am very fond of Valour.'

His smile faded. 'I will see to it.' He had no intention

great. We must do as Miss Blane suggests. Retreat for the moment and allow emotions to calm down.'

'He cannot make us marry.' Her face filled with anger again.

'When do you inherit?' he asked.

She looked at him suspiciously. 'In a little more than a year's time, when I turn twenty-one.'

'Twenty-one?' He was surprised. Most heiresses did not receive their inheritance until at least twenty-five.

'I know it is unusual,' she said. 'But that was how my father wrote the will. Why do you ask?'

'I propose we become betrothed, but we postpone marriage until after you are twenty-one. Once you have inherited, you can decide to cry off if you wish.' This way they could play Tranville's game and win.

Her brow furrowed. 'You propose to become betrothed only to thwart my uncle's manipulations?'

He still believed that marrying her was the only honourable thing he could do, but he could not tolerate her thinking he had done so to appease Tranville. Indeed, he could not quite imagine life without her. He believed that fate had brought them together. All they had to do was the right thing, the honourable thing and all would work out well.

He cupped his hand against her cheek. 'There is so much we have endured together that was not under our control. Let us put the issue of whether we marry or not into our hands and no one else's.'

close enough to hear. 'Do not pay a penny more than she's worth.'

He peered at them again. The woman seemed to be dressed in a fashionable frock and there was something familiar about the man. Edwin rose from the bench and edged closer.

Lawd. It was Landon.

Landon, that paragon of perfection, was attempting to purchase a woman's services. How very amusing.

The woman lifted her face and the sun illuminated her features.

It was his cousin!

Marian was in Brussels? How delightful she was here. Edwin greatly needed a friendly smile and some support and sympathy, just the sort Marian could provide.

He took an eager step forwards, but stopped. Why was she with Landon? Why this *intimate* conversation with him?

Landon kissed her on the lips and set off towards the Parc, a stern look on his face.

Edwin fumed.

Was everything in his life to be a competition with Landon? His father already relentlessly compared his skills as an officer to Landon's and, of course, Landon was never the one found wanting. He should not have to compete for Marian's attention too. Marian was not like other women. She was clever and had been the only woman who truly understood him.

She was his cousin, after all. He'd even thought that some day he might marry her, if he had to…. Some day, when he was ready. Good God, would he now be required to *romance* her better than Landon?

Marian stood at the doorway of the hotel for a long time, watching Landon walk away. Suddenly, she pulled open the door and went inside as if Landon had upset her. That was good.

Edwin rubbed his scar. What ought he to do next? Go in the hotel and see Marian? Or chase after Landon and discover what had transpired between them?

He decided to chase after Landon.

It was easy to spy him striding across one of the paths in the Parc. Edwin ran to catch up to him.

'Landon!'

Landon turned and scowled, but waited.

Edwin panted so hard he could barely speak. 'Where are you going in such haste?'

'Back to my rooms, if it is any of your concern.' Landon started walking again.

'I saw you with a lady just now.' He stopped to catch his breath. Lawd, he needed a brandy. Or more Belgian beer.

Landon glared at him.

Edwin straightened his spine. 'You were with my cousin and I demand to know what business you have with her.'

Landon stared down into Edwin's face. 'If you wish to know, ask her.' He turned away again.

Edwin seized his arm and pulled him back. 'I am asking you, sir.'

Landon winced and placed a hand on his shoulder. When he spoke his eyes glittered with acrimony. 'I am betrothed to her.' He pushed Edwin aside and strode away.

Edwin's jaw fell.

Betrothed? Marian was betrothed to Landon?

This was a matter not to be endured.

He headed back to the inn where he lodged. No beer this time. He needed brandy to calm his nerves.

He scratched his scar. Brandy first, then he'd return to his father's hotel and get to the bottom of this loathsome betrothal.

When Allan reached the Fentons' rooms a missive was waiting for him, asking him to report to the regimental office at the Place Royale the next day. They wanted him to rejoin the regiment in France as soon as possible.

He crumbled the paper in his fist.

He needed more time, time with Marian to sort out the mess he'd created by taking her to Tranville.

He wanted to marry her. It was, simply, the right thing to do. Tranville's interference and threats had tainted what should be something wonderful between them.

It was a good plan for them to wait. Allan needed to make something of himself before marrying her. He could not just live on her fortune. He had to bring something to their marriage. He had to *be* something.

With Napoleon's defeat at Waterloo, war was probably over and a future in the army was not likely. Besides, Allan had enough of battle.

He needed something. Some direction in life. Something to bring to a marriage with Marian.

He crumpled the missive from the regimental office in his hand and went off to tell the servants and the soldiers that Marian would not be back.

Edwin was very careful not to drink too much brandy. Marian had always been able to tell when he'd imbibed too much. He drank only enough to steady his shaking hand and settle his nerves before returning to the Hôtel de Flandres.

He supposed he must call upon his father before seeking out Marian, always a depressing prospect and one he'd almost totally avoided. Why pretend a filial affection he neither felt nor received? Landon had been right about one thing. Edwin would have been delighted if his father had died on the battlefield. Jack Vernon did him no favour by acting the hero.

At least his father's illness provided him the excuse of remaining in Brussels. Edwin was perfectly willing to pretend concern for his father in order to avoid marching to France with the regiment. He had already called upon his father once soon after Jack brought him back to Brussels. His father had been feverish and smelly and the detestable Mrs Vernon had hovered over him.

At this moment, though, it was expedient to make another visit to the sickbed and play the dutiful, concerned son. It was what Marian would expect of him.

He entered the hotel and walked up the stairway to his father's room.

He lifted his hand to knock on the door. 'Lawd, I hope that woman is not in there.' He hated encountering Mary Vernon, or any of the Vernons. He took a breath and rapped on the door.

Mrs Vernon's manservant opened the door.

'I came to see my father,' he snapped at the man.

'He is sleeping, sir,' the servant said. 'I would not suggest waking him.'

Thank God. Perhaps his luck was improving. 'Very well. I will call upon my cousin, then. Which room is hers?'

The man hesitated before responding, 'If you would be so good as to wait in the drawing room off the hall of the hotel, I will seek out Miss Pallant and send her to you.'

This servant was Mrs Vernon's man. He had no right to dictate to Edwin. 'Direct me to Miss Pallant's room.'

The servant stood his ground. 'I cannot. It is not my place to do so. Be so good as to wait below stairs.'

Edwin gave the servant a withering look, but turned and sauntered away. He descended the stairs and stopped the hotel attendant. 'Bring me a carafe of claret and two glasses, and put it on Lord Tranville's account.' At least if he must wait for Marian, his father could provide the refreshment.

The drawing room was reasonably comfortable and the attendant was prompt in delivering the wine. Edwin lowered himself into a chair and poured a glass, downing it in one gulp. He poured another.

No sooner had he done so than his cousin entered the room.

'Marian!' He stood and held out his hands.

She allowed a quick kiss on the cheek. 'I am happy to see you, Edwin.' No smile creased her face. 'I hope you are well.'

'I am,' he exclaimed, then thought better of it. 'As well as a man can be who has endured a battle.'

She sat in one of the chairs. 'Were you injured?'

'No.' He stroked his scar. 'At least nothing to signify.'

She gazed at him with some sympathy. Let her think him the worse for wear.

'So you were in the battle?' she asked.

He sat in a chair opposite her. Next to the table holding the claret. 'I carried messages for General Picton and for Father.' He lowered his eyes as if a pang of grief assailed him. 'That is, until Picton fell and Father was lost.'

'You carried messages?' She seemed to brighten. 'What a coincidence—' She waved a hand. 'Never mind.'

He narrowed his eyes. Landon had probably told her the same thing. At least it seemed Landon had not mentioned his absence in the battle.

'I understand Uncle Tranville had a very dramatic rescue.' She seemed to be making conversation with effort.

'Yes.' Edwin did not elaborate. He had no intention of glorifying Jack Vernon. 'Would you like a glass of claret? I took the trouble of ordering it, thinking it would please you.'

She nodded. 'That was kind of you.'

He poured claret into the empty glass and handed it to her.

He took a big drink from his own glass, wishing the claret were as warming and numbing as brandy or as smooth as the Belgian beer. 'I just learned today you were in Brussels.'

She barely sipped hers. 'I came with Domina and her family, but they have gone back to England now.'

'Domina.' He rolled his eyes. Marian's tedious friend.

'We came in late May,' she added.

None of this explained how she had become betrothed to Landon. 'I suppose you attended many parties.'

She nodded again and took another sip of wine, but glanced down at her lap, seemingly lost in thoughts that did not involve him.

He drained his glass of claret and poured himself another. Nothing for it but to be direct. 'I happened to meet up with Allan Landon earlier today—'

Her head rose.

He went on, 'He told me—'

'—that we are betrothed.' Her eyes flashed as if the idea made her angry.

He leaned forwards and grasped one of her hands. 'Why, Marian? I did not even know you were acquainted with him. Are you really going to marry him?'

She looked away. 'Oh, Edwin. It is very complicated.'

He donned an expression of devoted interest. 'I am at liberty to listen.'

She looked angry again. 'I do not wish to talk about it. Can you understand? It was a very sudden thing and not at all a certainty. It is too much to explain.'

Not a certainty? That was encouraging.

He squeezed her hand. 'I always thought you would marry me, Marian.' He tried not to sound resentful. 'I thought you knew that.'

She pulled out of his grasp. 'Oh, Edwin.' She looked at

him with dismay. 'We are much too close to be married. It is simply not possible.'

He was offended by her tone. 'Many cousins marry. The whole aristocracy is one inbred mess.'

She shook her head. 'But you and I grew up like brother and sister. I could never think of you any other way.'

But she could think that way of Landon? He poured himself the last of the claret.

She looked at his glass disapprovingly. 'Besides, you never said one word to me about marriage. Ever.'

'How could I? I was stuck in the army.' He drank his wine and damned her disapproval.

She made an exasperated sound. 'I have had enough of proposals, Edwin. Do not tease me about this further. You are my cousin and I love you as such. But that is all.' She stood. 'I must go back to my room now.'

He stood as well. 'Do not leave yet, Marian!'

'I must. I simply cannot talk about this any longer.' She started for the door.

He went after her. 'Tell me one thing, then.'

She stopped.

'Do you want to marry Landon?'

Her eyes were pained. 'Call on me tomorrow, Edwin.' She started for the door. 'Perhaps I will be better company.'

He pushed ahead of her and blocked the doorway. 'Do you want to marry Landon?' he demanded.

'I do not know,' she finally answered.

He stepped aside and she fled up the stairs.

Edwin returned to his chair and picked up his glass, draining it of its contents. Then he finished hers, as well.

Lawd, if Marian married Landon, Edwin's father would be comparing him to Landon from now until doomsday.

He slammed down the glass and stormed out of the room, back to the inn and the tavern that offered sweet oblivion.

The next day Allan called upon Marian and paced the drawing room, waiting for her. It was not long before she appeared, Miss Blane at her side.

'Good day to you, Captain,' Miss Blane said from the doorway. 'Do not fear, I have no intention of remaining in the room. It is too soon to speak to Lord Tranville again, by the way, so I would not advise you attempting it.' She closed the door behind her.

'Marian,' Allan whispered.

He had missed her. If possible she looked more beautiful than ever. Her dress was pale green, making the blue of her eyes even more vibrant. Her blonde hair was skilfully arranged, a dark green ribbon threaded through it. He could not take his eyes off her.

She walked gracefully towards him, reminding him

of the swans on the Thames. 'Why are you staring at me?'

He blinked. 'I am having difficulty believing anyone ever mistook you for a boy.'

Her face reddened. 'Had I been a boy, we would not be in such a fix.'

'It is not a fix, Marian.'

She averted her gaze. 'I suppose you are going to ask me to call you Allan.'

'Not if you do not wish to.' It only mattered a little that she did not wish this intimacy with him.

'Good.' She still sounded unhappy. 'I am not certain I can give up calling you Captain.' She glanced at him again. 'How are our soldiers?'

'All are doing well.' He added, 'They send their regards to you.'

Her expression softened. 'Please tell them all they are constantly in my thoughts.'

He nodded.

He ought to invite her to sit, but instead took a step closer to her. 'I am ordered back to the regiment.'

She looked surprised. 'When?'

'Tomorrow. Or the next day, if I find some excuse.' He lowered his voice. 'It gives us no time.'

She made a sound deep in her throat. 'Oh.' She took a breath. 'Well, there is nothing we must do.'

'I thought I might convince Tranville to remove his

threats, but Miss Blane is right. It is too soon, and now I will be unable to attempt it.'

She lifted a hand to her brow. 'I think talking to him makes matters worse.'

He took her hands in his. 'You are likely correct and I am regretful that I ever forced you into it. Now I am sorry I cannot be here to protect you from him.'

She glanced away. 'I plan to avoid him.'

He lifted her hands to his lips. 'We will sort this out, Marian, I promise you.'

She looked him in the eyes. 'I just feel this horrible sense of doom. It frightens me more than the French or the fire or the farmer's axe.'

His insides constricted in pain. He embraced her. 'No, Marian. We will find our way. You will know if you want to truly accept my real proposal of marriage. You and I will freely decide what we want.'

The door opened.

'There you are!' Edwin Tranville walked in.

Damned Edwin.

They stepped apart.

Edwin put on a sardonic expression. 'I am interrupting.'

Marian said, 'Yes, Edwin. You are interrupting. The captain and I are saying goodbye.'

Edwin brightened. 'You are leaving, Landon?'

'To rejoin the regiment,' Allan's voice turned sour. 'Are you not ordered to France, as well?'

Edwin smirked. 'Alas, no,' he drawled. 'I am to remain with my father. To render him whatever assistance he requires.'

Allan stiffened. Edwin had been drinking. 'Perhaps your father needs some assistance right this moment.'

Edwin slid into a chair, even though Marian was still standing. 'I've just come from him.'

'Did you want something, Edwin?' She sounded annoyed.

'Nothing at all.' He sighed. 'Except to see you.'

'This is not a good time,' she responded. 'Would you come back later?'

His eyes flashed. 'Very well.' He made no move to leave.

She waved an impatient hand. 'Edwin! Do not be tedious. Leave now.'

His expression hardened, but he got up and sauntered out of the door.

Allan was glad of his leaving, but Edwin's brief presence had already changed the mood between them.

'Are you fond of your cousin?' he asked her.

'We grew up together,' she said noncommittally. 'Do you dislike him?'

He clenched his jaw before answering, 'Yes. Very much.'

Allan needed to warn her about her cousin, especially since Edwin would remain in Brussels after Allan left. But how much could he tell her without speaking of matters he'd promised to keep in confidence? 'He drinks heavily.'

She sighed. 'I know it.'

He held her by her arms. 'Promise me to take care around him.'

She tried to pull away. 'You are acting like a husband. Telling me what to do—'

He held firm. 'That is not the point. I've seen Edwin when drinking. He is not safe to be around.'

'Not safe?' Her brows rose.

'I cannot say more, but I am serious. Promise me you will avoid him at such times.'

She lifted her eyes to his. 'Edwin does not concern me. I have always been able to handle him.'

Her gaze made him think only of the pain of leaving her, and his hands slid to caress her neck. There was so much more he wanted to tell her, if he could only work out how to put his emotions into words. How, in spite of Tranville's interference and his complete lack of fortune, he still desired her with every part of him, as strongly as that night when they'd shared the same bed.

He leaned down to take possession of her lips.

She made a sound deep in her throat and wound her arms around him, deepening the kiss into something more erotic than he'd dared dream. He held her firmly against him, wanting more, needing more.

She pulled away. 'I cannot—' She backed away from him.

He reached out to touch her again, but withdrew his hand.

She wrapped her own arms around herself. 'Perhaps we should say goodbye now.'

Now? He was not ready.

'Please, Captain?' Her voice rose to a higher pitch. 'I must do this in a hurry. It is too painful.'

It heartened him that parting from him was painful to her. It convinced him she was as attached to him as he was to her.

'As you wish.' Allan could not make himself move, however.

Her eyes creased and her voice turned low. 'Goodbye, then, Captain.'

'Goodbye, Marian,' he murmured in reply.

He bowed and forced himself to walk to the door.

'Captain!' She ran to him.

He opened his arms and caught her in a tight embrace. He held her as if he would never release her, never lose the scent of roses that surrounded her, or the softness of her curves, or her courage and resourcefulness.

'I am so used to being with you,' she murmured against him. 'I do not know how to go on without you.'

He held her close. 'I do not know how I will go along without you, either.'

She pushed away from him again. 'Go, please. I am all right now.'

'I will write to you.' It seemed like not enough to say.

'Yes. Yes. Just leave now.' Her voice cracked. 'Please?'

He leaned down and kissed her on the cheek.

She looked up into his eyes. 'Godspeed, Captain,' she whispered. 'Godspeed.'

Chapter Ten

A week later Marian felt pushed to the limits of her endurance. How ironic that a week at the Hôtel de Flandres had been harder to bear than all the danger and hardship she'd shared with the captain. Her nerves were frayed to ragged threads, and she wished only to scream and hurl breakable objects about the room.

She missed him.

It made no sense that his absence should create such a void. They'd known each other for so short a time.

It did not help that her uncle had insisted upon her presence so he could bully her and order her about. She hated being controlled by him.

He'd discovered that she'd offered to help care for the injured soldiers recuperating in the hotel. 'It is not seemly for a young lady and well you should know it,' he'd snapped at her. He'd also refused to allow her to visit the soldiers at the Fentons' house.

She'd barely existed to her uncle before this, but now she was someone to command, the only person he could command. He was too dependent upon Mrs Vernon to order her about, and her servants took orders only from her.

Miss Blane simply ignored him and did whatever she wanted. She was an intriguing person, very confident and secure in her betrothal to Mrs Vernon's son. If it weren't for Ariana Blane's connection to Uncle Tranville and the Vernons, Marian might have wished to make her a friend.

Marian's feelings about Mrs Vernon were very muddled. She could not forgive the older woman for the injury to her aunt, but, at the same time, Marian pitied her for remaining attached to a man such as her uncle.

Edwin was irritating, but a distraction. He called frequently and seemed to fall into his childhood habit of depending upon her for companionship. Poor Edwin! He'd inherited the worst from his parents. He was as weak as his mother and as selfish as his father. And he had no desire to improve himself or to help anyone else.

Edwin certainly made no effort to help with the battle's casualties. He did nothing useful as far as Marian could tell. The only useful task Edwin performed was to deliver his father's mail.

Each day he visited the regimental office and picked up any mail that came for his father in the regimental packets from London or Paris where the regiment was currently stationed. Then he returned to the office with whatever mail his father wished to send.

This day, Edwin brought his father a letter. Because Mrs Vernon was out on an errand, Uncle Tranville sent for Marian to write his reply.

It was an ordeal. If she asked her uncle to repeat a word, he protested that she should pay better attention. If she asked him to speak slowly, he shouted for her to write faster.

When the silly letter was completed, signed and sealed, he turned to Edwin. 'This goes back today, do you hear? I want it in the next packet to London.'

Edwin gave him a withering look. 'Do not be tedious, Father. There won't be another packet until tomorrow.'

Uncle Tranville sat up in the bed. 'I want it at the regimental office, *today*.'

'Very well.' Edwin's manner made it seem as if this was an onerous task instead of a short walk across the Parc.

'Do you have more need of me?' Marian kept her voice civil with effort.

'No. Go.' He waved her away. 'You've already wearied me excessively.'

She walked out with Edwin. When they were in the hallway, he asked, 'Would you like to share a glass of claret with me in the drawing room?'

'I would much prefer to be outside.' She was feeling

like a tethered falcon. All she wanted was to stretch her wings. 'May I walk with you to the Place Royale?'

'Can we have some claret first?' His voice rose in dismay.

'No, indeed. You drink too much as it is,' she scolded. 'Let us leave now.'

She fetched her hat and shawl, and they were off. Soldiers still lounged on the benches, but for the fresh air, not because they were forced to live out of doors. It heartened her that the men were recovering, that they were not abandoned.

Edwin also glanced at the benches. 'They should order them out of the park. These men have no rank. What if we wanted to sit down?'

'Edwin, have some compassion!' She pushed him.

He glowered, but Marian enjoyed the scent of the grass and swish of trees and being away from her uncle.

Edwin paused and regarded her with a weary expression. 'I almost forgot.' He reached in his coat. 'I have a letter for you, too. It was sent in care of Father in the packet from Paris. It's from Landon.'

'From the captain?' She snatched it out of Edwin's hands and gazed at the captain's clear, confident script on the envelope. 'I am going to walk back. I want to read it.'

'Read it here.' Edwin said. 'I'll make these fellows leave the bench.'

'No, you will not,' she responded. 'I'm not taking their seat.'

He lolled his head, like he always did when he thought she'd made a ridiculous statement. He pointed. 'There's an empty bench.'

Marian walked quickly across the path to reach it. She sat and immediately broke the seal of the letter. Then she began to read.

'Aren't you going to read it out loud?' Edwin asked in a sarcastic tone.

She poked him gently. 'Stop jesting. Be quiet so I can read.'

'This is a bore,' he complained.

Dear Marian, the letter said. *I have only a short time to write this note to inform you that I have successfully rejoined my regiment. We are in Paris, but there is no danger here. I believe the French are as weary of war as we are. There is much beauty in this city. Perhaps I will be lucky enough to have time to visit the museums and sights. I would be even luckier if I could bring you here with me some day. Yours, Allan Landon. P.S. Valour quite misses you, as do I.*

Why did it make her want to cry?

Perhaps because it sounded like him. It sounded so *dutiful.* So perfectly correct.

Except for the whimsical postscript.

'Let me read it.' Edwin reached for it.

'No!' Marian folded it up and, having no pockets, slipped it down her dress. Next to her heart.

Edwin rolled his eyes. 'I suppose it is all maudlin and full of declarations of love.'

Is that what she wished? Once she and Domina talked of such things.

She stood. 'If it were, I would not tell you. Let us be on our way.' She started towards the Place Royal.

He hurried after her. 'You never kept secrets from me before, you know.'

Oh, yes, she had. She had never confided in him. In fact, he had never been very curious to know what she was thinking or feeling. Or doing.

'Edwin, just stop it! You are making me cross.' She walked on.

He kept pace with her and kept his lips pressed shut.

They reached the regimental offices.

Edwin opened the door for her. 'Tell me one thing, Marian.' He looked angry. 'Are you going to write back to him?'

She could feel the paper of the letter crackling against her chest. 'Yes, I am going to write back and I want you to put it with the other mail going to the regiment.'

He glowered at her, but did not refuse.

She decided to give herself a day to think about a reply. At this moment she felt too agitated to know what to say to the Captain. The joy of hearing from him was great, but she still did not know if he wrote out of duty or true regard. She knew he cared about her. Everything in his behaviour told her so. She knew she could make him desire her in that physical way, but did he love her?

Tomorrow her thoughts would be calmer.

With that meagre comfort, she waited until Edwin gave Uncle Tranville's letter to the proper person.

When Marian's letter arrived, Allan was more excited than he would dare admit. The fact that she'd written back to him so quickly was some evidence of her attachment. Perhaps they could make theirs a real betrothal. Each day away from her persuaded Allan that he desired that above all things.

Her handwriting was as graceful and as beautiful as she was herself.

Dear Captain, she wrote.

I am very pleased to hear that you arrived in Paris without mishap and that the city offers some enjoyment for you. I remain in good health, but am quite ready to return to England. My uncle insists that I wait until he is able to travel.

She sounded so cold, so impersonal. His spirits sank dismally. He read on.

On the pretext of an errand Miss Blane and I went to check on our soldiers without my uncle's knowing of it. I am happy to report that they are all doing very well. Five of them have returned to duty. The others await passage home.

Bless Miss Blane. He was glad Marian had an ally in her, even though the actress was, he suspected, as defiant as Marian.

The letter continued. *Please tend to your own health, as well. I remain your friend, Marian Pallant.*

He rubbed his face. *Friend.* This was a dreadful letter.

There was a postscript, however. *P.S. Please tell Valour that she has quite spoiled me for other horses. Although I do hope she enjoys trotting around France, I wish she will not forget me.*

Allan smiled.

He immediately sought out pen and ink and sat down to compose a reply.

In the beginning half of this letter, he wrote the barest news of his activities with the regiment and asked dutiful questions about her health and the health of those around her. In the postscript, however, he let Valour tell of the various sights of Paris from a horse's point of view, of missing her, of wishing they were together.

Over the next few weeks several letters passed between them, the postscripts becoming longer and longer, teeming with humour and hopeful emotions that they might happily see each other again.

This was a new side of Marian to discover. Playful

and fanciful, and brave in its own way. Through Valour she more openly expressed her emotions, including worries that 'Valour' would tire of her some day, or that 'Valour' might feel duty bound to provide her a ride, merely because Marian had cared for her at the peasant's farm.

Allan-as-Valour wrote back, reassuring her that Valour's fondest wish was to carry both Allan and Marian on her back again.

Allan could hardly attend to his regimental duties and he bemoaned the free time he had, which seemed more and more difficult to fill. He passed the time by visiting the city's sights.

And writing about them to Marian.

Edwin Tranville rubbed the scar on his face as he paced the drawing room waiting for Marian. She rarely cared about seeing him these days. She merely wanted to either send a letter to Landon or see if he had sent her one.

She would not even talk about the letters with him. Hadn't read him a single one. He'd taken to intercepting them when he could, and had quite perfected the means to unseal and reseal them without her noticing the tampering.

The letters turned sillier as the weeks went on. They made him want to down gallons of Belgian beer. Talking through a horse, indeed. He'd never thought Marian could be so ridiculous.

He had to do something and quick.

There was no enduring having her marry Landon. Even now his father used Landon's name to jab at him. 'Landon knows his duty,' his father repeated often. 'He is a capital officer. Knows his duty to your cousin, as well…' Then his father would congratulate himself on his cleverness at so easily marrying Marian off, then he would lament that Edwin was not dutiful, brave or clever.'

Edwin was not greatly disappointed at Marian's refusal to marry him. She had become much too bossy and he had no wish to hear her proselytise about the evils of drink every day of his life. He'd formed a plan, though, to erase Landon from the scene, a brilliant plan, if he said so himself. He had no doubt he could pull it off and that she would fall for it.

The attendant brought a decanter of claret and Edwin downed two glasses right away.

Marian finally entered the hotel's drawing room. 'Hello, Edwin.' She smiled brightly. 'Any letters today?'

He seethed at her greeting, the only way she greeted him these days.

'No letter, I'm afraid.' He put on a serious face.

Her shoulders sagged.

'Do not tell me you are fretting.' He tried to sound concerned for her.

'I am not fretting.' Her voice turned low. 'There is no trouble in Paris, is there? What are they saying at the regimental office?'

He made himself grimace and turn away.

She ran to him and clutched at his arm. 'What has happened, Edwin? You know something. Is the captain ill? Has he been injured?'

He gave her a sarcastic smile. 'He is, in fact, very well indeed.'

She looked puzzled. 'Then what is it?'

He cocked his head. 'I am not certain I should tell you.'

She faced him. 'Tell me what?'

He turned away.

'Tell me what, Edwin?' Her voice had become frantic.

'Very well, but do not be angry at me.' He gave her a direct look. 'I heard something today.'

'About the captain?'

Edwin cringed inside. Landon was all she cared about.

'Yes.' He paused. He must make it seem as if he did not want to tell her.

'Edwin.' She raised her voice. 'I am losing my patience!'

'Very well,' he snapped.

Her eyes flashed at him. 'Go on.'

He donned his most sympathetic expression. 'Some of the fellows at the regimental offices were talking about him.' He could not help but relish this next part. 'Landon has apparently developed a *tendre* for a Frenchwoman. She consumes his time, and they are living as—' he smirked 'as man and wife.'

Her eyes widened and she stared at him a long time, so long that he began to wonder if she'd seen through him. He poured another glass of claret.

She spun away and stared at one of the walls as if there were something on it to fascinate, something besides a tedious Flemish landscape.

Finally she spoke. 'I cannot believe this. It is not like him.'

'Marian, how well do you really know Landon? I've served with him in the same regiment for years. I tell you, he is not always the person he pretends to be.'

She sank into a chair.

'I could have warned you, Marian,' Edwin said. 'But I didn't think you were seriously going to marry him. He is not the sort to let a mere betrothal bar him from the pleasures of a willing Frenchwoman.'

'It cannot be true,' she rasped.

He thought she would believe it more easily than this. He rubbed his scar and drank more claret. Realising he ought to share, he poured her a glass and carried it over to her.

He tried again. 'It is said Landon has boasted about

marrying an heiress and becoming wealthy. He is spending freely.'

'He would not say such a thing.' She placed the glass upon the table without even looking at it.

Edwin sat in a nearby chair, drumming on its arm with his fingers.

Time to be bold.

'If you do not believe me,' he said. 'I'll take you to the regimental office. You can ask the fellows there. More than one heard the tale in their correspondence.'

He gambled that she would not take him up on the offer.

She just stared at him, looking very unhappy indeed.

It was quite gratifying.

'No need for that,' she said in almost a whisper. 'But I would like you to wait while I write a letter. Do you mind? I'd like you to take it to the regimental office today to be included in the next packet.'

He pretended to be put out. 'Very well. I suppose I shall have to call upon Father anyway. See to his mail. Send word when your letter is ready.'

She stood and, without another look at him, walked out of the room with a determined step.

His victory was not entirely sweet. She had not fallen into his arms for comfort, but at least she had believed him.

He rose and finished the rest of the claret.

* * *

Allan eagerly opened this latest letter from Marian. He was in the stable, ready to give Valour a nice run. It seemed the best place and time to read it.

Besides, it had just been placed in his hands a few minutes before.

He stood in a ray of sunlight in Valour's stall and unfolded the paper.

He read:

Dear Captain,

I have given our situation a great deal of thought and have no wish to stand in your way. I know my own mind and have decided we will not suit.

Do not fear that my uncle will carry out his threats to you. His interest in managing my life has waned as his health improves. When he returns to England I am confident he will forget me and the betrothal.

This decision is a final one. You are herewith released from any obligation to me.

Wishing you continued health and future happiness,

Marian Pallant

P.S. Please do not write to me. Your duty to me is done.

'What?' he said aloud. He read the letter again. 'No!'

It was as if she'd run him through with a sword. The letter made no sense. It came without warning. Without explanation. What did *'stand in your way'* mean? What did any of it mean?

It must be a mistake.

He checked the date, thinking this might have been written before their friendly, flirtatious discourse, but, no, it was dated three days ago.

Valour whinnied.

Allan patted her neck. She was saddled and ready, but he could not think of anything but returning to his rooms and writing to Marian.

Over the next two weeks he wrote her three letters. Each was returned unopened. After the last one was returned, he heard that Tranville had travelled back to England. He had to think Marian had gone with him and his party.

It was dusk when he heard this news. Instead of returning to his rooms he walked along the Seine in the shadow of Notre Dame, the stone of its towers glowing gold in the setting sun. Boats of all sizes floated in the river as Allan imagined they'd done even before the old cathedral had had its first stone laid.

He walked until his thoughts were clear and his emotions quieted. It had been his duty to offer marriage, but it had always been her right to refuse him. A lady always had that right.

Allan would never know what might have happened between them had he not involved Tranville. He was convinced Tranville's interference had sounded the death knell to his future with Marian.

His only choice now was to withdraw like a gentleman and try to plan what next to do with his life.

Knowing she would not be in it.

Chapter Eleven

April 1817—London

Marian sat behind the desk in the small library of her townhouse near Portman Square.

She tapped at the papers the man had shown her. 'Are we truly going to make this happen, Mr Yost?'

The slim man, hair greying at his temples, cocked his head. 'There is a great deal of interest. Soldiers from all over the country are willing to march, and many others are willing to sign the petition. We have only to say the word to set the plan in motion.'

She needed this Soldiers' March. She needed something to occupy her mind and her passion.

The restlessness that had been her constant companion since leaving Brussels had been somewhat assuaged by plotting for this march. She had financed and organised it with the assistance of Mr Yost.

Marian had left Brussels almost two years ago. She'd returned to Bath to occupy her aunt's house where she and Edwin had been reared. Ariana Blane had returned to London. Edwin, her uncle and Mrs Vernon had gone on to her uncle's country estate in Dorset, the one he'd inherited when he become a baron.

As Marian had predicted, her uncle lost interest in her as soon as they reached the shores of England and he could look forward to more interesting matters, like lording it over an entire estate and the surrounding countryside. No more was ever said about the betrothal.

Mrs Vernon wrote to her that she and Uncle Tranville had married, and that he and Edwin had sold their commissions in the army. Marian sent her a dutiful letter in return and waited out the time until her twenty-first birthday.

While in Bath she'd read with great concern about the plight of the soldiers returning from the war. Mr Yost's essays about the Napoleonic war veterans in the radical newspaper, *The Political Register,* had made a great impression on her. When she moved to London, to her surprise the town house she purchased in Mayfair wound up being next door to Mr Yost.

He was also a friend of the liberal orator Henry Hunt. In early December she'd read of Mr Hunt's involvement in the demonstration at Spa Fields where ten thousand had gathered to protest high prices and to advocate parliamentary reform. Unfortunately the meeting had turned into a riot, something that must not happen in her demonstration.

'What does Mr Hunt say?' she asked Yost.

Hunt was still a powerful figure in the movement for reform. Since the Spa Fields riots, though, Mr Hunt had withdrawn from taking any active role in protests against the government. Still, his support and advice would be invaluable.

Mr Yost regarded her with a serious expression. 'He believes your plan can be implemented if done carefully.'

A *frisson* of excitement raced up Marian's spine. This felt so right, as if it had been her destiny to see first-hand the courage and sacrifice of the British soldiers, so she would understand their plight and have the passion to do something about it.

She sat back in her chair. 'Oh, Mr Yost. Ever since I came to live in London, it has greatly pained me to see our Waterloo veterans begging on the streets in their tattered uniforms. I am determined to assist them all.'

The soldiers had come back from war to the high prices created by the Corn Laws and few opportunities for employment. The government, it seemed, had simply abandoned them.

But Marian would not. She knew first-hand what they had endured. She'd bandaged their wounds and quenched their thirst.

And watched them die.

And had fallen in love with one of them.

'Hunt advises us to be careful,' Mr Yost said. 'The Seditious Meeting Act makes it illegal—'

Marian pulled herself back to the present. '—for a meeting of more than fifty people,' she finished for him. 'We must be very clever and lawful and peaceful.'

'The Spa Fields meetings were supposed to have been peaceful,' he reminded her.

She averted her gaze. 'I know.' She would never forgive herself if she led the soldiers into more violence and injury, as had occurred at Spa Fields.

Her idea was to craft their demonstration after that of the Blanketeers, weavers and spinners who, a month before, had been organised into a march from Manchester to London. They marched in groups of ten, precisely following the law. Unfortunately, their plan was thwarted before the marchers could reach London and later Parliament passed the Sedition Meeting Act making it even more difficult to carry out a demonstration, even a peaceful one.

She and Mr Yost would need to be even more clever.

He regarded her. 'In any event, Mr Hunt approves. What say you, Miss Pallant?'

'We proceed.' She handed the papers back to him.

The door opened and Marian's lady companion entered. Mr Yost glanced towards her and his colour heightened.

A smile flitted across her companion's face.

Marian smiled at the flirtation between Blanche and Mr Yost. 'Come in, Blanche. We are finished.'

'I came to warn you of the time. We need to leave soon if we are to arrive at your friend's house as expected.' Blanche lowered her eyes. 'How do you do, Mr Yost?'

'I am splendid, Mrs Nunn.' His voice turned rough.

Marian felt like applauding. This quiet romance blooming beneath her feet was delightful.

Blanche had sailed on the same boat back from Belgium as Marian. Her husband, a cavalry officer heavily in debt, had been killed at Waterloo, and the despondent Blanche had been attempting to jump overboard when Marian pulled her off the boat's railing. She offered Blanche employment as her companion. Uncle Tranville had approved, perhaps because hiring a companion gave him an excuse to leave her in Bath and forget about her.

Whatever the reason, Marian was delighted Blanche had accepted the employment and was now sharing careful pleasantries with Mr Yost.

Marian rose from behind the desk. 'I'll leave you two and fetch my hat and gloves.'

Mr Yost looked at her as if he'd forgotten she was there. He probably had. 'I ought to offer to escort you ladies, but I fear it would not be wise for Miss Pallant to be seen with me on the streets of Mayfair.'

Marian assured him, 'Reilly will walk with us.'

Reilly was the corporal from Captain Landon's regiment, their first patient in Brussels. He'd come to the servants' door, begging for work, and Marian had instantly recognised him. She'd insisted he come in to be fed and, before he'd eaten his fill, she'd hired him to work for her. Reilly was now Marian's butler and most loyal retainer.

All Marian's servants had some connection to the war. Her cook and housemaids were soldiers' widows. Toby, her footman, had lost a leg at Waterloo. He had been one of the soldiers she'd pulled from the burning chateau at Hougoumont and though there were many tasks his impediment prevented him from performing, he was a tenacious worker otherwise.

Because of their connections to Waterloo, none of Marian's servants would ever betray her. They were in support of the demonstration. Reilly and Toby both would take an active part in it.

Mr Yost reluctantly bade his farewell to Blanche—and to Marian—and returned to his house. Then Marian, Reilly and Blanche started out for Mount Street.

'It is a pity Mr Yost could not walk with us, is it not?' Marian remarked to Blanche.

Her companion blushed. 'Indeed. His company would have been most agreeable.'

Marian smiled. 'Most agreeable.'

The day was sunny, but so breezy they often had to grab hold of their hats to keep them on their heads.

The wind echoed a return of Marian's restlessness. She chastised herself. She was happy and free and her life had purpose. She had even received this invitation to again mix in society, something she'd done in only a limited way in Bath. She'd had her come-out in Bath, but never a London Season. That once had been a bitter disappointment, but since Waterloo mixing in society and wearing the latest fashions seemed unimportant.

Still, she could not refuse this first invitation to call upon Lady Ullman.

Her old friend Domina.

Domina's life could not have taken a more opposite turn than Marian's. Within a fortnight of arriving back in London from Brussels, Domina had married the widower Earl Ullman. Seven months later the new Lady Ullman gave birth. Marian read the birth announcement in the *Morning Post*. The Earl Ullman had a son by his new wife.

Marian had written a note of congratulations, and when she and Blanche moved to London, she sent another letter informing Domina of her new lodgings. She pitied Domina. Her marriage seemed even more tragic than Marian's might have been.

But Marian would not think of that, *could* not think of Captain Landon. She refused to do so. In fact, he rarely crossed her mind now. She rarely wondered where he was, if his wounds had healed.

If he had remained with that Frenchwoman.

'You've turned quiet, Marian,' Blanche remarked.

'Have I?' She blinked in surprise. 'I must have been woolgathering.'

'Are you concerned about this visit?'

Marian's brows knitted. 'I suppose I am. Domina and I did not part under the best of circumstances.'

'Indeed,' responded the companion.

Marian had already told Blanche about their escapade in Belgium, the plan to reunite Domina with Ollie before the battle and what had happened to Marian when they'd become separated. Marian had told Blanche everything except about Domina's pregnancy.

And about Captain Landon.

Marian walked on. 'I confess I am intensely curious about Domina. How she could marry so quickly.'

'I must own some of that curiosity, as well,' Blanche admitted. 'I could not have married so soon after losing my husband.'

Marian slanted her a knowing look. 'Ah, but time heals, does it not?'

Blanche blushed.

They reached Earl Ullman's townhouse on Mount Street. It was a great deal finer than Marian's snug little one.

'Domina has done well.' Marian craned her neck to see to the top floors.

Reilly sounded the knocker. 'I will wait for you nearby, miss.'

Her brows rose. 'Are you certain? Someone might offer you some refreshment if you come in.'

'I'm hungrier for the fine day.' He glanced at the sky. The April breeze had blown away the haze, revealing a rare peek at blue sky.

'Do as you wish,' she told him. 'We should not be long.'

Reilly stepped back as a footman in pristine livery opened the door and ushered them in to a marble-floored hall decorated with jardinières of daffodils and classical-themed paintings.

'How lovely the flowers are,' Marian whispered to Blanche.

The footman helped them off with their coats and passed the garments to a waiting maid. After leading them up an elegant marble staircase he crossed through a doorway framed in gilded moulding to announce them.

Domina bounced up from a pale-pink brocade sofa and rushed over to Marian, her arms extended. 'Oh, I cannot believe you are here! I have missed you so.'

'You look wonderful, Domina.' Marian meant it.

Domina's eyes sparkled, her skin glowed with health and her red curls were bright as ever. As she grasped both of Marian's hands, the skirt of her peach gown swirled around her ankles. The gown looked as new and fresh as its wearer.

Marian had expected to see evidence of suffering on

Domina's face, some indications she had endured the death of a lover, the birth of his child and marriage to a stranger.

Her friend looked perfectly radiant.

'I am splendid now you are here.' She squeezed Marian's hands as fondly as if she had never betrayed her and allowed her to be abandoned in Brussels.

'Let me present my companion…' Marian turned to Blanche and introduced her to the new Lady Ullman. Marian briefly answered Domina's polite questions about her situation. That she and Blanche lived on Bryanston Street. That they managed to keep themselves busy. 'Although I cannot say what we do,' she added truthfully.

'We must do something about your social life, mustn't we? I will see you get invitations from Ullie's friends.'

Marian started. '*Ollie*'s friends?'

Domina's smile faltered for a brief moment. '*Ullie*'s. Lord Ullman, but I call him Ullie. He likes it excessively.' She gestured for them to sit down. 'I've ordered tea. I have so much to tell you…'

Where Marian had been brief, Domina indulged in great detail, telling all about meeting Lord Ullman within days after she and her parents came to London directly after leaving Belgium. He had proposed quickly.

'After Ollie, of course, I felt I never could fall in

love again, but, you know, Marian, he looks a lot like Ollie—' The tea arrived, but Domina did not even stop to take a breath. 'Ullie is older, as you might expect, but that is not a bad thing.'

'How old is he?' Marian managed to break in.

'Forty-two, but he is quite robust. And he dotes on the baby, even though he has two children by his late wife.' She leaned forwards and whispered to Marian, 'It is fortunate that the baby looks just like him.'

Marian ought not to be shocked that Lord Ullman did not know the truth about the baby's paternity; it was a protection for both mother and child, after all. Still, she suddenly felt very sorry for Harry Oliver's parents. They would never know that a part of their son lived on.

'You have had a baby?' Blanche asked. Blanche loved children and lamented that she had never conceived by her husband.

'A son!' Domina said brightly. She avoided Marian's eyes. 'He is with his nurse, of course, but we miss him terribly. Nurse wrote to us that he is walking now.' She paused. 'We named him Harry.'

Marian felt another pang of sadness. Perhaps Domina was not as blissful as she wished to pretend.

There was no further indication of it as Domina chattered on. 'Little Harry is third in line for the title. Ullie is excessively wealthy so he shall have every advantage—'

Domina had done the very best she could for Harry Oliver's child. What right had Marian to judge her?

Domina went on to talk about Lord Ullman's money, his influence, his country estates, the dresses being made for her, the ball she planned during the Season. Marian and Blanche could only listen and sip their tea.

Marian occupied her mind with trying to invent a polite way to take their leave. Finally the door opened, and Domina stopped mid-sentence. A portly, balding man entered the room, and Domina leapt from her seat and into his arms. Another man stood behind him, but his face was obscured by the loving couple's reunion.

'Ullie,' Domina cried. 'Come meet my dearest friend in the whole world!'

'Delighted, my dear,' he said. 'My nephew is with me. We may both be presented.'

Lord Ullman stepped aside to reveal his nephew. Marian stood, stunned.

It was Captain Landon. *Her* Captain Landon.

She was too astounded to speak when Domina presented Lord Ullman to her and Blanche, but Domina took no notice. 'And this is Ullie's nephew, Mr Landon.'

'Captain,' Marian whispered.

He nodded stiffly. 'Miss Pallant.'

Gone was the mended red coat of his uniform. Instead he wore a deep blue coat of fine wool. His linen was pristine white, and buckskin trousers hugged his muscular thighs.

'Do you know each other?' Domina cried. 'How can that be?'

Marian answered. 'The captain was in Brussels, Domina.'

'Domina?' The captain looked astounded.

Domina put her hands to her cheeks. 'Oh, my. I remember now! We saw him in the Parc!' She tittered. 'I thought you were familiar when we met, Allan, but it was such a brief meeting I had no time to remember where I had seen you. In Brussels! And now you are a relation!' Before he could comment, she turned to Marian. 'But we were not introduced to him, Marian.'

Domina's parents apparently had not told her of meeting the captain in Brussels, nor of their sordid imaginings of what had transpired between them.

'I met him afterwards,' she explained.

Domina giggled. 'And here we all are now. What a coincidence.' She waved her hands. 'Do sit, everyone. I'll send for more tea.'

Her husband stopped her. 'Do not trouble yourself, my dear. Rest. Allan would prefer brandy, I am certain.'

'As you please,' the captain murmured. His eyes sought Marian again. 'I trust you are in good health, Miss Pallant.' They both remained standing.

'I am well enough, Captain.' Marian fought to keep her gaze steady and her nerves calm. Her whole body had responded to him just as if she'd this moment crawled into bed with him. She had to get away. 'We must leave, I am afraid. It is late.'

'Oh, no,' Domina cried. 'You just arrived!'

Even Blanche looked surprised.

'I assure you, we must go.' She turned to Domina's husband. 'It was such a pleasure to meet you, Lord Ullman. I look forward to a further acquaintance, but we must bid you good day.'

He held a glass of brandy in each hand. 'Do not hurry off.'

'We must,' she insisted. 'I—I have an appointment. I regret not having more time. Come, Blanche.'

Blanche was on her feet.

'I'll ring for the footman to show you out,' Domina rose to cross the room to the bell pull.

'Do not trouble yourself,' Marian said. 'We will find our way out. Please continue your visit with the captain.'

Marian walked briskly to the doorway, Blanche following.

Domina called after her. 'Come back soon, Marian. I will see you receive some invitations!'

Once in the hall it seemed to take forever for the maid to bring their coats and for the footman to help put them on.

They had almost made their escape when the captain appeared. 'I will walk you home, Marian.'

'No need,' she replied in a bright tone. 'My butler waits outside for us.'

'I wish to speak with you.' His eyes pierced her. 'Wait a moment for me.'

She could not flee from what was inevitable. If he was in London, she might see him again, somewhere, some time.

'Very well, Captain.' She turned to Blanche. 'You and Reilly may go on ahead. I will follow soon.'

She could tell Blanche was bursting with questions about this impressive-looking man and why he sought Marian's company, but Blanche simply said, 'Good day…Captain', and left.

Marian's heart was beating as if she were running a footrace. In her mind she'd convinced herself he was gone, as her parents were gone, as her aunt was gone, as the soldiers who died in her arms and those taken by the fire were gone.

She'd almost succeeded.

But now he was here, looking as handsome and intense as ever. Even in a gentleman's clothes everything about him was familiar, even the scent of him. It was as if almost two years had vanished.

Neither of them spoke while they waited for the footman to bring the captain's hat and topcoat. When finally they stepped out into the street, the breeze had calmed and the blue skies were already replaced with grey.

'I live near Portman Square,' she told him. 'Do you know where that is?'

'I am not a stranger to London, Marian,' he answered, his voice low.

She'd offended him. It ought not to matter. After all, he had offended her very deeply with his easy infidelity. She started walking and did not take his arm.

'I did not know Lord Tranville's town house was near Portman Square.' His voice turned more conciliatory.

'I do not live with Lord Tranville,' she responded. 'I am free of him, which does not matter to him one whit.'

Their arms brushed as they walked together, silent again. The silence lasted until Marian could stand it no longer. 'You obviously did not tell Domina that you knew me.'

His pace slowed. 'I had no notion my uncle's wife was Domina until you spoke her name. I only met her once, very briefly. Uncle Ullman never used her given name.' He slanted a glance at her. 'Did you know Ullman was my uncle?'

'I did not.' Indeed, what had she known of the captain? Almost nothing, as Edwin had said.

They walked on.

He added, as if it were an afterthought, 'Our former association seems largely unknown to anyone.'

True. The gossip and scandal the Fentons feared and that had so concerned the captain had never materialised.

'So I cannot imagine why you would wish to speak with me, Captain.'

'I am no longer a captain. I sold my commission.'

He had long ceased being *her* Captain—why did this news disappoint her?

'A decade of war was sufficient for me,' he added.

One day of war had been enough for Marian.

But that one day of war had also changed everything for her, and he had been a part of it. No matter how she tried to deceive herself, he would always return to her, whenever she saw a soldier, whenever anyone mentioned Waterloo.

If only they had parted like they'd met. In an instant. First here, then gone. How much better that would have been than the pain of the marriage proposal and its aftermath. Her chest hurt from it this very moment. No wonder it was called a *broken* heart.

She gave herself a mental shake. This kind of thinking was ridiculous. Any romance between them had existed in her own mind. They'd become attached because of the circumstances, nothing more.

'What happened, Marian?' he said suddenly, his voice deep with emotion.

'Happened?' She blinked, thinking for a moment he could read her thoughts.

'Your last letter,' he said. 'I wrote back for an explanation, but you returned my letters unopened.'

Her throat tightened. She had no wish to go through

this again. 'Surely there was no mystery, Captain. I was very clear.' Tears pricked her eyes. 'I explained it to you. I told you Uncle Tranville was no longer a threat. I told you I had made my decision.'

He still looked confounded. 'But, why?'

She could bear no more of this. 'Listen to me, Captain. My uncle had affairs right under my aunt's nose. I saw what it did to her.' Her father's infidelity had done worse, bringing illness into their house, leaving her an orphan. 'It was not the sort of marriage I desired.'

The line between his eyes deepened. 'What have your uncle's affairs to do with me?'

Her eyes flashed at him. 'Do not play me for a fool.'

They reached Grosvenor Square, the most fashionable square in Mayfair. He extended his hand towards Hyde Park, only two streets away. 'Let us cross through the park.'

His long quick strides gave her no choice but to follow, although it was difficult to keep up. He did not slow until they crossed through Grosvenor Gate and reached one of the walking paths.

Soon the carriages and curricles would crowd the park, but the afternoon was still early enough that the fashionable world had not yet arrived. At the moment, she and the captain were alone.

'Now answer my question,' he demanded. 'What did your uncle's affairs have to do with me?'

She made herself meet his gaze. 'I know about the Frenchwoman.'

'The Frenchwoman.' His forehead creased. 'What Frenchwoman?'

She gaped at him. '*The* Frenchwoman. Your mistress. Your *paramour.*'

He shook his head. 'Marian, I have no *paramour.*'

'But you did. In Paris.' Marian put her hands on her hips. 'Did you think I would not discover it?'

He stepped back. 'There was nothing to discover. I had no mistress. Not then. Not now.' His expression was earnest. 'Who told you this tale?'

'Edwin told me.'

'Edwin!' He spat out the name like a piece of rancid meat.

She straightened. 'Edwin heard it at the regimental offices in Brussels.'

He seized her arms and drew her so close she felt his breath on her lips. 'Impossible.' Just as suddenly he released her, only to dip down to her again with a disparaging laugh. 'It is not true. Edwin did not hear about it at the regimental offices, because it did not happen. Edwin lied to you.'

She rubbed her arms where his fingers had touched. 'Why would he lie to me?' She breathed.

She felt sick inside. Edwin must have lied. Why had he done such a terrible thing to her?

The captain held her again, more gently this time, so

that there were only inches between them. His scent made her feel as if she'd downed too many glasses of wine, and her senses flared as they'd not done since he'd held her in Belgium.

'You believed him.' His eyes bore into her. 'How could you think me capable of such a thing? I considered myself betrothed to you. I wanted no other woman.'

She tried to remain rational, but her emotions warred within her, wanting him to hold her, wanting to run away.

She steeled herself. 'How could I not think that of you? You were forced by my uncle into offering for me.'

'You forget I offered marriage before your uncle stuck his nose in it.'

'Out of duty,' she reminded him.

His grip tightened. 'After what we endured together— after how I behaved—it *was* my duty, even if your uncle had not threatened us. But did I not also say I *wanted* to be betrothed to you? That I would wait until you were free to accept or reject me? Does this sound like a man who would take a mistress?'

He was so close their breath mingled. She remembered the taste of him, remembered his hands caressing her. Why had she believed him capable of keeping a French mistress?

Men need women to bed, her teachers had instructed.

'It is what men do,' she cried.

A memory flashed through her mind—her father being kissed by the Indian woman. Her mother screaming at him before both fell ill and died. The pain returned.

She wrested her thoughts back to the present. 'Why should I think you any different?'

He drew her even closer. 'Because we spent time together in the most intimate of ways.'

Her knees turned weak. She wanted to melt into his arms and be comforted by him.

She pulled away. 'You were either ill or we were running from danger. That is not a courtship.'

'It ought to have been enough to take the measure of my character.' He turned from her and started on the path again.

She had to run to keep up with him.

She'd been blind to that simple reasoning. Edwin had chosen the one falsehood to which she was so vulnerable. Infidelity killed her parents and killed her aunt's spirit. There was nothing he could have said about Captain Landon that could have fed into worse fears.

Her body was awash with arousal and rage.

And regret.

What might have happened between her and the captain had her uncle and cousin not so cruelly interfered?

She followed the captain through Cumberland Gate.

He abruptly stopped. 'Which street is yours?'

'Not far. Bryanston Street.' She was surprised she could even speak.

They crossed Oxford Street and walked the short distance to tiny Bryanston Street, giving her time to calm herself.

'I know this street.' His tone changed completely. 'John Yost lives here.'

Her nerves went on alert. 'Mr Yost?'

'Are you acquainted with him?' His expression was intense.

She stopped in front of her town house and tried to casually point to the one next to it. 'He lives next door.'

Edwin had been right about one thing. She did not know very much about the captain. She did not know if he was Whig or Tory, if he believed in reform or if he thought it right for the government to favour the rich and neglect the needy.

Her heart pounded with this new concern. 'Why do you ask about Mr Yost?'

Chapter Twelve

Allan gazed down upon Marian, too many emotions battling inside him to make his thinking clear. Why had he asked about John Yost? What did he care about Yost at a time like this?

He suspected his mind forced the distraction upon him to keep him sane. His confusion and anger, his raw desire for her, he'd thought buried with his work.

Damned Edwin Tranville! Allan should have known Edwin was behind all this.

What did it say about Marian's regard for him that she believed Edwin so easily? Was her opinion of him so low that she could entertain such a lie? She had not even given him a chance to defend himself.

Marian looked accusingly at him now. 'Why did you ask about Mr Yost?'

He'd already forgotten about Yost.

Allan rubbed his forehead. 'No reason. His name came up in my work, is all.'

'Your work?' Her voice rose a pitch.

'I am employed by Lord Sidmouth.'

Her eyes widened. 'Lord Sidmouth?'

'The Home Secretary.'

'I know who Lord Sidmouth is.' She tucked an errant lock of hair back under her bonnet. 'Why does the Home Secretary speak about my neighbour? Does Mr Yost pose some danger to me?'

'No danger.' Allan regretted even mentioning the man. 'Yost is merely known as a liberal thinker who has written on various radical topics. It makes him of interest to the Home Secretary.'

She did not quite meet his eye. 'What work do you do for Lord Sidmouth?'

He shrugged. 'I attempt to uncover possible treasonable offences, such as if someone is inciting unrest or rioting or some such activity.'

She took a quick intake of breath. 'And Mr Yost? Is he inciting unrest and rioting?'

'Not that I know of.'

There had been talk, though, that Mr Yost had met with Henry Hunt recently. Sidmouth believed something could be afoot between the two men.

But Allan did not want to talk about this. 'Who lives here with you?' Another man, he meant?

She seemed distracted. 'Who lives here? Mrs Nunn, who is my companion, and our servants. Why do you ask me that?'

Their conversation had become even more stilted and difficult than when they'd been talking of the past.

'No reason,' he quickly countered. He was not about to admit he was worried that she'd taken a lover.

The door was opened by a looming manservant with the aura of a bodyguard.

The man laughed. 'Captain!'

Allan looked into his face. 'Reilly?' He could hardly believe his eyes.

Reilly made a congenial, if exaggerated, bow. 'Good day to you, Captain Landon.'

'He is no longer a captain, Reilly.' Marian entered the house and glanced back at Allan. 'Mr Reilly is my butler.'

Without thinking, Allan followed her inside, his hand extended to clasp Reilly's. 'By God, Reilly. I am astounded, but it is good to see you.' He asked Reilly about his wounds and listened to Reilly explain how Marian had taken him in and trained him to be her butler.

'In fact, we all have a connection to Waterloo here,' Reilly told him. 'Toby, our footman, lost a leg at Hougoumont. Mrs Nunn, Cook and the maids are all Waterloo widows.'

'Indeed?' Allan was impressed. He turned to Marian. 'You hired them because of Waterloo?'

She nodded. She remained by the door, her fingers clasping the doorknob.

'How did you find—?' He lifted his hand. 'I beg

your pardon. I am intruding, and you indicated an appointment you must keep.' He stepped back towards the door. 'I am glad to see you looking so fit, Reilly.' His glance went from Reilly to Marian. 'Good day to you, Miss Pallant.'

She leaned against the door. 'Good day, Captain.'

He walked out remembering their companionship in the house in Brussels. Her door now closed behind him, and he felt as empty as he had felt when reading her final letter.

Allan walked the streets with his head and emotions awhirl. He had half a mind to report Edwin's crimes at Badajoz to the Colonel-in-Chief of the regiment.

Except he'd given his word not to speak of it to anyone.

What would be the use anyway? Exacting revenge against Edwin would change nothing with Marian.

He passed a flower vendor with a large basket. She sang, 'Buy my fine roses… Buy my fine roses.'

The flowers' scent reminded him of Marian. He shook his head and walked on.

He crossed Oxford Street and walked past Hanover Square to enter the Coach and Horses Inn on Conduit Street, choosing a seat in a dark corner of the taproom. He'd done a fair amount of ale drinking in taverns and inns since working for Sidmouth, keeping his ears open for hints of sedition, but other than complaints about high prices and concerns about the numbers of unemployed in the streets, he'd heard nothing of impending discord.

At the moment, though, the conversations around him held no interest. He wanted to ease his own unrest.

Caused by Marian Pallant, the woman who had not believed in him, who had not wished to marry him.

He cursed Edwin Tranville once more.

After Paris, Allan had poured his energies into building a new future for himself. He still had the drive to make something of his life, even if it no longer was to be worthy of marrying her. He strived for something big—he wanted to run for a seat in the House of Commons. But first he needed to prove himself worthy and knowledgeable.

Allan was a second son and, though his family was well known in Nottinghamshire, he had few connections in London besides his uncle. Uncle Ullman had introduced him to Lord Sidmouth, and Lord Sidmouth had offered him employment. What could be a better situation for him than to work for the Home Office?

Allan believed passionately in Sidmouth's work. His father had been killed when a protesting mob had run amok. At Badajoz Allan had witnessed first hand the violence and destruction of men out of control.

Each day he worked to prevent a protest march or rioting in the streets was a day he avenged his father's death. And atoned for what his fellow soldiers, including Edwin, had done at Badajoz.

If this were not enough, his work also served to replace the passion he'd felt for Marian.

Almost.

Seeing her again brought it all back. She looked more beautiful than ever, and there was a new fire of determination in her eyes that made her even more tantalising.

The tavern maid delivered a tankard of ale. Allan wrapped his fingers around it and drank deeply, remembering the ale Marian had given him after his fever broke. He drained the tankard of its contents and ordered another one.

Maybe one more—or three more—would wash away his anger and regret.

Three days later Allan saw Marian again.

His uncle had arranged for him to be invited to Lady Doncaster's musicale, where many of society's influential people would be in attendance. As Allan walked from his rooms near St James's Square to Duke Street, mere streets away from where Marian lived, it occurred to him she might be there.

As soon as he entered the Doncaster town house and greeted his hostess, his gaze found Marian, standing with his uncle and Lady Ullman. Like a moth to flame, he crossed the room to them.

'Uncle, Lady Ullman, good evening.' He bowed.

'Allan!' cried Domina. 'You must call me Domina.

We are family.' She turned to her friend. 'I have brought Marian with us.'

Allan bowed to Marian. 'Good evening, Miss Pallant.'

'Capt—' she began, then caught herself. 'Mr Landon.' She dropped into a curtsy.

She was easily the loveliest woman in the room. A bit taller than was fashionable, but her hair gleamed like spun gold. Her gown was some gossamer confection as angel-white as the first gown he'd seen her in, its only decoration a simple edging of gold ribbon.

The memory of her dressed in boys' clothing dragging injured soldiers from a burning house flashed through his mind. He smiled.

The colour rose in her face, making her even lovelier.

Lord Ullman seized his wife's arm. 'Someone you must meet, my dear.' He whisked her away, leaving Allan with Marian.

Marian's eyes flickered with irritation as they so callously left her.

'Domina has abandoned you again, it seems,' he remarked.

Her lips pursed. 'And she knew this was my first real foray into society since Brussels. I know hardly anyone.'

Because Tranville had not bothered to see her properly introduced.

'Chin up, Marian,' he said quietly. 'You faced the French. Surely a few lords and their ladies cannot daunt you.'

Her eyes rose to his. 'I feel out of place.'

Out of place? Because she outshone them, perhaps.

Across the room a woman glanced towards her, then whispered something to a lady next to her. Both continued to gaze at her.

She sighed. 'I have not escaped gossip, it seems.'

'Perhaps they are merely envious of your gown,' Allan said.

She rolled her eyes, not even heeding his compliment. 'More likely they are saying I am woefully out of fashion. Everyone else is festooned with lace and frills.' Her voice turned to a whisper. 'Or perhaps it is you who have captured their interest.'

'Me?' He was surprised.

'An eligible man, surely women would notice.' She averted her gaze. 'Forgive me—for all I know, you may no longer be eligible.'

He spoke in a low tone. 'I am not married, if that is what you mean, Marian. I am not betrothed.'

Her eyes rose to his and that sense of connection they'd shared so often in Brussels returned.

She quickly looked away. 'Perhaps Domina has gossiped about me.'

He felt the distance between them again. 'Surely she would not have spoken about Brussels.'

She waved a hand. 'Not about Brussels, but she is very capable of chattering on about me living independently. The *ton* is not likely to favour that.'

He'd had the same thought. An independent woman was by definition suspect, unless she was a widow or an aged spinster. He wondered what those ladies might think of her if they knew she'd run into a burning building or swept out a barn.

He was about to make that remark when Lord Sidmouth approached.

'Good evening, Landon.' Sidmouth gave Marian a speculative look.

Allan obligingly presented Sidmouth to her.

Her eyes widened at the mention of his name. 'You are Home Secretary.'

'Am indeed, Miss Pallant.' Sidmouth nodded towards Allan. 'Landon works for me. Good assistant.'

'Yes, he told me.' Something in her manner changed and that glint of determination returned to her eyes.

'Mark my words. Landon will rise high. He's that sort.'

She slanted a glance toward Allan. 'Rise high?'

'My hope, Miss Pallant,' Allan explained, 'is to sit in the House of Commons some day.'

'Is it?' Her voice turned more sarcastic than impressed.

'Will succeed, too. Mark my words.' Sidmouth walked away.

The butler announced that the music was about to begin. Everyone made their way to the ballroom, which was set up with rows of chairs.

Allan caught sight of his uncle helping Domina into a seat next to another couple. 'Would you do the honour of sitting with me, Miss Pallant?'

She also had noticed her friend had seemingly forgotten her. 'Thank you, Mr Landon. That is kind of you.'

Kind? To sit with anyone else would feel unnatural.

Cards detailing the programme had been placed on each chair. An Italian soprano, Giuditta Pasta, would sing from *Figaro*, and a pianist would play some of John Field's works.

They settled in seats towards the back of the room. The performers were soon ready.

The first selection, one of John Field's nocturnes, had a certain sweetness and delicacy yet depth of mood that seemed to perfectly reflect Allan's companion. At first Marian sat very still and listened intently to the music. Eventually her gaze drifted, and Allan sensed her thoughts had travelled elsewhere, somewhere beyond this room, beyond the music and his company.

The Italian soprano was next. She walked into the room dressed in breeches. Her role in *Figaro* was Cherubino, an adolescent page always played by a soprano.

Allan exchanged glances with Marian, and knew she,

too, was reminded of her own disguise as an adolescent boy.

The soprano began to sing. Allan's Italian was limited, but he was able to translate the first line:

You, who know what love is, see if I have it in my heart.

The line ran through his mind during the rest of the musical evening. Seated next to Marian, Allan felt more attuned to her than to the music. He knew when she listened and when she drifted away. He wished he could drift away with her.

When the music concluded, the audience clapped, but immediately stood, ready to seek out the refreshments, which would be served in another room. Allan and Marian did not rise immediately. It took Allan a few moments to remember they were in the Doncaster ballroom.

When they entered the room with the refreshments, Marian's friend Domina rushed up to them. 'Marian! I thought I had lost you, but I was excessively grateful to know you were with Allan. I knew I need not worry at all. Have you enjoyed the performance?'

'I did enjoy it,' Marian said.

Allan wanted to deliver a set-down to Domina for abandoning her friend. Again.

'That is splendid.' Domina clapped her hands. 'Ullie has introduced me to so many wonderful people, people we would never have met in Bath. I shan't ever recall all their names, but it has been quite exciting.' She glanced over to where her husband kept an eye on her. 'I would ask you to join us, but there are no chairs.'

'You should—' He was about to tell her that she and his uncle should choose a table to include Marian, but Domina was off, her skirts sailing behind her. 'Your friend angers me,' he muttered.

Marian sighed. 'She angers me, too.'

They joined some people with whom Allan was mildly acquainted and talked of the music. It was an entirely pleasant time.

When Domina decided she wanted to leave, she sent a footman to alert Marian. Allan escorted her out of the town house to where his uncle and Domina, and others, waited for their carriages to reach the front of the queue. It had rained earlier in the day, but the night was fine, and Allan did not mind that the wait for the Ullman carriage dragged on.

Marian looked impatient. 'I could walk home faster than this.'

Allan was the only one close enough to hear her. 'I will escort you, if you wish.'

She glanced around. 'Will anyone remark upon it, I wonder?'

'We have darkness on our side. I will inform my uncle. If he has no objection, we can slip away.'

A minute later, they were crossing Oxford Street.

'Thank you for taking me home, Captain.'

He smiled. It felt good to hear her call him 'Captain' again. 'I enjoy the walk.'

'I did learn one thing this evening,' she said.

'What was that?' He liked this sudden camaraderie with her. It reminded him of better times.

'I have little need to mix in society.'

They walked side by side again, but he wished he could thread her arm through his. 'Are you certain? You cannot isolate yourself.'

She looked pensive. 'I no longer belong in such company.'

He could not believe it. 'You look as if you have always graced the fashionable world.'

It was her turn to look surprised. 'Why, thank you, Captain.' She shook her head. 'No matter. It holds little interest to me.'

He frowned. 'Because of Belgium?'

She slanted a glance. 'Yes. It changed me.'

He looked into her face. 'It changed me, too.'

Her lips trembled and he was lost again in a haze of wanting her, needing her, unable to conceive of being apart from her.

They stood on the Mayfair street, gazing upon each other. For Allan the moment stretched until he lost how long they remained there. Slowly he bent down, bringing his lips closer to hers.

She turned away and started walking again. The

moment passed and they began to talk of the musicale and the people there, about Domina's total self-absorption.

They reached her street and walked up to her door.

'Thank you again, Captain.' She extended her hand.

He took it and, wanting so much more, pulled her close enough to place a kiss upon her forehead. 'I enjoyed your company.'

She looked up at him, her eyes large.

Before he lost the thin tether on his restraint, he sounded her knocker. Reilly almost instantly opened the door and Marian rushed inside.

Allan nodded to Reilly and stepped away. 'Goodnight, Miss Pallant.'

From just within the threshold, she turned back to him. 'Godspeed, Captain.'

Allan had hoped to see her at other entertainments over the next few days but, even though his uncle and Domina were present, Marian was not a member of their party. He began to worry about her. Was she ill? Was some man not of his uncle's set entertaining her? Or was she merely turning her back on a society in which she felt she no longer belonged?

He told himself not to think of her, to concentrate on work instead. He filled his time checking in with

Sidmouth's sources, reading newspapers, visiting taverns and coffee houses.

This day he was in the office, seated at his desk, perusing a Nottingham newspaper. Some familiar names dotted the pages, making him wonder how they went on. Between the lines he read of much distress from lost jobs and high prices. It was like that throughout Great Britain.

Lord Sidmouth rapped on his door.

Allan lowered the newspaper and stood. 'Come in, sir.'

'Well? What have you found?' Sidmouth sat in a nearby chair.

'Nothing specific.' Allan folded the paper. 'Something has changed in the last week. I can sense it, although I've heard nothing and read nothing specific.'

'Have the same feeling,' Sidmouth said. 'What of Mr Yost?'

Allan shrugged. 'His name recurs, but in the context of people wondering if he will dare write another essay.'

Sidmouth pounded his knee. 'He's our key. Bet a pony on it.' He leaned towards Allan. 'I have an idea.'

'What is it?'

He leaned back again, lounging in the chair. 'You are acquainted with his neighbour. Pretty girl. Met her with you at Lady Doncaster's.'

Allan held his gaze steady.

'Miss Pallant,' Sidmouth went on. 'That's the name. Sizeable fortune. Father was with the East India Company. Lord Tranville's niece by marriage. Had some sort of falling out with him. Been living on her own since inheriting.'

Allan was appalled. 'You investigated her?'

A corner of the lord's mouth turned up. 'Asked a few questions here and there.'

Allan's fingers curled into a fist.

'Unconventional sort. Lives with a companion. Controls her own funds. Went to Brussels with Sir Roger and his wife. Something happened there. Don't know what it is yet.'

Good God.

Allan's eyes narrowed. 'What has this to do with Yost?' Why was Sidmouth digging into Marian's past? Did he know that Allan had been with her?

'Had this idea.' Sidmouth grinned in delight. 'Call upon her. Court her, even. Makes sense for you to court an heiress.'

Now he was sounding like Tranville.

'Court Miss Pallant?'

Sidmouth cocked his head. 'Only for show, if you like. Too uncommon for an MP's wife, I'd say. Look for a peer's daughter for that. Real reason is to get information about Yost. Watch his house. See what she knows, what her servants know. Servants talk, see everything.'

By God, this was callous.

Allan gripped the arm of his chair. 'You want me to use Miss Pallant in order to spy on John Yost.'

'That's the right of it.' Sidmouth grinned. 'Inspired idea, is it not?'

Allan stood. 'It is a detestable idea! Toying with a young lady's affections merely for information. It is dishonourable.'

Sidmouth's expression darkened. 'Then do not court her. Just call upon her. You are a friend of hers, are you not?'

Sidmouth had a way of manipulating people for his own ends. He apparently had no qualms about manipulating Marian.

Allan gave Sidmouth a direct stare. 'I want no part of this.'

Sidmouth rose and sauntered to the door, but he turned back. 'This is not a request, Landon. This is the job you agreed to perform when I employed you. If you care about your future and the future of your country, you'll befriend your Miss Pallant, court her, sleep with her, anything necessary to get information that prevents sedition. Do as I say and persist until you have something on Yost to bring to me.' He strolled out of the room.

Allan sank in the chair and ran his hand through his hair.

To do his job, to serve his country, to avenge his father, he had to take advantage of Marian.

Chapter Thirteen

Marian sat at her desk and riffled through the latest set of invitations. Domina had been true to her word. Invitations arrived every day to various events and Domina often penned notes offering to include her in their party. Marian found excuses to refuse, although each time she wondered if *he* would be attending.

He consumed her thoughts much too often, her *Captain*, but it was essential she stay away from him. He worked for the Home Secretary. His job was to thwart everything she was working hard to bring about.

She dropped the invitations on the desk and pulled out a sheet of paper to pen a conciliatory note to Domina, refusing yet another offer to accompany her to a breakfast, but promising to call upon her soon.

Blanche walked in. 'Do you need to speak with Mr Yost today?'

Marian put down her pen. 'I do not think so. Why?'

She blushed. 'I just met him outside when I was

coming from the shops. He invited me to walk with him in the park.'

Marian hid her amusement, wondering how long Mr Yost stood at his window watching for Blanche to return. 'If he needs to speak with me, he certainly may, but otherwise, enjoy the day.'

'You do not mind?' Blanche took her duties as companion so seriously she felt guilty ever leaving Marian alone.

'I do not mind,' Marian assured her. 'I have letters to write and much to keep me occupied.'

Blanche grinned at her. 'Thank you, Marian.' She started for the door.

Marian called after her. 'Invite Mr Yost to dinner, if you like.'

Blanche stopped. 'Indeed?'

'Of course. It will be pleasant.'

Blanche returned a grateful look. 'I will, then.'

'Tell Cook,' Marian added.

Blanche nodded and swept out of the room looking blissfully happy, the way a woman in love ought to look.

Marian rested her chin on her hand. Blanche renewed Marian's faith in romance. Mr Yost was a good man with a solid independent income. Both he and Blanche deserved happiness.

Something that eluded Marian.

Her own fault. What might have happened if she'd

even considered that Edwin had lied to her? What if she had opened one of the captain's letters instead of returning them?

Perhaps she would be wed to him and sharing his bed at night. She couldn't deny the fact that her body still yearned for him.

As did her soul.

She forced herself to pick up her pen, dip it in the inkpot and resume writing her letter.

One thing was certain, she would not be planning a soldiers' march if her husband worked for the Home Secretary. How then would the soldiers' voices be heard? She was determined to give them that voice. There was nothing more important to her.

She easily finished her correspondence and stood, stretching the stiffness from her muscles. She walked out to the hall just as someone sounded the knocker.

'I'll get it, Reilly,' she called out. 'I'm right here.' She opened the door.

The captain stood at the threshold.

'Captain!' She felt herself flush.

He removed his hat. 'I did not expect you to answer the door. Domina said you have refused several invitations—'

Now she understood. 'Domina sent you? I am sorry you have been put to so much inconvenience.'

He shook his head. 'She did not send me.'

He had come of his own volition? She flushed again, too instantly aware of him.

She stepped aside. 'Do come in.'

Reilly appeared, all smiles when he saw who it was. 'Captain! May I take your things?'

He handed Reilly his hat and gloves. 'How do you fare today?' he asked the butler.

A pleased expression lit Reilly's face. 'In good health, sir.'

'Well—' Marian clasped her hands together '—come to the drawing room, will you? Reilly, bring us tea.'

'Yes, miss,' he said.

She led the captain to the small drawing room on the first floor, the one that faced the front of the house. 'Do sit, Captain, and tell me why you have come.'

He stood until she lowered herself in a chair. 'I merely was in the neighbourhood and thought to see how you went on.'

'Why?' There must be more to it than that.

'Do I need more reason than the concern of a friend?'

They could never be friends, not even if they were not political enemies.

'Everything is splendid here.' She did not wish to be the topic of conversation. 'How is the Home Office?'

His eyes flickered. 'No Blanketeers at the city gates as yet.'

Had he been a part of thwarting the Blanketeers' march?

Marian tried to keep her voice even. 'Ah, but did not one of the Blanketeers make it through? The newspapers said he delivered his petition.'

'One man is not a riot,' he countered.

This irritated her. 'Not every protest is a riot. The papers said the men marched peacefully in small groups.'

The captain countered, 'Ah, but the intent was for them all to meet in a large gathering. When numbers are large, there is always the danger of riot.'

Her brows rose. 'Cannot large numbers of men gather and behave in organised, disciplined ways?'

'It only takes one spark to set a fire. One man, one mistake, and a riot might result.' His fingers tapped the arm of the chair.

She smiled stiffly. 'I was not thinking of marches upon Parliament. I was thinking of soldiers. Are soldiers not disciplined, even though their numbers are large?'

'Even soldiers can run amok.' His tone turned bleak and pain filled his eyes.

He witnessed such a thing, she realised. *In the war.*

She wanted to comfort him, to soothe away the pain of whatever it was he'd endured.

Would he want her comfort if he knew she was planning a soldiers' march? Her march would be different, however. *Her* soldiers would maintain discipline. There would be no arrests, no injuries. They would make the government pay attention, to recognise that if their needs were neglected they could indeed be a force to be reckoned with.

Reilly entered with the tea tray. After he left Marian was silent as she fixed the captain's tea, remembering from Brussels exactly how he liked it.

He took a sip and closed his eyes, as if savouring the taste. 'I have learned how to appreciate this luxury.'

Marian knew instantly what he meant. 'Yes. There is so much I no longer take for granted.' She handed him the plate of biscuits.

'Good food,' he said, taking a bite of a biscuit.

She touched her gown. 'Clean clothing.'

He seemed to be thinking for a minute. 'Absence of pain.'

That pierced her heart. 'No one brandishing axes.'

'Or shooting at us.'

'Dry shoes and stockings,' she added.

He lifted a finger. 'Speaking English.'

She smiled and patted her chair. 'Furniture.'

He smiled in return. 'A bed.'

Their gazes caught and held and he was slow to glance away. She remembered the night she had shared his bed, remembered the lovemaking they shared, remembered how she urged him to do more.

She stared into her teacup.

He spoke quietly. 'I only regret the suffering you endured.'

She glanced up at him. 'I do not regret even that.'

Marian regretted nothing between them, except the interference of her uncle and cousin. That she greatly regretted.

'It made me realise what is important,' she told him. 'It made me realise I can be strong.'

He looked at her. 'You were remarkably strong, Marian. To that I owe my life.'

She felt her cheeks burn. 'Say no more. You deserve equal credit.' She brushed a lock of hair off her forehead and latched on to a safer subject. 'We should give equal credit to Valour, you know. She saved us a time or two.'

He smiled. 'Indeed.'

'Where is Valour?' She would like to see the horse again, stroke her muzzle and whisper her thanks. 'Do you have her in London?'

'I do.' He took another sip of tea. 'I may have to send her to my uncle's country house, though. It is expensive to keep her here and I have little time to ride her.'

Marian lowered her gaze, reminded of his limited finances. 'She will not like being parted from you.'

'But she will enjoy galloping through the fields and breathing the fresh country air.'

The door opened and Blanche walked in, followed

by Mr Yost. 'We are back.' Blanche saw the Captain. 'Oh—forgive me. I did not know you had a caller.'

Allan stood. 'It is good to see you again, Mrs Nunn. I trust you are well.'

She curtsied. 'Very well, Mr Landon.' She turned to Mr Yost. 'Allow me to present our neighbour, Mr Yost. Mr Yost, this is Mr Landon, who was acquainted with Miss Pallant in Brussels.'

Marian's heart raced. She had not felt this level of anxiety since Waterloo. The captain was already suspicious of Mr Yost; he had said so that first day. He could make this meeting a very difficult one.

Instead he surprised her.

He strode forwards and extended his hand in a most gentlemanly manner.

Mr Yost shook it. 'You were in Brussels for the battle, then?'

'With the Royal Scots,' he explained.

'A momentous day in history,' responded Mr Yost.

Marian was still filled with anxiety. She needed to warn Yost. 'Captain Landon is now working for Lord Sidmouth at the Home Office.'

Mr Yost did not miss a beat. 'Are you, sir?'

'I am.' The captain smiled genially. 'I am no longer a captain, however, although Miss Pallant persists in calling me one.'

Marian doubted she could ever call him anything else.

She rose and walked towards the door. 'Do sit. I will ask Reilly for more tea.'

Once in the hallway, she leaned against the wall for a moment, trying to sort her disordered emotions.

She found Reilly nearby. 'You ought to have warned me Mr Yost was here, Reilly.'

He appeared chagrined. 'I could not, miss. Mrs Nunn asked where you were and I said the drawing room and she was already at the door with Mr Yost behind her.'

She pressed her fingers to her temple. 'Never mind. I suppose we need more tea. Can you bring some?'

When she walked back into the drawing room, the gentlemen started to rise, but she signalled them to remain seated.

As she returned to her chair, Mr Yost addressed the captain. 'Work for the Home Office, you say? I suspect you have heard my name spoken there.'

What was he doing?

'It has been mentioned,' the captain replied. 'I am afraid you have a reputation as a radical essayist.'

Yost was unapologetic. 'I dare say I have written what might be termed radical criticism of the government in my time. My views remain liberal, but the climate is too dangerous to publish them at the moment.' He leaned towards the captain. 'I am curious, sir, why you choose to work for the Home Office.'

The captain's eyes turned piercing. 'I know the carnage protesting mobs can do. I seek to stop it.'

Marian remembered. 'Your father,' she whispered, too low for anyone to hear. She was surprised she had not thought of it before. She raised her voice. 'The captain's father was killed by rioters.'

Yost lowered his head. 'My sympathies, Mr Landon. That is a great sadness to bear.' He raised his head again. 'Perhaps we can agree that violence helps no one's cause.'

The captain lifted his tea cup to his lips. 'On that we can agree.'

The tense moment passed and the two men continued discussing their differences, but in a quite civil manner.

Reilly, looking abashed, entered with the tea tray. 'Cook says dinner will be ready in an hour.' He hurried out.

Marian bit her lip, wishing she had not snapped at him.

The captain rose. 'I have overstayed my welcome, I fear.'

'Oh!' Blanche exclaimed. 'Right in the middle of your debate.'

He smiled at her. 'We are not likely to resolve anything no matter how long I stay.'

'But it is interesting,' Blanche went on. 'I should think you could talk even through dinner.' Her eyes brightened. 'Marian, might we ask Mr Landon to join us for dinner?'

Marian could not compose an answer. Had Blanche's wits gone begging?

Captain Landon glanced at her. 'I am not dressed for dinner.'

'Well, neither am I,' said Yost.

The captain's voice changed in tone. 'You are staying, sir?'

'Yes,' Blanche answered. 'You would make our numbers even and it would be like a party. Can we not include him, Marian?'

She was trapped. She turned to the captain. 'You are very welcome to stay to dinner, if you do not have another engagement.' Perhaps he would take the hint that she expected him to say no.

Instead he gazed into her eyes. 'I would be honoured to dine with you.' He smiled. 'I never take a good meal for granted.'

Marian felt herself flush. He was reminding her of their past hardships, hardships of which they'd so light-heartedly jested earlier.

'That is splendid, Mr Landon,' Blanche said.

Marian had never confided in Blanche about the exact nature of her acquaintance with the captain in Belgium, but surely Blanche knew not to keep the fox in with the chickens for longer than necessary.

More tea was poured and the conversation resumed, but about foods and favourite dinners, not politics.

* * *

Dinner was a lively affair and one Marian enjoyed more than she could have anticipated. Mr Yost and the captain listened attentively to each other and disagreed respectfully, much to Marian's relief and admiration. Both she and Blanche entered in the conversation, but Marian was careful to follow Yost's lead so she would not rouse Landon's suspicions. In many ways the captain's views were sympathetic to the people's suffering; he merely advocated different means to alleviate it.

'Change best happens within the boundaries of the law,' he said. 'If left to a mob, we risk the anarchy of the French Revolution.'

'But our government has been part of the problem,' Mr Yost countered. 'The Corn Laws, for example.'

The Corn Laws set high prices for grain and restricted its import. The laws protected the profits of large landowners, but also made bread, the staple food of the lower classes, very costly.

'Government makes bad decisions sometimes,' the captain responded. 'I am not saying the Corn Laws were bad. It is more complex than that. If the government makes too many mistakes, then one must elect a new government. That is working for change within the law.'

'You forget that only landowners can vote.' Yost stabbed the air with his fork. 'Who speaks then for those suffering souls who do not own land?'

'For that matter,' added Blanche, 'who speaks for women? We cannot vote no matter what.'

Captain Landon smiled at her. 'Do you advocate suffrage for women, Mrs Nunn? That is radical, indeed.'

She coloured. 'I meant only to make a point.'

Marian kept quiet. She strongly believed women should have the power to decide their own fate. Perhaps the captain would be shocked that she felt that way.

The captain speared a piece of meat with his fork. 'I believe that if good men are elected, they will do the right thing by everyone.'

The problem lay in recognising good. Marian gazed at the captain through lowered lashes. He was a man she'd once trusted with her life, yet now his job was to arrest organisers like herself and have them hanged for sedition. Would he see her hanged if he knew what she was about?

The discussion continued through the dessert and after-dinner tea, but Marian was more absorbed in observing the captain, yearning to be close to him again and at the same time wary lest she gave him cause to send her to the gallows.

The clock struck ten and the captain stopped midsentence. 'I had no idea of the time. Forgive me for staying so late.' He stood.

'I should go, too,' Yost said, but he made no effort to move.

'I'll walk you to the door, Captain.' Marian rose.

Their shoulders brushed as they walked to the hall. Marian could almost fantasise that they were companionable again.

The captain picked up his hat and gloves from the hall table. 'You did not need to walk me out, Marian.'

'Mr Yost and Blanche would have no time alone if I did not.'

His brows rose. 'He is courting her?'

She smiled. 'Oh, yes. It is quite a romance.'

He pulled on his gloves. 'I meant only to stay a civil fifteen minutes.' He glanced at her. 'But I much enjoyed dining with you.'

It had seemed right to her to see him seated across from her at the evening meal.

'I hope you did not think our neighbour too radical in his beliefs.' She meant she hoped he would not suspect Yost of more.

His expression turned serious. 'He was an interesting man. I liked him.'

She watched him adjust the fingers of the gloves and remembered when his bare hands had stroked her.

'I like him, too,' she replied. 'Which is a good thing, because of Blanche.'

He smiled.

She opened the door to a cool breeze that ruffled her skirt and cooled her face. He placed his hand on her arm and drew her closer. Her head tilted back and she closed her eyes.

Like before he placed a light kiss on her forehead and moved away slowly to step out of the doorway.

'Goodnight,' she managed, trembling with the need to be in his arms one more time.

He tipped his hat to her before placing it on his head and starting to walk away.

She hurried back to the drawing room and watched him through the window as he made his way down the street.

'To what do you owe that visit, Miss Pallant?' Yost asked, his voice grim.

'I do not know.' She was no longer able to see him.

Blanche leaned against the back of her chair. 'Well, I believe he has a *tendre* for you.'

Marian wrapped her arms around herself. 'I cannot think so.'

'He could be spying for the Home Office,' Yost said.

'I do not believe that!' Blanche cried.

Marian gave Yost a worried look. 'Do you think he suspects me?'

'I do not see how,' he replied. 'We keep your name out of everything. Likely he suspects me of something.'

'He is much too nice to be a spy,' Blanche insisted.

Yost laughed. 'Those are the kind one must worry about, my dear.'

Marian felt sombre. 'What shall we do?'

Yost lowered his brows in thought. 'It is best to act as

if you have nothing at all to hide. That was my strategy tonight, and I think it worked well.' He tapped his chin. 'I suggest you accept his calls. In fact, accept some of the invitations your friend sends your way. No one will think a society lady is the organiser of a protest.'

She touched the cool window pane. In two weeks her soldiers would march and the entire event would be over. She did not know what would happen after that, how she would fill her time.

She did not know if Captain Landon would be a part of it.

The next day Lord Sidmouth summoned Allan as soon as he walked in to the Home Office.

'Well?' Sidmouth looked up from his desk as Allan entered. 'Did you call upon her?'

Allan scowled. 'I did.'

'And?' Sidmouth persisted.

Allan shrugged. 'I spent a pleasant evening. I even met John Yost. He was a guest of Miss Pallant's companion. Our conversation was lively and interesting.'

'Interesting, eh?' Sidmouth brightened. 'What did you learn?'

Allan gave him a direct look. 'Nothing we did not already know. Yost freely discussed his views, but said nothing to make me suspect him of sedition. He was a thoughtful, intelligent, reasoned man.'

Sidmouth made a derisive sound. 'Delighted you like

the fellow. Go back. Keep digging. Keep your eyes and ears open.' He waved him off.

Allan started for the door, then turned. 'Sir, I cannot help but feel my continuing to call upon Miss Pallant is toying with her sensibilities—'

'I care nothing about her sensibilities!' Sidmouth replied. 'Your job is to gather information and this is the way it is done. Yost is the key, I tell you. I feel it.'

Allan left the room.

He waited two days before calling upon Marian again. A grey-haired maid answered the door this time, obviously one of Marian's war widows. She showed him into the drawing room and went to fetch her mistress from some other part of the house.

He heard the mumbling of voices. A door closed nearby and footsteps sounded in the hallway. A moment later she walked into the room.

'Captain,' she said with an edge to her voice. 'Good afternoon.'

He bowed to her. 'I hope I did not take you from something important. I had an impulse to call.' Less like an impulse and more like a command.

Still, a part of him gladdened to see her, to hear her voice again, to smell the scent of roses.

'I was finished,' she said, not explaining. 'Do sit. I've ordered tea again.'

They sat in the same chairs as the previous visit.

'This time I promise not to stay so long,' he said.

She averted her face.

He had difficulty dreaming up conversation. 'Where is Reilly today?'

'He and Toby—the footman—are doing errands for me.'

She did not seem inclined to elaborate so he had to come up with something else. 'And the lovebirds? Where are they?'

'Blanche and Mr Yost?' She glanced towards the door. 'Blanche went to the shops.' She paused briefly. 'I would not be surprised if Mr Yost also finds a sudden need to shop.'

'This sounds like a serious romance.' And also an opening for him to do Sidmouth's bidding.

She smiled. 'Yes. Is it not lovely?'

'As long as Yost's political beliefs do not cause him trouble.' He felt like a cad, but tried to cover it by matching her light tone.

Her smile fled and her expression turned serious. 'Will *you* cause Mr Yost trouble for his beliefs, Captain?'

'A man is still free to believe as he wishes.' He hated trying to pump her for information. 'But what he does must be within the law.'

'Within the law,' she repeated solemnly. 'I do not forget you work for Lord Sidmouth.'

Neither do I, he thought. 'I am sorry, Marian. I like Yost even if we disagree on some matters—'

He was about to ask her what she knew of Yost's

activities when the knocker on the front door sounded and loud voices came from the hallway. Allan started for the door when it burst open revealing the maid.

'This man came in!' the woman cried. 'I opened the door and he came in and would not leave.'

Allan ran out of the room with Marian behind him.

A man was seated on the stairs, his head leaning against the banister. Allan rushed over and turned him around to see his face.

'Edwin!' Marian cried.

Chapter Fourteen

Marian stared down at her cousin. His clothes were rumpled and he smelled of spirits and vomit.

He opened his eyes, but they seemed unable to focus. 'Greetings, Marian!' he slurred.

She glared at him. 'You are drunk.'

He made a soundless laugh. 'Drunk as a wheel-barrow.'

'Get up.' The captain pulled Edwin off the stairs.

'Whoa!' Edwin pushed him away and grabbed for the banister. 'Can do it m'self.' Comprehension dawned on his face and he pointed at the captain. 'You! You are not 'sposed to be here.'

The captain seized Edwin's coat lapels and leaned close. 'Thought you were rid of me, did you?'

'Yes!' Edwin's reply was high-pitched.

The captain dragged him to the door.

'Leggo!' Edwin shoved the Captain away and staggered towards Marian. 'Marian, wanted to see you.'

'Not like this, Edwin!' She was furious at him. For

coming to her house drunk. For lying to her about the captain, but she could not discuss it will him in such a state. 'You have to leave.'

The captain grabbed for his arm again, but Edwin twisted away.

'Can't make me go!' Edwin pointed to the captain again. 'Make him leave.'

'He is not drunk,' she retorted. 'You are. I want you out.'

His scarred face contorted. 'No! Want him out. I stay.'

He lunged at her and she cried out in alarm.

The captain seized him from behind and pulled him away from her. Edwin landed on the floor. His face contorted in anger and he rose up again, a frenzy of fists, wailing like a child. He groped for the captain's throat, but the captain shoved him away. Edwin staggered back, hitting the wall and falling against a table that shattered beneath him.

He lay still.

'Oh, my God!' Marian stared at him. 'Is he dead?'

The captain leaned down and felt for a pulse. 'Passed out.'

Marian sank down on the stairs. 'What am I going to do with him?'

The captain still laboured to catch his breath. 'I can put him in a hackney coach and send him home.'

'I have no idea where he is staying.' She had not even known Edwin was in London.

'Would he not be staying at your uncle's town house?'

'I cannot think he would be. He and my uncle had a big row.' Last she heard from the former Mrs Vernon, now Lady Tranville, was that Edwin was not welcome in any of his father's houses.

The captain straightened his coat. 'I could carry him into the park and leave him on a bench.'

'Surely not.'

He gave her a direct look. 'I'm quite serious.'

She was so angry at Edwin she could almost agree with this plan.

She stood. 'I am tempted to say yes, but something might happen and I would never forgive myself. I suppose he must stay here until he sobers up.'

The captain gave her a steady look. 'Marian, that is not wise.'

She waved a hand in exasperation. 'What choice do I have?'

'He cannot stay here.' His tone was insistent.

'No one could possibly object,' she went on. 'Edwin is a relation of mine. Besides, who would know? My servants will not talk of it.'

The captain rubbed his brow. 'That is not the point.' He crossed the hall and placed his hands on her shoulders, forcing her to look into his eyes. 'You cannot have him here because he is dangerous.'

'He's unconscious!'

His grip tightened. 'He might rouse at any moment. You saw him! And he could get much worse. The alcohol makes him out of his mind.'

She looked down at Edwin. 'I have seen him deep in his cups. He becomes silly or maudlin.'

The captain stared at her for a long time before speaking in a low voice. 'I have seen him become violent.' His fingers pressed into her shoulders. 'You must believe me.'

She remembered the captain had warned her of Edwin before. 'I believe you, Captain. But I have no choice. I cannot leave him in the park to attack someone else.'

He released a frustrated breath and let go of her. 'Post Reilly outside his door, then.'

She looked up at him with chagrin. 'Reilly is out of town and will not return until tomorrow.' Reilly was delivering messages about the march to their contacts outside the city. 'Toby, my footman, will be here, but he is a small man and he has only one leg.'

'That won't do.' Allan stared down at the floor before directing his gaze back at her. 'I will stay.'

'No—' she started to protest, but he placed his fingers on her lips.

'If Edwin's presence would remain unknown, then

mine will, as well.' His gaze pierced into her. 'I will stay.'

His closeness made Marian light-headed, as giddy as if she'd been spun around. She inhaled deeply. 'Very well, Captain.'

He smiled at her.

Her eyes narrowed. 'Why are you smiling?' Had he noticed his effect on her?

'You persist in calling me Captain.'

'It is how I know you,' she murmured. It was how she preferred to think of him, not as a man doing Sidmouth's work. She cleared her throat. 'There is a spare bedroom above stairs, but how do we get him there?'

'I'll carry him.' He crouched down and hoisted Edwin over his shoulder as if he'd done such a thing before.

The maid peered around the corner. 'Has he gone?'

'No, but it is safe to come out, Hannah,' Marian told her.

The maid crept into the hall and saw the captain carrying Edwin up the stairs. 'Oh, my goodness!' she exclaimed.

'He is quite harmless now,' Marian assured her. 'He is my cousin and I'm afraid he must stay here to sleep off the drink. Run ahead, please, and put fresh linens on the bed in the spare bedroom.'

Hannah rushed past the captain, who'd reached the first flight of stairs. She'd managed to strip the old covers from the bed and tucked in a fresh sheet by the

time Marian led the captain into the room to unceremo-
niously drop Edwin on to the bed.

'He smells foul.' Marian covered her nose with her
hand. 'Can we take off his clothing?'

'I'll do it,' Captain Landon said.

Hannah put a hand on his arm. 'I'll help you, sir.
After raising two boys of my own, I won't see anything
I have not seen before.' Hannah had lost one of those
sons to the war, in addition to losing her husband. The
other son still marched to the drum.

'Thank you, Hannah,' the captain said.

'I'll find some nightclothes.' Marian would not intrude
upon Reilly's or Toby's rooms without their permission,
so she ran next door to Yost's house, even though she
knew Yost was out.

She and Yost had been meeting to discuss the march
when the captain called. At Mr Hunt's suggestion,
Marian and Yost had organised the marchers into small
groups. Yost, Hunt and Marian's household were the
only ones who knew of her involvement. A few more
men knew of Yost's, but they'd organised the groups
in such a manner that, if betrayed, no man would have
more than one or two names to provide. After leaving
Marian, Yost intended to rendezvous with one of his
contacts, who would spread the final information about
the time, place and scope of the march.

After all that, Marian expected Yost to seek out
Blanche.

Yost's valet was at home, however, and he agreed to lend Marian fresh nightclothes for Edwin.

In clean clothing and put to bed, Edwin curled up and slept like a baby. Until Toby returned, Marian felt obligated to sit with the captain in Edwin's room, where they talked quietly through the afternoon.

The Captain asked her about her life in India before her parents died. She told him about happy memories, such as when her *amah* took her into the market place with its colourful fruits and fragrant spices. Or to visit her *amah*'s relatives in tiny homes with much laughter and exotic cooking. Or to the silk shop, a fairy land of colourful, fluttering cloth.

'How did your parents become ill?' he asked her.

She again saw the woman kissing her father in the carriage, but that part was too painful to relate.

'My father came home with a fever, and soon nearly everyone in the house died of it.' Her mother. Her father. Her *amah*.

She changed the subject. 'Tell me about your family.'

He told her about growing up in Nottinghamshire on his father's estate, of exploring the countryside as a boy or spending time in the nearby town with his childhood companions, getting into one scrape after another.

He laughed. 'My father would put his hands on his hips and ask me if I had windmills in my head. "Can you not just do what is right?" he would say. Those were wise words, but hard for a boy to heed.'

'I am sympathetic to you as a boy. How does one know what is right, especially if there are two sides to something?' His strong convictions about right and wrong made no sense to her. 'Is it not often a matter of one's point of view? For example, you are so certain the Spa Fields demonstrators and the Blanketeers were wrong, but surely if I'd asked them, they would have said you were wrong.'

His eyes narrowed. 'You are sounding like Mr Yost.'

She'd gone too far. He was the last person with whom she should debate politics.

'Oh, my!' she cried. 'I am repeating his views, am I not?' She tried to act as if the notion surprised her. 'But he is as convinced he is right as you are.'

'A man's opinions are never wrong, but what he *does* can be right or wrong. Those men at Spa Fields were right that there were many hardships that ought to be changed, they were wrong to break the law.' He paused and his expression turned even more serious. 'Do you think Yost puts his opinions in action?'

Her nerves flared. 'What do you mean?'

'Would he organise men to demonstrate or to march on London?'

'Surely he would not.' She took a breath. 'Would you see him arrested if he did?'

He frowned. 'I would be compelled to do so.'

Edwin stirred and mumbled something, instantly capturing their attention. He turned over and became quiet again.

Marian made certain they talked of other things thereafter and when Toby returned they locked Edwin's door and posted Toby in a chair outside the room with instructions to alert the captain if Edwin stirred. By dinnertime, Blanche and Yost had arrived from the shops and the four of them again shared a pleasant meal and evening together.

When the hour drew late Mr Yost took his leave. The Captain insisted Toby should go to bed and took up position in the chair outside Edwin's door. Marian brought him a footstool so he could prop his feet up.

The spare room was right across the hall from Marian's bed chamber, so the captain sat right outside her door. How was she to sleep knowing he was so near?

Their time together had been so companionable, almost like Brussels when they'd cared for the soldiers. She could almost pretend they could bridge the huge gap that had grown between them.

Until they began discussing Mr Yost and protests and arrests.

By the time the clock struck one, Edwin's snores rattled the windowpanes. Marian sat up in her bed.

It was not the cacophony coming from Edwin's throat that kept her awake, but the captain. Sleep was impossible when he was so near.

Exasperated with herself, she dangled her legs off the side of the bed. With sudden decision, she slipped off and padded to the fireplace. From one of the glowing coals she lit a taper and carried it to the door, opening it a crack to see if the captain was sleeping.

He immediately stood. 'Marian?'

She opened the door wider. 'I woke you. I am sorry.'

He rubbed his face. 'I was not asleep.'

A loud atonic sound, like blocks of wood scraping across a bare floor, came from behind the locked door.

'It is a wonder any of us can sleep,' Marian said. 'I never heard such snoring.'

'Even Blanche was awake.' He stifled a yawn.

She also covered her mouth with her hand. 'Blanche? Did you speak with her?'

'No. She may have thought me asleep. She hurried down the servants' stairs.'

'The servants' stairs?' That was odd. A drop of hot wax dripped on to Marian's finger. 'Oh!'

'You've burnt yourself.' The captain took the taper from her hand and used it to light a candle in a nearby sconce.

She placed her burnt finger to her mouth.

He pulled it away. 'Let me see.'

'It is nothing,' she said, suddenly finding it hard to breathe as he examined her finger.

Still holding her hand, he led her to the chair. 'Sit with me.'

She lowered herself on to the footstool.

He yawned again.

She glanced towards her bedchamber door. 'Would you like to lie down in my bed?'

His eyes grew wide. 'Share a bed again?'

A thrill shot through her, a thrill she dared not nourish. 'I meant that I would sit here and wake you if Edwin causes trouble.'

His lips turned up at one corner. 'I was hoping you meant we would share a bed like we did at the inn.'

'Hoping?' Her voice rose, remembering her moral lapse. 'I thought you disliked me for it.'

His brows rose. 'Disliked?'

She moved the stool away. 'Let us not discuss this.'

He leaned forwards and reached for her hand. 'I did not dislike what passed between us.'

She tucked her hands beneath her arms. 'You were appalled by it.'

'I was not.' He reached out again, holding her chin so she could not look away. 'I was appalled by my own weakness, Marian. I wanted nothing more than to—' He broke off.

'But that was because I made you.' She moved away again. 'I seduced you.'

She disliked remembering how wantonly she'd behaved, how much she'd wanted the captain to show her what could exist between a man and woman.

She wanted it even now.

'I had better go back to bed.' She fled into her room.

He followed her, catching her and spinning her around to face him. 'Marian? Do not be distressed.'

His arms encircled her and she buried her face in his coat, realising she had been desperate for his embrace. 'I am ashamed of how I behaved. Like a strumpet.'

She felt him laugh. 'A strumpet?' He continued to hold her and spoke in that low voice that might be her undoing if he did not stop. 'You'd guarded your emotions so long when we were in danger. The danger was past, and you...you needed comfort.'

His heart beat beneath her ear, soothing her. 'That does not explain my feelings now. I am in no danger now.'

He released her and lifted her chin. 'And you feel such urges now?'

She nodded.

'As do I.' His eyes darkened as he continued to stare down at her.

'Do not look at me,' she protested. 'I do not know what you are thinking.'

A slow smile creased his face. 'I am thinking of kissing you.'

His words set her body aflame. It was all she could do to wait while he slowly dipped his head until his lips touched hers. His kiss was gentle at first, then, like a fire that finally ignited, it flamed and devoured and demanded. Feeling as if her own passion might consume her, Marian kissed him back.

'Marian,' he murmured.

'Captain,' she whispered in response.

He swept her into his arms and carried her to her bed. Together they tumbled upon it. He kissed her again, playfully this time.

The wonder of it! She'd no idea there could be so many kinds of kisses. Playful, hungry, demanding. She tried another version, a kiss to tell him she did not want him to pull away this time. With that kiss the room blurred and sounds seemed to echo as if in a dream.

Boldly she pulled off her nightdress and knelt on the bed, letting his eyes savour her. She could hardly breathe.

His boots were already off and, with her eager help, he made quick work of the rest of his clothing. Feeling his bare skin against hers was both familiar and new. One moment she felt like the most experienced courtesan, knowing what she wanted, what she needed, and the next she marvelled at the experience, like the virgin she was.

He covered her with his body, dipping down to kiss her as she parted her legs and prayed he would not delay in fulfilling her desire for him. When the male part of him touched her most sensitive place she thought she might cry out. She wanted more, much more.

But he stopped.

She wanted to weep. Not again!

He looked her directly in the eye. 'Are you certain of this?'

'Yes. Yes,' she cried.

'Do you know what to do to prevent a baby?' he asked.

A baby could be prevented? She'd had no idea.

'Of course I know,' she lied.

Not even the risk of a baby would make her stop now.

She thought how glorious it would be if a baby grew inside her from this. His baby. This might be her only chance. Tomorrow she could ask Blanche what women did to prevent babies.

She stared into his eyes. 'I am very certain of this.'

He stroked her skin until she felt like bursting with the pleasure of it. His hand closed on her breast and sensation shot straight to between her legs where the aching grew more intense. She gasped in delight.

He slid down her body and his tongue tasted her nipple, causing sensations she never could have imagined. She buried her hands in his hair and hoped he would not stop. Writhing beneath him, she heard sounds of pleasure escape her lips.

His hand flattened against her abdomen, and she remembered the magic his fingers created when he'd touched her most intimately. Part of her yearned for him to repeat that bliss, now—but even more she wanted to give him pleasure. Would a man find touching as thrilling as she did?

She decided to find out. 'Lie on your back,' she whispered.

He glanced at her in surprise, but complied.

'Your turn,' she murmured.

Her hand shook before she touched his skin and dared to explore him as he'd done to her. His skin was rough with the dark hair that peppered his chest and his arms and legs. She remembered how firm his muscles had felt beneath his skin and again savoured the strength they represented.

The light was dim in her bedchamber, coming only from the glow of coals in her fireplace and the flame of the sconce in the hall, but she could see what a beautiful man he was. She wanted to rejoice aloud that she was again feasting upon the sight of him, revelling in the feel of him, and that she was soon to be joined with him.

She felt giddy with excitement at what was to transpire between them. No longer afraid to be wanton, she relished each sensation. She was unafraid of offending him or seducing him. Let him prose on about duty this time; she would not listen to it.

She cared only that he said he wanted to make love with her. He said he'd hoped for it. He desired her, he said. She'd take him at his word, because she wanted this and wanted nothing to stop her from getting the pleasure he could bring.

She slipped her hand down the length of his chest to where his male member had grown large and hard for her. She clasped him in her palm and explored that most mysterious part of him.

He groaned. 'That is torture.'

'Oh!' She released him. 'I did not know it would hurt you.'

He took her hand and pressed her fingers around him again. 'I did not say to stop.'

So she did not stop until he took her hand away and turned her on her back. 'I cannot wait.'

'Then do not,' she murmured. Indeed, she was eager for what came next.

She parted her legs and his fingers slipped inside her and she began to understand what he'd meant about torture.

She, too, did not wish this torture to stop.

Suddenly he withdrew his fingers and was on top of her, ready to enter her. Her heart raced in panic or excitement, she didn't know which, as he pushed into her, little by little, gentle strokes that she somehow knew she didn't need or desire.

She lifted her hips and suddenly he pushed inside her, filling her completely.

Yes, she felt like saying. *At last,* but words were impossible in the moment.

He moved against her, and she marvelled at the new feeling, something else that had been beyond her imagination. She wanted it never to stop, this exquisite agony, this tormenting bliss.

Somehow she knew to move with him, and a rhythm formed between them, like a dance for which she'd never needed lessons. Their dance grew faster and faster and more and more frenzied, and her need grew as well, until it suddenly seemed unbearable.

She wanted to weep and wail that this almost-pain, almost-pleasure was too difficult to bear. She wanted it to stop, but was incapable of stopping.

Then, all of a sudden, there was an explosion of sensation, inconceivable waves of pleasure, leaving her gasping and writhing beneath him. He pushed into her even harder and she felt him shudder inside her, spilling his seed.

When his body relaxed he slid to her side, but still held her close. 'Marian,' he moaned.

She sat up on an elbow so she could look at him. 'Was that how it was supposed to be?'

'That was how it was supposed to be.' He was still breathing hard. 'But much, much better.'

She lay back with a satisfied sigh.

From the other room, Edwin's snores again reached their ears. They both burst into laughter.

'I dread him waking,' she murmured.

'I should resume my post before he does,' he said.

'No. Stay with me.' She snuggled against him, and he held her close.

Marian felt a lassitude that was again new and unexpected. Her eyes grew heavy and she felt at peace, but she fought sleep. She did not want to miss a moment of being next to him.

'Marian?' His voice rumbled in his chest.

'Mmm?' she responded.

'We must marry.'

She opened her eyes and looked at him. 'Not again.'

'I can explain my reasoning.'

She sat up and gathered the linens around her. 'I know your reasoning. You will say you have a duty to marry me because you made love to me, even though I freely chose to do so.' Could he not merely savour the experience? Must he spoil it?

The captain sat behind her, tucking her close against him and enfolding her in his arms. 'It is the right thing for us to do.'

'No, Captain.' Her voice cracked with emotion.

'Why not?' He nuzzled the sensitive skin of her neck.

She moved away and climbed out of bed. 'Too many reasons.' She groped for her nightdress and slipped it over her head.

'Name one of them.'

She walked to the window. The main reason was one she could not tell him. She was planning an act of sedition and it was his job to hang her for it.

She searched for another explanation. 'I have no wish to be the sort of conventional, society wife you will need if you wish to be an M.P.'

He was silent for a long moment and she knew he was forced to agree with her. 'Perhaps that will not matter so much,' he finally said.

She leaned her head against the cool glass of the window. This time there was no Edwin or Uncle Tranville to shatter their plans. This time it was Marian putting the sledgehammer to the glass.

'It is hopeless, Captain,' she whispered.

Allan embraced her from behind, treasuring the feel of her skin against his, even as he forced himself to listen to what she said. True, her unconventional, impulsive nature was not an asset in gaining a seat in Commons, but she was not a social pariah either. Voters would accept her. Perhaps they would even love her as he did.

She could not deny that they belonged together. Fate had brought them together because they completed each other, filled each other's empty spaces. Whatever else threatened to separate them, they would simply have to conquer, because, even if a battle raged around them, even if flaming roofs caved in on them or farmers threatened them with axes, they were better together.

This time he refused to give up. 'Allow me to court you, Marian. Let us see what happens.'

Before she could answer him, footsteps sounded on the street below. He leaned forwards to see out the window.

Two men approached Yost's door.

'What is this?' Why would men come to Yost's door in the middle of the night?

'I do not know,' she replied breathlessly, although he'd not meant to direct the question to her.

Allan's muscles tensed as he waited to see if the men would be admitted. He could only see the tops of their heads from this high vantage point, but he heard the door open and they seemed to converse with someone. They were admitted and, at the same time, a woman left the house.

'It is Blanche!' Marian whispered.

Allan moved away from the window and searched for his clothes. 'I am more concerned about the men entering his house than Blanche leaving it. Do you know of any reason he should have callers in the middle of the night?'

'Of course I do not know.' Her voice was clipped. 'He is merely a neighbour and dinner guest.'

Allan managed to don his trousers and shirt as he heard Blanche's footsteps on the servants' stairs. He stepped out into the hall to grab his boots.

Blanche appeared and froze when she saw him. 'I—I could not sleep. I was below stairs for a while.'

'You were at Yost's,' Allan said.

'Yes, I visited Mr Yost.' She averted her head.

Marian stood in the bedroom doorway.

'Am I discharged?' Blanche asked her.

Marian went to her. 'Oh, Blanche, of course you are not discharged! What should I do without you? If you and Mr Yost are lovers, I am certain that is a fine thing.'

'What do you know of his activities, Mrs Nunn?' Allan asked. 'Who were those men?'

She glanced at Marian before answering. 'I do not know what you mean. I do not know those men or why they knocked on his door.'

The sconce's candle illuminated her anxious expression.

He gave her an intent look. 'If Yost is involved in something nefarious, I would not like for you to be caught up in it.' This was true enough, just not his main motivation.

Blanche looked from him to Marian and back. 'Did you see the men from up here?'

Her implication was clear. She knew he had been in Marian's bedchamber, and, to judge by his present appearance, not entirely clothed at that.

The silence after her question was suddenly broken by the rattling of Edwin's doorknob.

'Hey, there,' Edwin called from within. 'Unlock this door.'

Chapter Fifteen

'Do not open the door,' Allan whispered. 'Talk to him first. See if the drink is worn off.'

The doorknob rattled again, more violently this time. 'Where am I?' Edwin cried. 'I heard voices. Open the door! Somebody open the door.'

Marian leaned against it. 'It is Marian. And I am not opening the door unless I know you are in your right senses.'

'Marian?' He sounded surprised. 'I'm sick, Marian. My head hurts like the devil.' He rattled the knob. 'Why is the door locked?'

She looked at Allan.

He shrugged. 'He slept a long time, and sounds safe enough.' He edged towards her room. 'Best he not see me.' Especially half undressed. 'I'll duck in here. I'm close enough to come to your aid, if need be.'

'One moment, Edwin,' she said through the door.

Allan stepped inside Marian's room and kept out of sight while he searched for his coat and waistcoat.

He heard Marian turn the key in the lock.

Edwin's voice became louder. 'Why did you lock me in there, Marian?'

'Because you came to my house out of your mind with drink, that's why,' Marian replied sharply. 'That was very bad of you, Edwin.'

'Stop yelling,' he whined. 'My head hurts. I need something to make it feel better. Do you have any brandy?'

'I am most certainly not giving you brandy!'

Blanche spoke up. 'Perhaps a little ale would do? A little watered-down ale used to help my husband the day after drinking. Shall I fetch some?'

Not too much, Allan thought. He found his neckcloth and just draped it around his neck. He donned his waistcoat and coat without bothering to button them.

'Very well,' Marian answered Blanche. Marian addressed Edwin again. 'Go into the room and sit. I'll be in as soon as I've put on a robe.'

'Do not lock me in again,' he demanded.

Allan stuffed his stockings inside his boots.

'I won't.' Marian told him. 'See? I'll leave the door open a crack. Go inside and light some candles from the fire.'

A moment later she slipped into her bedchamber.

Allan caught her arm. 'He seems controlled enough,' he whispered. 'I'm going to sneak out before he discovers I am here.' He wrapped his arms around her. 'I intend to court you, Marian. And marry you.'

'Captain—' she began in a warning tone.

'No argument.' He gave her a swift kiss.

Allan peered out of the door to make certain Edwin was not in the hallway, and gave Marian one more glance before slipping out of the room. Carrying his boots, he quickly made it to the servants' stairs he'd seen Blanche use earlier.

When he entered the hall, he encountered Blanche carrying the ale and a candle. He liked the woman and certainly did not wish to see her be hurt if her lover was a saboteur.

He nodded to her.

'Wait a moment, Mr Landon.' She placed the ale on the stairs. 'I will lock the door behind you.'

He lifted his boots to show her he needed time to put them on. He sat upon the stairs to do it.

She watched him silently.

He crossed the hall as quietly as he could and she opened the door for him.

'Take care, Mrs Nunn,' he said.

He started to leave, but she put a hand on his sleeve. 'Mr Landon, I will tell no one about you being in Marian's room.'

'Thank you.' He could at least promise not to tell Sidmouth she was Yost's lover.

When she closed the door behind him, he took a few

steps and stopped in front of Yost's house. There was no sign from the front of a candle burning, no sign anyone was there. He decided to check the back. If he could get close enough, maybe he could see the faces of the men through a window.

He found the backs of the row of houses. Yost's house was the third from the end, Marian's, the second. All had walled gardens.

'In for a penny, in for a pound,' he said to himself, climbing the first wall.

Allan made it to the top. The easiest way to reach Yost's garden was to walk along the top of the walls. If anyone happened to be looking out their window at this hour, they'd easily see him.

He decided to try none the less.

Holding his arms out like a rope walker, he followed the narrow wall to the third garden and flattened himself on the top so he would be less visible. One window showed the glow of light.

He jumped down from the wall and a cat screeched. His heart nearly seized. Shrinking back into the shadows, he watched the lighted window to see if the curtains moved. They were still. Releasing a tense breath, he picked his way to the back of the house.

The window was too high and there was nothing he could climb on to peer in. He hated to turn back now. He sidled to the back door and tested the knob.

It was unlocked.

Before he thought too much about it, he slipped inside the house and found his way to the first floor. Finding the room where Yost and the two men were talking was not difficult. Its door was slightly ajar and the voices carried into the hallway.

Allan recognised Yost's voice. 'So, you will meet the other organisers at the appointed place in two nights. The date is set.'

He heard chairs scrape against the floor. They were leaving! Allan ducked into a room across from this one. Its darkness concealed him. Yost carried a candle into the hallway, and Allan caught a glimpse of the two men's faces. They walked on to the stairway.

Allan waited as they descended. He could make out from the barest outline of a table and chairs that he stood in the dining room. Where Yost would take his meals. And serve invited guests.

Of which he was not one.

Allan had invaded another man's house, just as Luddites had once invaded his father's house. He felt sick.

Hearing Yost bid his guests farewell in the hall, Allan roused himself to make a dash for the back stairway, hurrying all the way to the ground floor and out the back door. He crept along the wall until finding a place to climb it. Then running, as if he were on the ground and not a surface the width of a brick, he retraced his steps. At the last house, he jumped down and brushed off his clothing.

At that moment, the two men turned the corner and Allan shrank into the shadows. They crossed Quebec Street and headed towards Oxford Street. Still feeling as if he ought to be hauled before a magistrate, Allan followed them.

They walked to a tavern in the North Bruton mews near Berkeley Square. Allan waited several minutes before following them inside. With luck he found a table nearby with a wooden barrier between so they could not see him. He ordered ale from the bar and carried it to his seat.

Much of the conversation between the two men was in tones so hushed Allan could not hear them. As they continued to drink, their voices became louder.

'The day is near,' one said. 'Let us drink to our success.'

'To our successful march!'

As he suspected: a march was planned.

They began to speculate as to who was the organising force behind the march, the real leader of it.

'It is not Yost, that is certain,' said one. 'He always speaks of someone else.'

His companion responded. 'Well, the leader is not Hunt. Hunt is staying out of it.'

'Has to be Yost,' the first man said firmly. 'Even though he denies it, he is it. Who else could it be?'

Indeed. Who else? Allan cupped his tankard of ale and stared into its contents. He didn't want to report Yost. He liked the man.

And he was Marian's friend, her companion's lover. How was he to turn in Yost? Would Marian ever understand? This would just be one more impediment to their being happy together. A huge one, if she saw her friend arrested for sedition.

Marian sat across from Edwin at the breakfast table. Hannah had laundered and brushed off his clothing, and Marian had badgered him to wash himself, so he looked—and smelled—a great deal better than the day before.

Still, he was ashen and his hand shook.

'Eat something, Edwin,' she demanded.

'Does it not look as if I am trying?' He lifted a piece of toast for her to see. 'Stop being so cross. It is very disagreeable.'

'I have reason to be cross.' She glared at him.

He rolled his eyes. 'Just because I had too much to drink—'

'Too much to drink!' she cried. 'You came to my house corned, pickled and salted. And you were rowdy, as well.'

He tossed off her words. 'Do not speak cant, Marian. It is most unbecoming. Besides, you cannot fault my coming here, because I did not even know I was doing it.'

'That makes it worse!' she retorted. 'You drink entirely too much, Edwin.'

He folded his arms over his chest. 'I do not need you to harangue me over it. I can handle myself very well without your scolding.'

Marian clamped her mouth shut. Edwin finished the piece of toast and held up another so she could see he was eating. A little colour returned to his face.

She chewed her lip, uncertain whether she should bring up the only topic she wanted to discuss with him. She took a breath. 'I have seen Captain Landon here in London, Edwin.'

He looked surprised, then resumed his cynical expression. 'Landon? Too bad.' He lifted his cup to his mouth.

'He told me there was no Frenchwoman in Paris.'

Edwin's hand stilled, the cup at his lips. 'Frenchwoman?' He placed the cup in its saucer and suddenly looked as if understanding dawned. 'Ah, the Frenchwoman. I had forgotten. Do you mean the woman in Paris was not French?'

'There was no woman, he said.'

Edwin laughed. 'As if he would admit such a thing. Do not tell me he is dangling after you again, although I suppose he still needs a wealthy wife.'

She averted her gaze. She had never once considered that the captain might be interested in her fortune.

No. She could not believe he was talking of the captain. The man who'd made love to her was not a fortune hunter.

She faced Edwin again. 'I am furious with you for making up that story. Did you do it to keep me from marrying the captain? Did you think that it would make me marry you?'

He gave her a withering glance. 'Do not insult me, Marian. After the set-down you gave me, I am not likely to propose to you again.'

She twisted the edge of the tablecloth with her fingers. Edwin was not behaving like a man telling a lie. What was she to think?

Edwin stood up again. 'You were correct. I do feel better for having eaten. I believe I shall try some of the ham.' As he stood at the sideboard his back to her, he said, 'I merely passed on information about Landon I received at the regimental offices, you know. I had no reason to doubt its veracity.'

She had to let the subject drop. She did not want to believe her cousin had lied to her about something so important. As weak in character as he was, he was still her only living blood relative.

She rubbed her forehead. 'Where are you staying?' Because he was certainly not welcome to stay with her.

And she did not want him near if the captain called again.

Perhaps he would come to her tonight.

That thought filled her with excitement, even though she knew there was no future with him.

And Edwin brought doubt back again.

Edwin's back was to her. 'I'm staying at the Adelphi.'

She'd heard of it. Rooms popular with young gentlemen. 'What are your plans?'

He sat down again. 'Plans? What do I need with plans? I sold my commission when Father did. He gives me a good allowance. I can do whatever I wish.'

'You must have something useful to do.' She could not imagine the captain being so idle. 'Something other than drinking, that is.'

His eyes flashed. 'Do not start on that again, Marian.'

She glared at him. 'You were terrible, Edwin. You broke my table.'

His brows rose. 'I did? I cannot remember.'

'See? You should not drink like that.'

They went round about this again. Finally Marian said, 'Well, do not call upon me unless you are sober. I mean it, Edwin. I will turn you away.'

He pressed his temple with his fingers. 'Very well, Marian, but stop yelling. My head still aches.'

She let the subject drop and watched him drink his tea.

'What are you going to do today?' he asked between sips.

'I have an appointment this morning and this afternoon I have to call upon Domina.' And she hoped to see the captain that night.

'Domina.' He made a face. 'Lawd. Is she in London? She married Lord Ullman, I read. It should not surprise me. After he was jilted by Jack Vernon's sister, I suppose he had to settle for Domina.'

'He was jilted by Nancy Vernon?' This was new information.

'I was with him when he met her at the Egyptian Hall, of all places.' He gave a derisive laugh. 'She ran off with some penniless architect friend of Jack's.' He paused to rub his eyes. 'What a time that was. Such drama. Ariana Blane cuckolding Father and sleeping with Jack. You should have been there.'

Miss Blane and Uncle Tranville? Miss Blane never told her this when she and Marian shared a room in Brussels. She'd acted as if her connection to Uncle Tranville had been through Mrs Vernon.

Edwin laughed. 'I wonder if Domina knows she's got Nancy's leavings. It would be amusing to tell her.'

'Don't you dare!' Marian cried. 'She is actually quite happy, and I will not have you spoiling it.'

'Rich and titled. No wonder she is happy.' He continued eating. 'I believe I shall come with you.'

'To call upon Domina?' She wished he would not. 'Why?'

'I am that bored.' He bit into a piece of ham.

She tried to think of a reason to discourage him. There was no use in refusing. He would show up anyway, just to prove he could. 'You will have to change your clothing and return looking presentable. And *sober.*' She put emphasis on the word sober. 'And do not tell her about Jack's sister.'

He swallowed 'We'll see. Where is your appointment?'

'Here.'

'What is it about?' He spoke with his mouth full.

She narrowed her eyes. 'About *my* business, not yours, Edwin.' She rose from the table. 'I need to prepare, but do stay and eat as much as you wish.'

He nodded. 'What time will you call on Domina?'

'Perhaps around two.'

The visit was her attempt to improve her attendance at social events, as Yost had suggested, but Edwin coming along made it all the worse.

'I'll come back at two.' His voice was muffled with another mouthful of ham.

Allan walked into the Home Office in the late morning, still battling with guilt and indecision.

Sidmouth accosted him right away. 'I hope your tardiness means you have some information for me. Did you discover anything about Yost?'

Too much. But he was not ready to report it, even if his sworn duty to Sidmouth was to tell him what he knew.

'I have discovered nothing of consequence,' he said.

Except that the leader of the movement he was sworn to thwart was a friend of the woman whose bed he shared the night before, the woman he was determined to marry.

Sidmouth looked disapproving. 'Did you question Miss Pallant's servants?'

'I never had the opportunity,' he answered honestly. Good God. He did not want to involve Reilly in this.

Sidmouth frowned. 'Make opportunities, my boy. I have a new fellow in my employ who has discovered a great deal more than you have in half the time.'

'A new fellow?' This was a surprise to Allan. 'Who is it?'

'Hah!' Sidmouth laughed. 'A fellow who knows what he is about. Used him before. Makes things happen. Does what needs to be done and then some.' He clapped Allan on the shoulder. 'You need not know his name.'

Allan's eyes narrowed. Why keep the man's name from him?

He had heard the rumour that the man giving testimony

about the Spa Field Riots had been a provocateur in Sidmouth's employ. He had not believed it at the time.

He'd accepted employment with Sidmouth because it meant protecting the government and enforcing the laws, but it seemed to him that much of what Sidmouth wished him to do skirted the boundaries of honourable behaviour. Spying on people, trespassing, betraying people who trusted him.

'Did you even see Yost last night?' Sidmouth demanded. 'Talk to him like before?'

'He was Miss Pallant's dinner guest, as was I,' Allan told him.

'Again?' Sidmouth leaned forwards in interest. 'What does this mean?'

Allan tried to maintain his composure. 'He is a single man in need of feeding.'

Sidmouth's face fell. 'That cannot be all.'

Allan's gaze remained steady. 'I believe Miss Pallant and her companion enjoy company and conversation at dinner.'

Sidmouth's brows rose. 'What do we know of this companion?'

'She is an impoverished widow quite grateful for employment.' And Allan could curse himself for even mentioning her to Sidmouth.

'A war widow? She could have connections.' Sidmouth stroked his chin.

'Or not.' Good God. Allan could not allow Sidmouth's suspicions to fall on Marian's companion.

'There's the pity, Landon.' Sidmouth clucked. 'You see only what people want you to see. You need to develop a more suspicious nature. Not going to succeed, if you do not. Remember, the crown depends upon this office to thwart any threats to the sovereignty and the peace of the citizenry.'

Allan believed in those duties of the Home Office wholeheartedly. He'd agreed to use the woman he loved to get information, had he not?

And now Sidmouth had hired someone who *does what needs to be done and then some.*

Allan flexed his fingers into a fist. 'What did this man of yours discover?'

Sidmouth gestured for Allan to come in to his office and have a seat. He lowered himself in the chair behind his desk and folded his hands in front of him. 'Someone—and I suspect Yost—is organising unemployed soldiers to march upon Parliament. The organisation is spreading around the country, and my man says it is imminent.'

'To what end? What are they seeking?' Allan asked. This all rang true. Yost had spoken of his concern for the plight of the soldiers.

'Jobs. Food. Compensation for their injuries in the war.' Sidmouth spoke as if these were unreasonable requests.

Of course his fellow soldiers needed such things. 'Are they advocating force?'

Sidmouth pursed his lips. 'Would you expect soldiers to be peaceful? Come on now. Been one yourself. Who else would take what they want by force?'

Allan gave him an even stare. 'Do you have evidence that they advocate violence against the Crown?'

Sidmouth restacked the papers on his desk. 'Not as yet, but I will.'

Edwin slouched in his chair, bored to tears with Domina's incessant chatter about Lady So-and-so's breakfast or ball or the latest play at Drury Lane. At least Ariana Blane—Vernon, he meant; she'd married Jack, for God's sake—was not performing. Word was she'd had a baby. Lawd.

He munched on a tray of raspberry tarts and sipped tea when his thirst demanded a more robust beverage.

Marian made a more successful show of appearing interested in Domina's drivel. In fact, she gave Domina a great deal more of her attention than she had him. Just because he'd arrived at her town house a little drunk.

Well, *very* drunk, he had to admit.

He touched his cheek. He often drank a great deal, but he did not often lose the ability to remember where he'd been and what he'd done. Like the time he'd awoken with a gash across his face. He'd gone into Badajoz during the sacking, his father had told him, and Landon had carried him out.

Landon.

He wondered if Landon had told Marian about Badajoz. He might not remember what happened in that city, but it would certainly make him look bad and Landon look good, if she were told he'd needed rescuing. Having Landon look good was nothing he could desire.

He detested that Landon was back. Courting her, no doubt. Edwin thought he'd convinced Marian to rebuff Landon entirely with the little story he'd created, but now she was wavering again, he could tell. He'd be damned if he let Landon make a fool of him.

Edwin gazed over at his cousin. The ladies had begun discussing gowns and that was enough to make Edwin wish for a pistol to shoot himself, the talk was so tedious. Having neglected to carry his firearm, Edwin regarded his cousin instead. She was a handsome enough woman, but more so, she could be depended upon to take care of him, no matter what. He liked the certainty of that. He did not want Landon around to change things. See how she'd cosseted him, even after he'd apparently broken her table in his drunken state.

He did not mind so much that she did not want to marry him as long as she did not marry Landon.

Just once he would like to show Marian, his father and everyone else that he could do better than Landon.

The door opened and Lord Ullman walked in.

'Ullie!' Domina cried, jumping up from her seat and into his arms.

Edwin almost choked on his tart. Finally Ullman recognised Marian and then him. 'Edwin, my boy, good to see you.'

Domina still held on to her husband's arm. 'Ullie, my love, would you mind entertaining Edwin for a while? I want to show Marian the new gowns you purchased for me.' She nuzzled Ullman's nose in apparent gratitude for his anticipated generosity.

'Of course, I do not mind, my dear.' He reached in his pocket and pulled out a velvet box. 'Show her this as well.'

Domina opened the box. Its contents sparkled with some kind of jewels. 'Ullie!' She wrapped her arms around him again, then skipped over to Marian. 'Look, Marian. Is it not the most beautiful thing you have ever seen?'

'Dazzling,' Marian said.

'Come!' Domina took her hand. 'I want to show you all the wonderful things Ullie has given me.'

The two ladies swept out of the room.

Ullman watched his wife's retreat. 'I love to indulge her.' He clapped his hands and turned to Edwin. 'How about some brandy, eh?'

'I would be delighted,' Edwin responded. Brandy was preferable to shooting himself in the head.

They chatted over various things, finishing one glass and pouring another. Edwin savoured how the brandy burned going down his throat, how it spread warmth even to his extremities.

'So tell me,' Ullman said, pouring Edwin a third glass. 'Is anything happening between my nephew and your cousin? I say, when last I saw them together, I was certain he would court her.'

Edwin pressed his fingers tightly around the stem of his glass. 'I know nothing of it.'

'Allan would be a good catch for her,' Ullman went on. 'My nephew is a man who can rise high. His work with Lord Sidmouth—'

'The Home Secretary?' This was news to Edwin. 'What the devil does he do for Sidmouth?'

'Important work.' Ullman beamed. 'He's investigating possible sedition. His job is to stop it before trouble erupts and to arrest those responsible for inciting riots.' He took a sip of his brandy. 'I dare say this will get him a seat in the Commons some day.'

'Lawd. Is that what he wants?' Such high aspirations. Some day Edwin would have to sit in the Lords, though he looked forward to that tedium as much as Domina's conversation. With his luck Landon would rise to be Prime Minister by that time and he'd still look bad.

Edwin no longer listened to Ullman. He was hatching a plan to call upon Lord Sidmouth and show everybody he could do the job a great deal better than Landon,

whatever it was. Then he'd get the glory. Maybe he'd even stand for an election for M.P. instead of Landon.
  This time he'd show them all.

Chapter Sixteen

Marian saw him from a distance.

She and Edwin strode down South Audley Street coming from their visit to Domina. He was standing there, waiting for them, and she could feel his eyes upon her even at this distance. She felt a flush of excitement and imagined her face was filled with colour, betraying some of the confused emotions inside her.

It was clear to her that she must not marry the captain, no matter how her body and soul yearned for him. She could not tolerate marriage to a man who worked to imprison men fighting for what was due them. Eventually he would imprison her spirit, if not herself, as well. She needed to be free to prevent suffering wherever she could. Who could not feel that way after witnessing men dying, burning in flames?

All her lofty ideals were vital to her, but ever since she'd confronted Edwin, what nagged at her the most was the matter of the Frenchwoman. She'd feel completely duped if the captain had lied to her about having a mistress in Paris. If she must ultimately part from him, she at least wanted to believe he was really the man she thought he was.

She'd stopped listening to the drone of Edwin's voice as her cousin approached him, closer and closer.

'Lawd,' Edwin muttered in a disgusted voice, when he, too, noticed who waited for them.

When they reached him, the captain removed his hat and bowed. 'Good afternoon, Marian.' His voice was warm, as if he, also, savoured the memory of their night together. He straightened again and nodded coldly to her cousin. 'Edwin.'

'Captain.' Marian's tone was shriller than she'd intended it to be.

The Captain ignored Edwin and spoke directly to Marian. 'I came to call upon you and learned you were at my uncle's.'

She had difficulty looking at him. 'We just came from there.'

'Dreadful bore,' Edwin drawled.

'Be quiet, Edwin,' Marian said sharply. She'd reached the limits of her patience with her cousin.

The captain frowned at Edwin. 'Have you been drinking?'

Edwin gave him a disdainful look. 'Is it any concern of yours?'

Marian answered for her cousin. 'Yes, he has been drinking. And he promised me he would not.'

One corner of Edwin's mouth lifted in an attempt at a smile. His scar merely made the effort look distorted. 'As I have explained to you, Marian, I promised I would not drink before calling upon Domina. I did not promise to refuse a drink when there. Ullman offered brandy and it would have been inhospitable to refuse.'

Marian turned away from him. This was what plagued her. Edwin's explanations always sounded reasonable, whether about his drinking or about the captain in Paris.

The captain spoke, 'May I speak with you alone, Marian?'

Edwin held up a hand. 'Have no fear of offending me, Landon.' His tone was sarcastic. 'I actually have an important matter that requires my attention.'

Allan ignored him and waited for her answer.

She nodded and turned to her cousin. 'Do not come to my house if you have been drinking. I mean it. I will turn you away.'

Edwin made an exaggerated bow. 'I have learned from my one mistake.'

He sauntered away and the captain turned back to her. 'I am glad you remember my warning about his drinking.'

'Indeed,' she said stiffly.

Her disordered emotions about him made it difficult for her to even think.

He looked at her with concern. 'Marian, what distresses you?'

She wanted to believe in the captain, but both he and Edwin had been so convincing. 'Edwin has tried my patience. He has confused me, but I cannot discuss it now.' She forced herself to meet his gaze. 'What did you wish to say to me?'

She could see flecks of brown in his hazel eyes as he searched her face. Suddenly his expression relaxed and the ghost of a smile lit his lips.

'Do you have some time?' he asked.

She felt breathless. 'I am not expected anywhere, if that is what you mean.'

He took her hand. 'Come with me. I will take you to see an old friend.'

He led her to a line of hackney coaches on Oxford Street. He helped her into one and she heard him tell the jarvey to take them to somewhere on Knightsbridge Street. The hack left them off a short distance from Hyde Park Corner in front of a stable.

Marian seized his arm in excitement. 'You are taking me to see Valour!'

'An old friend, I said.' He smiled.

They walked into a large, well-kept stable with lines of stalls housing beautiful riding horses.

A stable lad greeted them. 'Saddle your horse, sir?'

'No need,' the captain replied. 'We are merely making a social call.'

The man gave him a bewildered look, but went on with his chores.

The captain led her to Valour's stall. The mare bobbed her head and shuffled in excitement.

'Oh, Valour!' Marian pressed her face against the horse's neck and stroked her. 'How I have missed you.'

For the moment all Marian's worries fled in the pleasure of seeing the horse again.

'There is a yard nearby,' the Captain said. 'We could give her a little walk.'

She beamed at him. 'Oh, yes. Let's do.'

He held the string to her bridle as they led her around the yard.

Marian turned to gaze at the mare. 'I feel sorry for her being so confined.'

The Captain nodded. 'I try to ride her as often as possible.'

'Do you ride in Hyde Park?' she asked, wanting desperately to merely enjoy the moment, the three of them together again.

'In the early morning mostly. Hyde Park gives her a good run.'

She felt wistful. 'I have never ridden much, but that sounds lovely.'

'You have not ridden much?' He sounded surprised.

'Not living in Bath.'

He continued to lead Valour around the small yard. 'You rode well enough in Belgium,' he remarked.

She shook her head. 'If I had been any kind of horse-woman, I would never have fallen off the horse I shared with Domina. I think Valour deserves most of the credit for me remaining on her back.' She lowered her gaze. 'Valour and you, of course. You held on to me.'

He glanced back at her. 'We made a good team, you, Valour and I.'

She almost smiled. 'We did.' She held back to pat Valour's muzzle.

Marian relished the memory of their days together, though they were fraught with hardship and danger. In many ways it had been as if no one else in the world existed but her, the captain and Valour. As they took another turn in the yard, the memories of Belgium returned. None of the memories fitted with Edwin's version of him in Paris.

She took a breath. 'I must ask you something, Captain.'

'Of course.'

All her distressed nerves returned. 'And you must tell me the truth.'

'I will.' He looked tentative, as if he was wary of what she would ask.

The clip-clop of Valour's hooves echoed in the yard before she could speak. 'Did you have an affair in Paris?'

He halted and it seemed as if his entire body tensed.

She went on, 'Because Edwin still claims you did, and I cannot determine which of you to believe.'

He seemed to glare at her. 'Are you asking me to prove it to you?'

She watched him, suddenly fearful of what he might say.

'I cannot prove it.' Pain flashed through his eyes. 'If I produced witnesses, Edwin would merely say they were lying for me. I can prove nothing.' His voice turned low. 'Upon my honour—' he touched her arm '—upon my *honour*, since meeting you there has been no other woman. I want to marry you, Marian. I want only you.'

She drew in a breath and felt tears sting her eyes. 'Oh, Captain.' It was the answer for which she'd hoped, but it only brought back the other barriers between them. Perhaps it would have been easier after all, if he'd been a man who'd deceived her all along.

'Believe me, Marian.' He touched her cheek and slid his fingers down to gently lift her chin.

Her heart pounded within her chest. Before she knew it, she closed the distance between them, twining her arms around his neck and pulling his head down into a kiss that overtook her senses, made her feel lighthearted, made her want more. He held her against him and she cared not one whit if someone walked into the yard and saw them.

Valour trotted up and nuzzled them, nickering low. They broke apart.

'Valour is jealous, I think,' he said.

Marian still clung to his arm. 'Come home with me.'

They returned a disappointed Valour to her stable and fussed over her a bit before Marian gave the horse one last goodbye hug.

'You will see her again, Marian,' Allan promised. 'In fact, you can ride her one morning.'

'I would like that.' But she knew that would never happen. She'd follow Yost's advice and continue to allow him to court her to deflect any suspicion of her, but after the march she must release him.

Arm in arm, they walked to Hyde Park Corner where they caught a hackney coach to carry them back to Marian's house. He held her as they rode.

'What saddens you?' he asked as the swaying of the coach and his arms lulled her.

'I am not sad,' she said.

He frowned and she knew she'd not convinced him.

The coach delivered them to her door, and Marian pulled her key from her reticule and handed it to him. She could make an excuse and bid him goodbye on her doorstep.

Instead she said, 'Reilly is still away and I suspect the other servants are busy.'

His eyes darkened. 'And Blanche?'

She whispered, 'With Mr Yost, of course.'

His expression changed for a moment, as if he'd had an upsetting thought, but he turned the key in the lock and swept her into an embrace as soon as they entered and closed the door behind them. His kiss sent her senses reeling and filled her with a desire she had no intention of denying.

He must have had the same thought, because he lifted her into his arms and carried her above stairs to her bedchamber. Before he even set her on her feet, she pulled off her hat and tossed it away. He sat her upon the bed and kissed her again as his hat, too, came off and he unbuttoned his coat.

As the captain stepped away to pull off his boots, Marian kicked off her shoes and took off her pelisse. She undid the bodice of her dress and slid the garment off, letting it fall to the floor. She turned her back to him, and without her asking, he loosened the laces of her corset.

Soon she was clad only in her shift and he in his shirt. She lifted the garment over her head and let the sunlight in the room reveal her nakedness.

He stilled and his eyes seemed to drink her in.

Perhaps if she were very lucky this would not be the last time with him. She could not be certain, however.

She took a deep breath and resolved to remember every tiny detail. His glorious masculine body. The feel of his hands and lips against her skin. The incandescent pleasure she knew would come.

Allan let his gaze touch every part of her, from the luxurious blonde tresses escaping their pins, to her kiss-reddened lips, the graceful curve of her neck.

The fullness of her breasts.

Her skin was smooth as cream and seemed to shimmer from the sunlight pouring in the room. He was glad they made love in the light, as if there were no secrets between them.

He should have guessed her change in mood had been Edwin's doing. Would he always have to battle the doubt Edwin seemed to know how to plant in her mind? If so, he would fight valiantly for her to believe him.

There was no woman but her for him.

His gaze continued, feeling reverent as he savoured her narrow waist and perfect navel. She remained boldly still, even when he took in the dark hair between her legs.

She became shy then, moving back upon the bed, lying against the pillows. He tore off his shirt and joined her, taking her head in his hands and leaning down to again taste her lips.

When he released her mouth, she sighed. 'I wish—' She broke off.

He tasted the tender skin beneath her ear. 'What do you wish?'

'You and I,' she murmured, not finishing her sentence.

He remembered then, the secrets he was hiding from her and felt ashamed after she'd exposed herself so openly to him.

He tensed. 'Marian, I have something to tell you—'

A tiny line formed between her brows. 'Then tell me later.' She reached for him and pulled him down upon her again.

He wanted to soothe her, to reassure her all would be well, but he knew his news of Yost would cause problems between them.

He stroked her skin, trying to calm her and himself, as well. He felt her desire grow under his touch. He kissed her again, one long, needful kiss, full of both promise and regret.

She opened to him and he entered her, savouring the warmth of her against him, of how they fit together with such perfection. To move inside her felt staggeringly wonderful. He moved slowly, wanting this sensation of joining with her to last as long as possible.

Desire overtook him and control fled. He drove into her with intense need. She met his pace, as if she responded to some inexplicable urgency. The sound of their joining and their breathing filled his ears until he was no longer able to compose a coherent thought. He was aware only of her. The pleasure of her. The intense need of her, a need that would never cease.

She cried out, and he felt her release spasm around him. She pushed him over the edge, shattering him with pleasure as he spilled his seed inside her.

She whimpered and tears shimmered in her eyes. He lifted his weight from her and rolled to her side. 'My God, did I hurt you?'

She covered her face with her arm. 'No. No. It was all I could desire.' She rose on an elbow and slid herself on top of him, her mouth finding his.

She quickly aroused him again with heated kisses and he showed her that he could enter her while she straddled him. She was a quick pupil because once more they moved in perfect accord, this time without the strange intensity of before. This time was quieter, a solace where before had been urgency. Together they again climbed to the pinnacle, slow and steady, until the end which was every bit a frenzy of bliss as before.

She collapsed on top of him and Allan felt awash in perfect contentment. Perfect union.

A cloud crossing in front of the sun darkened the room. Soon the servants and Blanche would return.

Their interlude had come to an end.

'I should dress,' Allan said, facing a reality he could not like.

'We both must.' She moved out of his arms and sat up. Her golden hair tumbled over her shoulders and more hairpins fell, joining others that now peppered the bed. 'Blanche will be home soon. She invited Mr Yost to dinner.'

Yost.

Allan could delay this no longer.

Marian rose from the bed and turned to him, before donning her shift. 'Would you like to stay for dinner?'

She would withdraw the invitation when he finished what he had to say to her.

He put on his shirt and trousers.

She sat at a dressing table and ran a brush through her hair. 'You did not answer. Would you like to stay for dinner?'

He walked over to stand behind her, meeting her gaze through the mirror that faced her. 'I have something of importance to tell you.'

She froze, brush poised in the air.

'I discovered something,' he began.

Her brows rose slightly.

He girded himself. 'I discovered that your neighbour, Mr Yost, is planning a march on London—a soldiers' march.'

She averted her gaze and continued to brush her hair. 'Do not be ridiculous.'

He looked down on her. 'It is true, Marian. I heard it myself, and Sidmouth knows as well.'

She gaped at him. 'You informed on Mr Yost?'

'No, another man did that.' An unscrupulous man, Allan feared.

She put her brush down with a trembling hand. 'Why do you tell me of this?'

He crouched down so he could look at her directly. 'Because he is your friend and Blanche's lover. And he is in danger of arrest.'

'You will arrest him?' Her eyes hardened.

'If the march takes place, or if there is some proof of his conspiracy, like a letter with his name on it, I may be forced to.' He touched her arm. 'The Seditious Meetings Act makes it a crime.'

'It is unjust.' Her eyes flashed at him. 'Besides, it sounds as if you only have rumours and speculation. You cannot arrest Yost on those grounds.'

'We do not need a reason to arrest him.' With the suspension of habeas corpus they could detain anyone they chose. 'Sidmouth will want to wait until he knows more before arresting Yost. Such as the time and place of the march and others who can be implicated in the planning of it.'

'And you think I can tell you who that is?' Her voice turned cold.

He jerked back. 'Not at all.' At least, not until this moment. His eyes narrowed. 'If you do know something, Marian, I would beg you to tell me.'

She lifted her chin. 'I would tell you nothing. If I knew something, that is.'

His mind was turning, calculating the timing of events. Yost's writings about the plight of the soldiers were printed months ago, yet the Home Office heard no rumours of Yost planning some demonstration until about a month ago.

Allan stood. 'How long have you been acquainted with Yost?'

Her face became like a mask. 'Are you interrogating me, Captain?'

He put his hands on his hips. 'Answer the question, Marian.'

'We met him after moving in, of course.'

That told him nothing except that she was being evasive. Why? He'd expected her to be upset at this news, but, by all signs, she'd not been surprised at it.

Allan's mind turned quickly. Besides the plight of the soldiers, Yost had written fervently about other radical issues, taking up the cause of the weavers, writing against the Corn Laws, all manner of topics. What had induced him to settle on the soldiers' problems? And how did he go from merely writing essays to becoming the leader of a soldiers' march?

Allan knew of only one person who so single-mindedly embraced the soldiers' cause. In fact, she would run into a burning building for them.

He stared down at her. 'You are in on this, are you not, Marian? You are in the thick of it with Yost.'

She shot to her feet. 'Now you *are* being ridiculous.'

He seized her arms. 'Good God, Marian. How deep in are you?'

She tried to pull away. 'Release me, Captain.'

He tightened his grip. 'First tell me! How deep?'

She met his eye with defiance. 'If I were involved, I would be a fool to tell you, would I not?'

He shook her. 'You risk arrest every bit as much as Yost. The penalty of sedition is death.'

Her face flushed with colour. 'Are you threatening me, Captain?'

'I am warning you, Marian.' He released her.

She glared at him. 'You accuse me of sedition. I accuse you of betraying men who fought and suffered at your side during the war. I cannot believe you are saying these things to me.'

'I am not betraying them.' He raised his voice. 'I am supporting the law.'

'A law that would put me to death for encouraging men to demand help?' She strode away from him, but turned back. 'It is said that Sidmouth hired provocateurs at Spa Fields and that *they* caused the violence, not the protesters. Is Sidmouth in danger of hanging, or would it merely be me?'

He looked her in the eye. 'He has hired men this time as well. You cannot go through with this. It is too dangerous.'

'I am no stranger to danger, am I, Captain?' She lifted her chin. 'Besides, I might have been speaking hypothetically. Will you arrest me for speaking hypothetically?'

Must he arrest her? She had all but admitted she had a part in this.

By God, no. He could never do such a thing. Her intent would never be criminal. Foolish, yes, but not criminal. Sidmouth would not care about that distinction, however. Allan could not stop Sidmouth from arresting her if he knew this much.

'Tell Yost to call off the march,' he demanded. 'It is too risky now. Stop it before it is too late for all of you.'

He turned away to stamp on his boots and don his waistcoat. He thrust his arms through the sleeves of his coat. The emotions between them filled the room like smoke from a blocked chimney.

Her voice was barely audible. 'Perhaps you ought not stay for dinner after all.'

Allan felt sick inside.

Marian laughed, but the sound was mournful. 'And again I free you from your obligation to marry me, Captain. I suspect that a threat to arrest and hang me is an indication we would not suit.'

'Marian,' he murmured, at a loss to say more.

She opened a drawer and pulled out a robe, wrapping

it around her and walking to the door. 'Take what time you require to dress and then leave my house.'

She walked out.

Chapter Seventeen

Marian, clad in only her shift and a silk robe, ran down the stairs to her tiny library. She closed the door and fled to the large leather chair that faced the cold fireplace.

She curled up in the seat, the leather chilly against her bare feet and through the thin fabric of her robe. Tears stung her eyes, but she refused to shed them. She'd known he would ultimately not wish to marry her when he understood the depth of her views, but she had not guessed that he knew so much about the march.

She covered her face with her hands. To be fair, he did not really want to arrest her. He wanted her to call off the march because of the danger to her and to Yost.

His footsteps sounded on the stairs and soon after the front door closed.

He was gone.

At least no one in the house had known he'd been there.

Marian hugged her knees to her chest and tried not to

think about how it felt to make love with him. She must think only of how he was working against her cause.

'Oh, no!' She shot out of the chair and paced the room.

She'd forgotten to ask Blanche what to do about preventing a baby.

How could she admit to Blanche that she'd bedded the captain when she must also tell her the danger he posed to her and to Mr Yost?

She glanced at the bookshelves. She'd purchased the house with most of the furniture and books in it. Perhaps the previous owners had owned a copy of *Aristotle's Masterpiece* or, if not that well-known book about all things sexual, *Culpeper's Complete Herbal*. Those books surely would explain how to prevent a pregnancy.

She found Culpeper's book and pulled it off the shelf. The light in the room was dim so she carried it over to the window and opened the leather-bound volume.

There was no table of contents. No index.

'They are listed alphabetically!' It would take her hours to pore through the pages of herbs and their uses. She closed the book again and leaned her forehead against it.

Could having a baby out of wedlock be any worse than leading a march on Parliament? At least she would not be hanged for having a child.

She pictured herself holding a tiny baby in her arms and felt like weeping again.

The baby would be *his.*

With a groan, she returned the book to the shelf and walked out into the hall.

Blanche had just come in and was removing her hat and gloves.

'Marian?' Blanche gaped at her undress.

'I—I took a nap and just returned a book to its shelf.' How easily she lied. She took a breath and forced a smile. 'I think Hannah must be out. Would you help me dress?'

A few minutes later Marian again sat at her dressing table, but it was Blanche with her instead of the captain.

Blanche drew a comb through Marian's hair. 'I am surprised that you did not remove the hairpins before napping.'

Hairpins had not seemed important at the time. 'It was silly of me.'

Blanche pulled her hair into a tighter knot. 'Well, I do not mind arranging your hair. I enjoy it and it gives me time to speak with you.'

Marian glanced at Blanche through the mirror. 'We have not had much time of late, have we?'

Blanche looked distressed. 'I have not been a very good companion.'

Marian reached up and squeezed Blanche's hand. 'I did not mean that. You are always here when I need you, and I do not begrudge the time you spend with Mr Yost.'

Blanche blushed. 'I do spend a great deal of time with him, do I not?'

Marian patted her face with a blotting paper. 'Is he dining with us tonight?'

'If you do not mind,' Blanche said uncertainly.

Dinner was time enough to tell them what the captain had said to her. 'Of course I do not mind! I enjoy his company.'

'Is Mr Landon dining with us, too?' Blanche asked, twisting a lock of hair and pinning it in place.

'No,' Marian answered in a sharp tone. She softened it. 'No, but I did see him briefly. He—he escorted me home when I called on Domina.'

'Did he?' Blanche gave her a knowing look through the mirror. 'That is three days in a row you have seen him.'

'Three days,' she mumbled. She wanted to divert the conversation away from the captain. 'What did you want to talk to me about?'

'About last night—' Blanche began.

Marian held up a stilling hand. 'You need not explain. I have seen you blossom under Mr Yost's attentions these few weeks. He brings you happiness. That is all I care about.'

Blanche's cheeks turned pink again, but she shook

her head. 'I meant what transpired between you and Mr Landon.'

Marian stilled. 'Because the captain was in my room?'

Blanche nodded.

Marian pressed a hand to her abdomen—where a baby might be growing. 'It was innocent, I assure you. I heard a sound outside and he came in to investigate. It—it was the two men coming to see Yost.' That sounded plausible. She hoped.

Blanche gave her a worried glance. 'You never mentioned meeting Landon in Brussels.'

'I did not think to mention it.' Marian could feel her pulse beating fast.

Blanche's brow creased. 'I am concerned for you.'

'Why?' Marian made her voice light. 'There is no reason for concern.'

Her friend seemed not reassured. 'I am persuaded you have little experience with men. And you have told me nothing about Mr Landon—'

'Because there was nothing of consequence to tell,' Marian said defensively.

Blanche attended to another lock of hair. 'Did you know him before Brussels?'

'No.' She did not want to discuss the captain. 'Do you have a point, Blanche? Because I wish you would make it.'

Blanche put her hands on Marian's shoulders and

met the eye of her image in the mirror. 'It takes time to know a man. To know if your heart is safe with him.' Her expression turned bleak. 'I—I just want to warn you that a man can deceive you. Seem one thing and be another entirely.'

Marian could feel the pulse in her body accelerate. What else was she to learn about the captain this day? 'Do you have some information about the captain, something I should know?'

Her companion looked surprised. 'No. Goodness, I know less of him than you do.' She swallowed. 'I am speaking about my husband, I suppose. He was a charming man and he quite swept me off my feet. He—' Her voice cracked. 'We were married very quickly after meeting, and it was not until later I discovered his fondness for cards and for drink.' She glanced down to pick up a hairpin. 'I merely wanted to warn you to not give away your heart too quickly.'

This warning was too late.

'I do appreciate your concern.' Marian's voice was stiff, but only because she was attempting to keep tears from flowing. 'But you do not have to worry about me.'

Blanche stepped back. 'I hope you will forgive my speaking so plainly. I know it is not my place.' Her face became the picture of distress.

Marian regretted her clipped tone. She stood and

gave Blanche a quick embrace. 'I thank you for caring about me.'

'I hope Mr Landon is every bit as gentlemanly as he seems. I like him,' Blanche said.

So did Marian. In fact, she loved him in spite of what he could do to them. To her.

Allan returned to the Home Office.

It was the only thing he could think of to do.

He walked in and went to his desk. The newspapers he'd left there that morning were missing. He opened the drawers looking for them, but they were not there.

Sidmouth appeared in the doorway. 'Walked out, did you? Wondered if you'd come back.'

'A matter of importance required my attention.'

Marian.

'Matter of importance, eh?' Sidmouth pursed his lips. 'Thought the Home Office was important.'

'That is why I returned,' he replied. 'To work some more today.'

Sidmouth was behaving oddly. Allan often left the office during the day. Most times it had been to follow up on some lead.

Sidmouth slapped his thighs. 'Well. Good news, Landon. Found another gentleman to assist.'

'Another?' Who this time?

He pointed at Allan's chest. 'Need a man willing to do what needs to be done. Found just the fellow.'

Allan disliked the sound of that. Was he hiring pro-vocateurs after all? Perhaps the rumours of Spa Fields were true.

'More men, more information. Need to know the day and location. Who else is in on it. Coming soon, I'll wager.'

Allan felt his anxiety rise. Would this new man dis-cover Marian's part? 'Who is this person?'

'Son of a baron. Not afraid to dirty his hands a bit.'

Son of a baron? A wave of trepidation washed over Allan.

Sidmouth gestured for him to follow. 'Come, Landon. Fancy you know the fellow.'

They walked to Sidmouth's office where, lounging in a chair reading a newspaper, sat Edwin Tranville.

Edwin stood when he saw Sidmouth, his expression smug when he rested his gaze on Allan. 'Twice in one day, Landon. What did I ever do to deserve this?'

Sidmouth clapped Allan on the back. 'Trust you to fill in young Tranville here on your efforts so far.' He left before Allan could say a word.

Edwin lifted the newspapers. 'I borrowed these from your desk. Boring stuff, mostly.'

Allan glared at him. 'Cut line, Edwin. What the devil are you doing here?'

'Why, engaging in gainful employment.' He smirked. 'As you have done.'

Allan stepped closer, making the most of his taller stature. 'Sidmouth said you were not afraid to dirty your hands a bit. What did he mean by that?'

Edwin's smirk did not falter, but he backed away. 'You would have to ask him, but apparently there is another fellow I am to work with. You are on your own, it seems.'

'Why are you doing this, Edwin?' Allan demanded.

Edwin placed a chair between them. 'Because I can do a much better job than you, Landon, and I'm going to prove it.' He rubbed his scar. 'Sidmouth valued my connection to Marian. It was one of the factors in my favour.'

Allan changed his tone. 'Listen, Edwin, you must take care about Marian—'

Edwin's nostrils flared. 'I always take care about Marian. Besides, she will not know I'm spying on Yost.' His eyes narrowed. 'Unless you tell her.'

Allan doubted she would listen to him long enough for him to tell her anything.

He advanced on Edwin again. 'You will spend much of your time in taverns, I warn you. You cannot allow yourself to get so drunk that you cannot remember what you have heard.'

Edwin rolled his eyes. 'Lawd, Landon. I can hold my drink.'

There was no reasoning with him. Disgusted, Allan strode out.

* * *

A week later Marian and Blanche waited in Marian's bedchamber for Lord Ullman's carriage to arrive and take them to Domina's ball. Domina had insisted upon sending the carriage, and Edwin had volunteered to escort them.

Marian stood at the window. 'I dread this event.'

Blanche turned from checking her gown in the mirror. 'Oh, Marian, I know you do.' She lowered her voice. 'Is it because Mr Landon may be there?'

Blanche persisted in thinking Marian's heart had been broken by the captain. Marian had done her best to convince her it was not so, that she considered the captain more of a threat to the soldiers' march than a lost suitor.

Marian forced a dry laugh. 'I hope the captain does attend. He will see me acting like a lady of the *ton*, interested only in parties and gowns and gossip.'

Marian had increased her attendance at various entertainments, mixing in society as much as possible to dispel any notions that such a frivolous creature could be the mastermind behind a march upon Parliament. She had no illusion about fooling the captain about her efforts, but, if he told anyone, who would believe him?

She went on. 'It is difficult to pretend to enjoy such triviality when the day of the march is almost here.'

'I think you should forget about the march and enjoy

yourself.' Blanche checked her image again. 'I confess, I am very excited. I never thought to wear such a beautiful gown in my life.'

Marian smiled at her. 'You look lovely in it. I'm glad we purchased it for you.'

The deep garnet of the gown enhanced Blanche's complexion and brought out the red tones in her brown hair. Marian made certain both her gown and Blanche's were the very latest fashion to suit the role she played. Her modiste had been delighted. Marian's gown was made of ice-blue silk with a bodice covered in lace and tiers of lace at the hem. The blue complemented her eyes.

And to be entirely truthful she hoped the captain would admire it.

'I am glad for the carriage,' Blanche went on. 'Although it seems like the rain has stopped for the moment.'

It had rained all day, matching Marian's mood and filling her with memories of the rain before Waterloo.

'Has Mr Yost seen your gown?' Marian asked, wanting to turn her mind away from those memories.

Blanche blushed. 'I will show him later.'

Yost no longer shared dinners with them and he rarely walked with Blanche. Reilly created a small opening in the wall that separated their gardens, though, so he could pass through unseen and consult with Marian about the plans. Blanche used the opening almost every night to be with him.

Marian heard a sound outside. 'Here's the carriage.' She reached for her wrap.

The ladies descended the stairs. Edwin was already waiting in the hall.

He bowed, hat in hand. 'Good evening, Marian. You are very prompt.'

Marian peered at him, looking for signs he'd been drinking. He'd seemed on exceptionally good behaviour of late. He'd called upon her a few times and had always appeared sober. Still, something was going on with him, she could tell. Once, in the middle of the night, she thought she saw him standing across the street, which made no sense at all.

'You look ravishing tonight, Marian,' he told her.

It bothered her that he said nothing about Blanche's appearance, but then he always treated Blanche as a mere servant.

'Thank you, Edwin.' Marian wrapped her shawl around her shoulders. 'I suppose we might as well leave now.'

There was a crush of carriages the closer they came to Lord Ullman's town house. They merely inched along. The captain would have suggested they walk the rest of the way, but such an idea would never occur to Edwin.

'Domina will be in raptures if the ballroom is as crowded as these streets,' Edwin drawled. 'This is her first big event.' He emphasised the word 'big' with a grand gesture of his hands. 'I suppose everyone will be scrutinising the flowers, the food, the…' He paused. 'The wine.'

'She has been talking of little else for several days,' Marian responded.

'Has she?' Edwin rubbed his scar. 'What a dead bore.'

He went on, trying to guess who would attend and who had refused the invitation. Marian barely listened. Out of the window of the carriage she had a clear view of the front of Domina's town house and could see who arrived.

She watched for the captain.

He'd not attended other social events where Marian had been present, but surely he would attend his uncle's ball. Perhaps he would not even speak to her. If he did, she knew how to play her part. She did not know which circumstance to hope for.

Their carriage reached the end of the street. They were mere steps away from Domina's house.

Marian could stand it no longer. 'Let us get out here. It will take a quarter of an hour to reach the front of the house if we do not.'

Edwin sent her a scornful look. 'Really, Marian. We are not tradesmen.'

They waited until the carriage reached the front door.

Domina and Lord Ullman stood near the entrance of the ballroom, receiving their guests. Edwin greeted them with a bored expression and limp handshakes.

Marian followed him. 'You look splendid, Domina,' Marian told her friend.

Indeed Domina had never looked better. Her gown, all white lace and silk, was trimmed with pearls. She wore a pearl-and-diamond necklace to match and a turban with a white feather.

'Thank you, Marian.' Domina's eyes sparkled. 'I am so excited I can hardly stand still. I do hope I get to dance.'

Lord Ullman patted her hand. 'No fear of that, my dear. I claim the first set.'

She squealed. 'Is he not wonderful?'

Domina turned to greet Blanche, and Edwin went in pursuit of a servant carrying a tray of champagne. Marian scanned the room and immediately spied the captain.

To her surprise he walked directly towards her. Her breath caught. There could be no more impressive a man than he, elegant and masculine in his formal attire.

Blanche came to Marian's side and spoke first. 'Why, Mr Landon. How good to see you.'

He bowed to her and to Marian. 'You are looking exceptionally beautiful tonight, Mrs Nunn.' His eyes shone with genuine appreciation.

Blanche flushed under the compliment. 'Thank you, sir.'

He turned to Marian, his expression guarded. He nodded. 'Marian.'

'Does not Marian look lovely tonight, as well?' Blanche asked.

His eyes flickered over her. 'As always.'

Marian felt her body awaken under his gaze. She fought the sensation. 'Captain.'

A fleeting sadness shone in his eyes, before he turned to Blanche again. 'Would you do me the honour of the first dance, Mrs Nunn.'

Blanche glanced at Marian.

Marian smiled. 'Goodness, do not refuse him, Blanche.'

'I do not like to leave you alone,' Blanche said.

Marian laughed and let her gaze sweep the room. 'In this crowd? I shall not be alone. Besides, we have just walked in. I may yet find a partner.'

'Then, yes.' Blanche beamed at the captain.

'I will find you when the dancing starts.' He bowed and walked away.

'Do you really not mind?' Blanche asked.

'Of course not!' Marian replied a little too brightly. 'You love to dance.'

On the contrary, when the captain had asked Blanche to dance, Marian warmed to him. Being engaged for the first dance by such a man would increase Blanche's social consequence. As a lady's companion, she might have easily not been asked at all, but she did look so lovely, Marian expected she would not want for partners this night.

She and Blanche walked through the room, exchanging pleasantries with people with whom they'd lately become acquainted. At the same time, Marian searched the room for the captain or fancied his eyes upon her when she looked away.

When it was announced that the dancing would start, his gaze merely touched hers before he took Blanche and led her on to the dance floor. As it turned out, Marian did not have a partner, so she watched them from her spot against one wall as the captain took Blanche's hand and, with the other dancers, formed two circles, one moving inside the other. The captain performed the dance without effort. His footwork was not perfect, but he danced as if he cared less for his own feet than for the enjoyment of his partner.

Marian envied Blanche.

Edwin sidled up to her. 'Oh, Lawd. Look at Ullman.'

Lord Ullman danced energetically, but was stiff and very slightly off the beat. He beamed adoringly at Domina, however.

'He appears to be enjoying himself very well,' she said to Edwin.

'He's a buffoon.' Edwin held a glass of wine in his fingers. He drank the contents in one gulp.

Marian glared at him. 'You are drinking!'

He sniffed. 'It is one glass of wine. A man might have one glass without getting drunk.'

She looked into his eyes. His returning glance was steady. 'Take care, Edwin. Do not drink too much.'

He rubbed his scar. 'I will not drink too much. It was just that one time. Have I repeated it?'

'Not in front of me,' she admitted. 'Not yet.'

He glanced around. 'Where is your companion? Isn't she hired to keep you company?'

Marian inclined her head to the dance floor. 'She is dancing.'

'I'm affronted for you. You should be on the dance floor and she should be—' He gazed at the dancers and stopped talking. 'I see her,' he finally said.

Blanche was asked by another man to dance the next set, a quadrille. Marian danced the next set, as well, and the one after that, a Scottish reel. Her dance partners were perfectly charming gentlemen, but Marian was more attuned to where the captain was at all times than to their company.

She was standing out in a line dance when she caught Edwin snatching a glass of wine from a passing footman and drinking it straight down. Later, at the supper, his voice carried across the room. She watched him sway as he walked towards her table, another glass in hand instead of food. He carefully lowered himself into a chair next to her.

Lord Ullman and Domina had stopped by Marian's table, but Domina had dispatched Lord Ullman to fetch her one of the tiny cakes from the buffet.

'Did you ever think that I would be giving such a grand party?' she chattered on to Marian. 'Does not the ballroom look transformed? Ullie said I could spend whatever I wished so I filled the room with flowers. It is a wonder we had space to dance. Are not the musicians grand? Ullie says they have played for the Prince Regent and were once engaged to perform at the Regent's palace in Brighton. You know, his Royal Highness is having the palace entirely redone. Ullie says we shall be invited there to see it—'

'Well, won't that be grand, Domina,' Edwin said with great sarcasm and in much too loud a voice.

'There you go being a nuisance again, Edwin,' Domina countered. 'Some people never change. Tell me, who is beating you up these days?'

'You always were a shrew—' Edwin began.

Marian interrupted. 'Domina, I think your husband needs your help at the buffet. He just looked back here for you.' He had not done so at all, of course.

'He needs me?' Domina shot out of her chair. 'I must go to him at once.'

When she had gone Marian turned to Edwin. 'You are behaving very badly,' she told him in a fierce whisper.

He merely laughed and gazed around the room with

a vacant eye. She twisted away completely and joined Blanche in conversing with the other people at the table. When she glanced up she found the captain watching her from across the room.

It was announced that the dancing was about to resume, and a gentleman approached Blanche to engage her for the set. Marian followed them into the ball-room with Edwin right on her heels. With an apologetic glance, Blanche left her to take a place on the dance floor.

Edwin gazed around the room. 'You should dance with me.'

She did not even look at him. 'I think not.'

'C'mon.' He seized her arm. 'I want to.'

'You are too drunk,' she whispered.

'Have to have a couple of drinks or it is no fun. C'mon.' He pulled her.

'Release me, Edwin. You risk making a scene.' She tried to wriggle away from him.

His grip tightened and his voice turned to a growl. 'Are you refusing me, Marian? In front of all these people?'

Someone appeared behind him.

Captain Landon!

'Ah, there you are, Miss Pallant,' he said in a clear voice. 'We are engaged for this dance, I believe.'

She was almost too grateful to speak. 'Yes, Captain, I believe we are.'

Edwin was still gripping her arm when she put her hand in the captain's.

'If you will excuse us, Edwin,' he said loud enough for others to notice and to turn curious glances towards them.

Edwin released her and backed away, an angry sneer on his scarred face.

The music began, and Marian and the captain joined hands and marched into place. He bowed and she curtsied, and he took her in his arms at the precise moment the music of the German waltz required him to sweep her around the room.

She gazed up at him. 'You have rescued me again, Captain.'

His eyes were dark and warm. 'I suspect we are even.'

'Even?' Her brows rose.

'You saved my life at least twice.' He twirled her under his arm and then held her again. 'Once by tending my wounds and once from the peasant's axe.'

'You cannot do sums,' she countered. 'You picked me up when the whole French army was chasing me. You pulled me out of the burning château. And you saved me from Edwin once before…in my hall.'

'Then you owe me.' His voice deepened. 'How shall you repay?'

Her body came alive to him and ached with wanting more. 'How may I?'

The waltz was once considered scandalous because the man held the woman, albeit at arm's length. The captain breached propriety and drew her close so their bodies almost touched.

He whispered in her ear. 'Do not risk a hanging.'

Chapter Eighteen

The fire inside Marian cooled. She tried to pull away, but the captain held her firmly as he twirled her around the room. 'Abandon this plan, Marian. Make Yost call it off. Sidmouth does not yet know the time or place, but he is getting close.'

A *frisson* of fear ran up her back, but she forced herself to ignore it. 'I will not abandon our soldiers.'

'There are other ways to help them,' he insisted.

She shook her head. 'This is the way I have chosen.'

He resumed a proper distance, but she remained in a swirl of emotions. Was he truly warning her out of his concern for her, or did he simply want to stop the march? Did he care about her or about his job?

She did not know. She only knew that she felt captured by his gaze and quite helpless to look away. She yearned to be making love with him, to be held by him in bed, but he was her enemy, intent on foiling her plans.

His eyes seemed like mirrors, reflecting identical longing and regret. Time ceased and the room blurred and she could see nothing but the captain, her *Captain* again, the man who'd captured her heart.

The music stopped and he reluctantly released her.

It was too much to bear. She curtsied and stepped away from him. 'Excuse me, Captain—'

She fled into the crush of people, to the ladies' retiring room, waiting there long enough for him to have asked another woman for the next dance. When she ventured out again she threaded her way through rooms where guests talked to each other in small groups. Lord Sidmouth, in a deep discussion with another gentleman, approached from the opposite direction.

Loathe to be forced to even greet him, Marian ducked behind a huge jardinière of flowers. To her dismay, the two men paused next to the flowers, within two feet of her.

She heard Sidmouth's companion ask, 'How did you learn so much about Yost?'

Sidmouth replied, 'Sent in a spy. Knew his neighbour…' The men continued walking.

But Marian had heard enough.

Allan completed his second circuit of the ballroom and made his way back to the hallway, searching for her.

Not that he expected her to dance with him again or even speak to him. He merely wanted to keep her in sight, as if that alone would save her.

He closed his eyes as the pain of his helplessness washed through him. All he could do was try to convince her to get the march cancelled before Sidmouth discovered her involvement. With Edwin in Sidmouth's employ it was even more dangerous for her to be a part of this.

He took a deep breath and opened his eyes.

And saw Marian advancing on him like charging cavalry.

'I would speak with you alone, Captain,' she demanded.

He nodded and led her to a niche near the stairs where they could be private. 'We can speak here.'

Her eyes flashed. 'You used me.'

'I never—' he tried to protest.

'You only pretended to love me.' Her voice was low and angry. 'I overheard Sidmouth. You used me to spy on Mr Yost.'

His worst fear had come true. 'Listen to me, Marian. It is not that simple—'

'Simple? Do not say you have some complicated explanation, some convincing denial.' Her breathing accelerated. 'Like your very convincing denial of a Frenchwoman in Paris.'

'That was the truth—'

She would not allow him to continue. 'Truth? Do you expect me to believe you now? You deceived me. You were *sent* to call on me. I was merely part of a task you were assigned to perform.' She made a strangled sound in her throat. 'What did Sidmouth say, Captain? "See if she will whisper secrets into your pillow?" Or did you merely seek entry to my room to see out of the window?'

'Marian—'

She held up a hand. 'Say no more. I will no longer believe any of it. And I am not stopping the march. So arrest me if you must.'

'I do not wish to arrest you.' He emphasised each word.

Her eyes flashed. 'Oh, but you might be *forced* to.'

He seized her by the shoulders. 'Enough!' He leaned into her face. 'Remember that *you* involved yourself in this danger, Marian. Not me. I am trying to extricate you from it. I'm trying to keep you from hanging by your neck.'

Her lips quivered and apprehension flickered in her eyes. 'I cannot stop it now,' she whispered.

Their gazes caught briefly. Allan released her and Marian again fled from him.

He pressed his forehead against the wall. How was he to save her now?

His only hope was to learn what he could about the march. Perhaps Yost could be persuaded to stop it if Allan could show him that Sidmouth knew the time and place and would be ready to arrest them all. Allan now had no illusions about Sidmouth. He was convinced the man employed agent provocateurs, and suspected that Edwin had agreed to become one.

Allan was no longer in Sidmouth's confidence. He had no guarantee he could learn enough to save Marian. He did not know how much time they had before it would be too late.

He walked back to the ballroom. Marian had retreated to one of the chairs against the wall. He stood on the other side of the room, unable to resist watching her. The last dance ended and the guests filed out.

Allan followed and, in the crush of people waiting for hats and cloaks, saw a drunken Edwin approach her. Marian seemed to be speaking hotly to him.

'Carriage for Miss Pallant,' the butler announced.

Edwin seemed to glue himself to Marian's side as she and Blanche walked out. Allan pushed his way through the crowd, reaching the pavement just as a footman assisted Blanche inside the carriage. Marian continued arguing with Edwin. She ascended the carriage step, but Edwin was right behind her.

'I'm coming with you,' Edwin slurred.

She turned to him, framed in the carriage doorway. 'No, Edwin.'

'I'm coming.' Edwin demanded. He shoved her inside.

Allan surged ahead and seized Edwin by his coat collar, pulling him off the step. 'Not so fast.'

Edwin swung around with fury in his eyes.

'I have need of you, Edwin,' Allan said to him, not wanting to cause Marian any embarrassment.

Her gaze caught Allan's as the footman closed the door and the carriage moved away.

Allan took hold of Edwin's arm and walked him away from the other guests.

'See here, Landon!' Edwin cried. 'You take your hands off me!'

Allan released him. 'You are too drunk to be fit company for ladies.'

'She's my cousin!' Edwin cried, as if that meant anything at all. He made a show of straightening his coat and brushing off imaginary dirt from where Allan had gripped his sleeve. 'Trying to act the hero, eh? We'll see how important you are when this march business takes place. For once everyone will congratulate me and you will be nothing to them.'

Allan seized the front of his coat. 'What do you know, Edwin?'

Edwin shrank back. 'Wouldn't tell *you* if I knew something.'

Allan released him.

The next afternoon Marian sat behind her desk, curling and uncurling a small piece of paper. She looked up to her two most important allies, Mr Yost and Reilly. 'Where do we stand?'

'All is set,' said Reilly. 'The men know it is to be

Charing Cross at dawn.' They had withheld the location until the very last minute.

'And they know there are likely to be provocateurs?' she asked.

Reilly nodded. 'Each man has sworn to be disciplined, to stop anyone who creates havoc.'

Mr Yost drummed his fingers on the arm of his chair. 'Your friend Landon called upon me this morning.'

'He spoke to me, too. Very early,' Reilly said. 'Came to the door while you and Mrs Nunn were still asleep.'

'He came to the door?' Her nerves skittered.

Yost shrugged. 'He asked me to stop the march. I didn't admit even knowing what he was talking about.'

Reilly nodded. 'Me, too, miss.'

She twisted the paper. 'He is persistent.'

Yost rubbed his forehead. 'I confess, he seemed genuinely concerned about you and desired I keep you out of this.'

'You cannot believe what he says to you.' She took a breath. 'He cares only for the Home Office.'

Yost raised his shoulders. 'He did inform us there would be agent provocateurs. That would seem counter to what the Home Office would wish.'

'He's passing the same message through his contacts,' Reilly spoke up. 'Some of the men heard him speak of his concerns as to the danger of the march.'

'He is trying to scare them,' cried Marian.

Yost pursed his lips. 'Perhaps, but it seems odd to me.

Why would he want to stop it? Wouldn't he want it to take place so arrests could be made?'

Marian stood. 'It does not matter why the captain does what he does. All we need ask ourselves is if the plan will still work.'

Reilly straightened. 'The men know what is expected.'

Smoothing out the paper only to twist it again, Marian went over the plans in her head. The march was intended to be merely a show of force, a warning that the soldiers' needs should not be ignored. At the exact time of the demonstration, Yost and another man would leave the list of demands at Parliament. Reilly and Marian would be with the other protesters at Charing Cross. The early dawn traffic through the busy intersection would be momentarily halted by the crowd. No speeches would be made, but the group would be led in a cheer. Three loud *huzzahs* and then the crowd would disperse. A brief—and hopefully safe—show of force.

'How many men do you think we have?' Marian asked.

'At least five hundred,' Reilly told her. 'Maybe more.'

Five hundred men willing to risk arrest. They would move into place very quietly throughout the night. They knew to plan their way to escape.

Would it work?

She inhaled a nervous breath. 'We must hope that

the Home Office is kept in the dark, but we prepare as if they know the whole plan. Does the captain know when the march is to take place?'

'I do not think so,' Reilly said. 'He is still asking for information in the taverns, but everyone knows who he is and what he wants. He almost got into fisticuffs with your cousin at the Coach and Horses Inn the other night.'

'My cousin?' Marian gaped.

Yost added, 'Your cousin is often seen in the taverns, as well, and not always in the company of gentlemen.'

So much for Edwin's promise to cut down on his drinking. At least he no longer called upon her, although that must mean he was very deep in the cups.

She looked down at the piece of paper, now hopelessly creased. 'My cousin is of no consequence. It is the Home Office and Captain Landon we must fear.'

But not for much longer, because by this time tomorrow, it would be all over.

Sidmouth sent Allan to the taverns that evening to search for Edwin. Neither Edwin nor his nefarious partner had reported in to the Home Office all day.

Unlike when Allan had searched for Edwin at Badajoz, this time there was no gunfire, no riotous shouting. No agonised screams, but something was afoot. Allan sensed it. His heart pounded with the same foreboding as it had in Badajoz. The sense of anticipation was so strong it was almost palpable.

He enquired after Edwin wherever he went. Not truly caring whether Edwin went to the devil or not, he really also sought information on the march. No one would tell him anything of that, but several men had seen a man fitting Edwin's description. Reports were that Edwin had been drinking heavily and had been in the company of a Mr Jones—Lord Sidmouth's man, no doubt.

Allan followed Edwin's trail from one dark taproom smelling of hops and sweat to another. As the night wore on, the sense that something was in the air intensified. More men eyed him with suspicion. Fewer men sat drinking. More wandered the dark streets.

Hairs rose on the back of his neck as shadowy figures passed him in the night. Memories of Badajoz filled his mind.

He felt himself grabbed from behind and swung around ready to put a fist in the man's face.

'Whoa, Allan! It is me. Gabe.'

Gabriel Deane. His friend from the Royal Scots.

'Gabe!' He clasped his friend's hand and shook it. 'I did not know you were in London.'

'I arrived not long ago.' Gabe rubbed the back of his neck. 'The battalion disbanded, Allan. I'm at a loose end at the moment.'

'Disbanded?' Allan frowned. 'I'd heard rumours that might happen. What will you do?'

Gabe shrugged. 'Pay a visit to Manchester.' Gabe had grown up in Manchester. His father and brothers were prosperous cloth merchants there. 'After that, who knows? And you? How do you go on?'

Three men slipped past them, eyeing them suspiciously.

'What the devil is going on here?' Gabe asked. 'I've been seeing men on the streets everywhere.'

Allan pulled him aside and explained about his employment with the Home Office and about the march he was trying to prevent. 'I am loathe to admit this to you,' he added, 'but I am in search of Edwin Tranville again.'

'Edwin?' Gabe cried.

'He's in the thick of it, causing trouble.' He peered at Gabe. 'Come with me, if you are at liberty. I'll explain the rest.'

Gabe laughed. 'I am quite at liberty.'

Allan went into more detail as he led Gabe to the next tavern. He explained about the Home Office, Sidmouth, about Yost and Edwin and about the provocateurs. He did not speak of Marian, telling himself he was merely protecting her by leaving her name out of it. Perhaps, though, he feared the pain of explaining to his friend what he'd almost had with Marian. And lost.

They left the third tavern without success.

'One more,' Allan said. 'If Edwin is not there, I'm

going to simply follow some of these men to see where they ultimately are bound.'

'One more tavern,' Gabe agreed.

They entered a tavern near Hyde Park Corner, dark like the others with chairs filled with men who examined Allan and Gabe as they scanned the room.

No Edwin.

They were about to leave when a man raised his head from a table near the back of the room.

'More brandy,' the man cried, holding up a bottle. Enough light hit his familiar scarred face.

They'd found him.

Allan and Gabe crossed the room and Edwin lay his head back down on the table.

Allan looked down on him. 'Edwin.' He spoke as if issuing orders.

Edwin looked up and it seemed to take time for his eyes to focus. 'Lawd, it is you.' His filmy gaze turned to Gabe. 'And *you*. I s'pose you'll want to drink with me.' He waved his hand to the weary tavern maid again. 'Two bottles, wench. These fellows are paying.' Edwin laughed as if he'd said something extremely amusing.

Allan gestured for the woman to leave them. He sat and leaned close to Edwin so others could not hear. 'Something is afoot. What have you learned, Edwin? Where is Jones?'

Edwin looked around. 'Where *is* Jones?' he said too

loudly. He slapped his forehead. 'That's right. He left. Went to make the report.'

'What report?' Allan demanded.

Edwin drained his glass and poured another bumper of brandy from the bottle. He gave Allan a smug look. 'Not going to tell you.'

Gabe seized Edwin by his coat and hauled him to his feet. 'Tell him what he wishes to know if you value your neck.'

Edwin's face contorted. 'Very well. Very well. I'll tell. What do I care about it?'

'Then speak up now,' Gabe ordered.

'Jones left. Told me to go to the devil.'

Allan took Edwin's face in his hand and forced Edwin to look at him. 'Where is the march to be? When is it scheduled?'

Edwin squirmed in Gabe's grip. 'This morning. Not going to tell you where. Not going to tell you when. You'll grab all the glory.' He tried to pull away, but Gabe restrained him from behind. 'Going there myself. T'watch the Horse Guards. Told Jones I'd meet him there.'

The Horse Guards? Did Sidmouth plan to release the Horse Guards on the protestors? The soldiers would not stand a chance.

Allan leaned into Edwin's face. 'Tell us where. What time this morning?'

Edwin slumped and Gabe must have loosened his

grip, but all of a sudden Edwin broke free, flailing his arms. He swung out at Allan before Gabe grabbed him again.

'Leggo!' Edwin shouted. 'I'm gonna report you to Sidmouth. Have you arrested. You wait and see!' He struggled, but Gabe held him tight.

Allan moved to another table, asking the two men seated there, 'Do you know where the demonstration will be? Do you know what hour?'

'Go away,' one man growled.

He addressed the entire room. 'Tell me, any of you. Where is the demonstration to be?'

They only glowered at him.

He went back to Gabe. 'I have to find out more, but I cannot let him get to Sidmouth.'

'He'll cause no mischief.' Gabe shook Edwin like a rag doll. 'I'll make certain of that. Do what you must.'

Allan nodded his thanks and rushed out. All he could think was that he had to warn Marian that she was walking into a trap. Bryanston Street was too far to walk, and finding a hackney coach might take time.

More men filled the streets, sauntering in the direction of Westminster Cathedral. Were they headed there or to Westminster Palace? There would be few avenues of escape if the march was on Parliament.

Allan went to the stables where Valour was kept. He shouted for the stable lad to let him in and to saddle his horse.

A few minutes later he was astride Valour, skirting Hyde Park to reach Marian's town house. The first slivers of dawn were peeking through the sky.

He dismounted in front of Marian's house and pounded on her door. 'Marian! Open the door! Open the door!'

Her house was dark. He glanced at Yost's. It was dark, too, but that did not mean that they were not awake in the back, preparing for the march.

He pounded again. 'Open the door! It is urgent!'

He heard a frightened voice through the door. 'Go away, sir.'

'Hannah? Hannah, is that you? It is Captain Landon.' He used his army rank without thinking. 'I need to see Miss Pallant immediately! Let me in, Hannah.'

'I dare not!' she cried. 'She's not here, anyway.'

He heard another woman's voice. 'What is this, Hannah?'

Blanche.

'Mrs Nunn,' Allan cried. 'You must let me in. I have news of grave importance.'

There was a pause, then the door slowly opened. Blanche's face appeared in the gap. She held a candle. 'What is it, Mr Landon?'

'Let me in, please,' he said to her.

She stepped aside and he entered the hall. Hannah held a hand to her mouth, looking frightened.

'I'm not going to hurt anyone,' he assured her. He turned to Blanche. 'Where is Marian?'

The women looked from one to the other.

'Has she already left for the march?'

Their eyes grew wider.

Allan took a step closer to Blanche. 'You must tell me where she is going. I have to stop her. She's walking into a trap.'

'A trap?' Blanche cried.

'The Home Office knows where the march will be and when, but I do not. You must tell me before it is too late.'

Hannah spoke to Blanche. 'You cannot tell him. Miss Pallant said we were not to believe him.'

He faced Blanche, placing his hands on her arms. 'You must believe me. I want only to protect her. And the men, if I can. And Mr Yost. Good God, Mrs Nunn, they are calling out the Horse Guards.'

She blinked.

'Mrs Nunn, listen to me—'

'Don't listen,' Hannah cried.

Allan went on. 'She is walking into a trap. You must help me stop her.'

Blanche searched his face. She blurted out. 'Dawn. At Charing Cross. She should be there already.'

He spared her only a quick grateful look, running out the door to mount Valour and race down Bond Street to Piccadilly.

The sky had lightened. Dawn would come within minutes. On Haymarket Street wagons and carriages stood at a full stop. Valour made her way through them.

When he finally reached the intersection known to all as Charing Cross, it was filled with soldiers, hundreds of them. They kept their voices low, collectively producing a low hum.

He searched for Marian, slowing Valour to a walk. The men barely parted for him.

'I say we give them a good fight,' he heard one man say, his voice louder than the others.

'We gave our word, man,' another responded in a Scottish brogue. 'Stubble it or we'll mark you for a provocateur.'

Allan continued to pick his way through the crowd. How hard could it be to find a woman among all these men?

He glanced down Whitehall towards Westminster Palace. Years of war had made his eyesight keen.

He saw movement.

The Horse Guards were forming their ranks, preparing for the charge.

Chapter Nineteen

Marian stood at the base of the statue of Charles I inside the wrought-iron fence, dressed once again as a boy. Surrounded once again by soldiers. Her nerves bunched in her throat, making it hard to swallow. Soon she'd know if they'd be successful or hanged for traitors.

Reilly climbed on to the statue. 'Is it time now, miss?' He would lead the cheer.

Three huzzahs and they would be done.

The sky was light, light enough for Marian to catch sight of the man on the horse, the man searching the crowd.

The captain.

She turned away from him. 'Yes, Reilly, now, I think.' *Before he arrests us.*

She should have known the captain would come. He'd warned her he would.

Reilly climbed a little higher and cupped his hands so his voice would carry. 'Soldiers!' he shouted.

The crowd went silent.

'Prepare to cheer!'

'No!' The captain swivelled around on Valour and pointed towards Whitehall. 'Horse Guards! They are coming!'

Marian scrambled up the statue to see rows of uniformed soldiers on horseback starting their charge. She remembered from Waterloo. They started slow and gradually built speed. They would burst into the intersection like a fire-breathing dragon.

'Cheer!' she cried at the top of her lungs. 'Cheer!'

'Huzzah!' Reilly lifted a fist in the air.

'Huzzah!' Five hundred fists rose. 'Huzzah! Huzzah!'

'Run!' boomed Allan. 'Run now!'

The men ran. From her vantage point on the statue they were like water splattering in all directions.

The Horse Guards built their speed.

Marian climbed down from the statue, and Reilly lifted her on to the iron fence surrounding it. 'Do not wait for me, Reilly. Get out of here.'

Reilly easily climbed to the other side. When his feet hit the pavement, he reached for her.

'No,' she cried. 'Go.'

He glanced behind him.

'Get out of here, Reilly!' It was the captain.

The captain's strong arm plucked her off the fence and on to Valour's back. Reilly ran, disappearing into the remnants of the crowd. She prayed he would escape.

'Hang on,' the captain told her.

She seized Valour's mane in her fingers and pressed her knees tightly to keep herself from falling. Rather than turn away from the Horse Guards, the Captain headed straight for them, but veering off and heading into St James's Park instead. She expected to hear horses' hooves behind them, but soon the only sounds were the chirping of early morning birds. The water of the lake peacefully sparkled as the sun finally rose.

'I didn't see Yost.' The Captain sounded worried.

'He wasn't there.' With luck, Yost had delivered the list of demands to Parliament safely. She could only hope for the others as well. 'Do you think they got away?'

'I think they very well might have.' He sounded as if he was glad of it.

She turned to look at him. 'You warned them. You warned the soldiers to run.'

He did not answer, merely put an arm around her as he had done when they fled the peasants' farm.

The park seemed quite deserted as if nothing had ever disturbed its tranquillity, not even a nearby demonstration that almost ended with a cavalry charge. 'Captain, I want to stop. Might we stop a while?'

He swivelled around, checking the area. 'Let us find a place where we won't be seen.'

He left the trail and found shelter under a weeping willow tree next to the lake. They dismounted and

Valour ambled over to dip her nose into the water to drink.

Marian sat upon the ground at the trunk of the tree.

'I am reminded of our resting place after running from the peasants' farm,' the captain remarked as he joined her.

She remembered every moment of their being together, but now was not a time for memories. 'Why did you warn us about the Horse Guards?'

He looked surprised by her question. 'So the soldiers might get away. If not, there would be injuries and arrests. I never wanted that.'

She shook her head. 'You did not want the march to take place at all.'

'There is no fear of arrest if no one breaks the law.' He spoke as if this should be self-evident.

'But then the plight of the soldiers could be further ignored.' She lifted her palms, realising she was starting their old debate. 'Did you not risk arrest by being there?'

He glanced away, then met her gaze. 'I had to save you.'

Valour ambled over and nudged her. She reached up and patted the horse's neck until Valour spied a spot of grass nearby to nibble.

Marian turned back to the captain. 'I never wanted anyone to be arrested. Or hurt. That is why I planned it the way I did, to only show that the soldiers could be a force to be reckoned with if their needs were not met—'

He interrupted her. 'You *planned* it?'

She nodded and went on. 'There was to be no rabble-rousing. No speeches. Just a demonstration of force and the delivery of a list of demands.'

He touched her arm. 'You were the leader?'

'It was my idea. All my idea,' she admitted. 'I involved others only because I knew no soldier would follow a woman.'

'You enlisted Yost?'

She would not answer him.

He shook his head. 'I am not spying now, if that is what you fear. In fact, today I shall resign from the Home Office.'

'Why?' she asked, astonished.

He leaned back against the tree. 'I kept hearing my father's voice telling me to do what was right. I finally decided to listen to him.' He glanced away for a moment. 'Sidmouth's tactics were not right.'

'But you knew he was doing nefarious things like hiring provocateurs and still you worked for him,' she accused.

His eyes narrowed. 'I needed to protect you. I could only do that by remaining with the Home Office and learning what I could from Sidmouth and his men.' He took a breath. 'I did not believe the rumours of Sidmouth's provocateurs, that is, until he hired Edwin.'

Her jaw dropped. 'He hired Edwin?'

The captain nodded. 'Edwin boasted of being hired as a provocateur.' His expression turned doleful. 'But I do not suppose you will believe any of this now.'

A day before she would believe nothing he said, but everything seemed different under this tree, next to the water, no one else around. 'Did Sidmouth truly ask you to use me to spy on Yost?'

He stared at her. 'Yes. And I agreed.' He gave her an anguished look. 'But once I'd been with you, I knew I would tell him nothing I learned at your house.'

She waved that away. 'Did he ask Edwin to use me to spy on Yost as well?'

He nodded. 'I fear so.'

She dropped her head into her hands for a moment. 'Why on earth did Edwin wish to work for Sidmouth?'

The captain rubbed his brow. 'I have no idea.'

Marian felt as if her insides were shredding into bits. Her own cousin had been working against her. Not the captain.

He added, 'Edwin never knew you were involved. I am certain of that.'

Would Edwin have cared? she wondered. At least the captain's work with the Home Office had been grounded in his beliefs about government and law. Edwin had no such strong convictions. She doubted Edwin would have experienced any conflict over using her to get what he wanted. She believed the captain genuinely had. She, on the other hand, had been as single-minded as Edwin.

Marian's thoughts and emotions were a jumble. 'I risked too much, did I not?'

He searched her face. 'What do you mean?'

'I was outraged by the government's neglect of the soldiers, so I planned something grand to show they had better pay attention. I see it all differently now. I thought I was so clever, that I had thought of everything. My march would not be violent like Spa Fields. My march would succeed, unlike the Blanketeers.' She paused. 'I did not think of the cost, that men might be arrested and hung because of my vanity.'

He took her into his arms and held her close. 'It was not vanity, was it? I would never doubt your loyalty to the soldiers.'

She nestled against him. 'Do you think some men were arrested?'

'I think they all scattered in the nick of time.' His voice soothed her. 'I see things differently as well. My work had as much to do with ambition as the lofty principle I espoused.' He lifted her face with his finger. 'Perhaps I am as vain as you are.'

She smiled and settled against him once more. 'Well, I have learned my lesson. I will think of others from now on, not myself.'

'You make it sound as if you are like Domina.'

They both laughed.

She felt him take a deep breath. 'We need to get you home before anyone sees you dressed as a boy.' He helped her rise and they walked over to Valour. 'I will tell you that I am still ambitious, Marian. I still want to become an M.P., but not at any cost. It is now more important for me to do what is right. As my father said.'

She hugged him close.

He broke away, but she felt a camaraderie with him that surpassed even what they'd had in Belgium.

'Come.' He smiled. 'I will take you home, then busy myself composing my letter of resignation.'

When he moved to help her mount Valour, she stopped him. 'Wait a while before resigning from the Home Office.'

'Why?' he sounded surprised.

'If you resign today, Sidmouth might blame this failure of the Horse Guards on you. Wait a while and find some other excuse to resign.' She thought some more. 'In fact, if anyone reports seeing you at the march, you must explain that you were the one who broke it up. That is the truth, and you might as well take credit for it.'

He gaped at her. 'By God, you are scheming to rescue me again.'

Her brows knitted. 'I was thinking of your desire to become an M.P. This must not ruin it. I could not bear it.' Then she smiled. 'And I do owe you a rescue or two.'

She threw her arms around him again, holding on tight and pressing her cheek against his chest. 'I am so sorry, Captain. So sorry for doubting you. So sorry for the things I said to you.'

He lifted her chin. 'Then perhaps you must make it up to me.'

'How?' she cried. How could she possibly repay him for what he'd done for her?

'Marry me,' he murmured.

Her eyes widened and she took a breath. 'I will not marry you to make it up to you.'

He turned away with an expression of pain.

She clutched him to her, rising on tiptoe. 'I will marry you because I love you, and nothing will stop me this time.'

An urgent sound escaped his lips before he crushed them against hers in a kiss that made her forget about spies and marches and everything but him.

'Take me home, Captain,' she whispered. 'And never be parted from me again.'

Epilogue

Marian took a seat on the bench in the back of St Stephen's Chapel. Mr Yost sat beside her in the place designated for members of the press who report on the proceedings of the House of Commons. She stared down at her knee breeches, stockings and boy's shoes. Yes, she would pass as a boy once again. No one would remark upon Yost bringing an errand boy with him.

She glanced around the room and thought of how much had changed in the three years since she had organised the soldiers' march.

She'd never had any reassurance that her march made any impact at all. No news of it ever reached the newspapers; Sidmouth had seen to that. Still, she had to believe someone had read the petition; someone must have realised the significance of ignoring the soldiers' plight, of what soldiers could do if they chose.

In three years not enough had changed, but Marian

had not lost heart. Her very reason for sneaking in to the Commons showed she continued to have hope. She kept to her promise to abandon grand schemes, instead now using her money to invest in ways to help individual soldiers find work, or to fund relief.

Other things had changed as well.

She glanced over at Yost, making notes on a sheet of paper. He had begun reporting on Parliament's activities for a new daily newspaper, one with neutral political views. He refrained from writing seditious material, now that he had a wife and twin sons who depended upon him. Marian smiled when she thought about how blissfully happy Blanche was to be Mrs John Yost.

Blanche still worried about her excessively. Her brow had creased in worry when Marian told her she intended to dress as a boy and accompany Yost to this place.

It was forbidden for women to attend these sessions in the Commons, but Marian had been determined not to miss this day. It was said that Caroline Lamb once disguised herself as a page to witness her husband's speech at the opening of Parliament. If Lady Caroline Lamb could do so, so could Marian.

This was the day Marian's *Captain*—her husband— now Mr Allan Landon, M.P., would make his maiden speech in the august body.

Her gaze took in the room with its wainscoted walls. It seemed dark and exclusive, a place where important things happened. The lavishly gilded Speaker's chair and majestic columns only reinforced this impression. In the spectator seats she spied Jack Vernon, now a successful portraitist, and Gabriel Deane. Gabe winked at her and grinned.

A door opened and suddenly the benches began to fill with countless important-looking gentlemen, and Marian shivered in anticipation.

Finally her captain entered and took his seat. Her chest swelled with pride. He'd denied being nervous, but she'd known he must be, just as she knew he would deliver an impressive speech and set the tone for what she was certain would be a great career in Parliament.

As he promised in his campaign, he would advocate for an improved pension programme, employment and housing for England's soldiers. Ironically, it was his passion for helping the soldiers that helped him get elected in a Whig stronghold; his brief stint at the Home Office was not held against him.

Yost took notes during other speeches and business, but at last the time had come.

The captain stood and walked to the front of the chapel.

'Mr Speaker,' he began.

Marian could not help but rise from her seat so she could see better.

'Members of Parliament…' His gaze swept the crowded chapel, but suddenly halted.

His eyes caught hers.

She would undoubtedly be in for a severe scold from him for this latest escapade. It made not a whit of difference to her. Nothing would have stopped her from being present to see and hear him speak. Nothing could make her regret it.

But she held her breath.

He smiled, just a fleeting smile, but one she had no doubt had been meant for her alone.

'Members of Parliament,' he repeated. 'I stand before you a wounded veteran, but one more fortunate than many, one whose life was saved—' he looked directly at Marian '—and I will speak to you today so I may help other men who fought tyranny for you and now suffer…'

He had no illusions that one speech would create change, but it was a start. Marian's heart burst with pride for him.

Who would have ever known that the lark of a foolish girl would lead to this day, this place, this *life*?

When his speech ended and several members cheered, her applause was the loudest of all.

* * * * *

Author Note

The soldiers' march depicted in the book is a mere figment of my imagination, although the plight of the soldiers after Waterloo was real enough. The Blanketeers and the Spa Field Riots did occur and Lord Sidmouth, the Home Secretary, was accused of hiring provocateurs to cause the trouble at Spa Fields. Henry Hunt was a genuine liberal orator, but Mr. Yost did not really exist.

Today we take for granted the freedom to criticize the government and demonstrate for causes, but with the Seditious Meetings Act of 1817, it was illegal for groups of more than fifty people to gather together. It also became illegal to write, print or distribute seditious material. Lord Sidmouth had been a strong advocate of these measures, but they proved to be a blight on Lord Liverpool's government and ultimately ushered in a more liberal Tory government in 1822.

Next in my Three Soldiers series is Gabriel Deane's story. From the moment he, Allan and Jack rescue the

Frenchwoman from Edwin Tranville at Badajoz, Gabe is captivated by her. When he meets her again in Brussels they begin a scorching affair, but when Gabe asks her to marry him, she refuses.

Then they meet a third time in London....

HISTORICAL

Large Print

COURTING MISS VALLOIS
Gail Whitiker

Miss Sophie Vallois has enthralled London Society, yet the French beauty is a mere farmer's daughter! Only Robert Silverton knows her secret, and he has other reasons to stay away. However, Sophie is so enticing that Robert soon finds that, instead of keeping her at arm's length, he wants the delectable Miss Vallois well and truly *in* his arms!

REPROBATE LORD, RUNAWAY LADY
Isabelle Goddard

Amelie Silverdale is fleeing her betrothal to a vicious, degenerate man, while Gareth Denville knows that the scandal that drove him from London is about to erupt again. In Amelie, Gareth recognises a kindred spirit also in need of escape. On the run together the attraction builds, but what will happen when their old lives catch up with them?

THE BRIDE WORE SCANDAL
Helen Dickson

From the moment Christina Atherton saw notorious Lord Rockley she couldn't control her blushes. In return, dark and seductive Lord Rockley found Christina oh, so beguiling… When Christina discovered that she was expecting, Lord Rockley knew he must make Christina his bride…before scandal ruined them both!

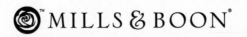

MILLS & BOON